70062

Johnson, D.
Loving hands at home.

DATE DUE	
MAY 1 0 1996	SEP 1 6 2003
FEB 0 5 1997	MAR 0 6 2004
MAR 2 1 1997	MAY 1 1 2004
MAY 1 3 1997	JUN 2 4 2004
JUL 1 8 1997	DEC 0 1 2005
SEP 2 3 1997	
DEC 0 6 1997	
JAN 2 0 1998	
MAR 0 4 1998	
DEC 2 2 1998	
MAY 0 1 1999	
JUL 1 9 1999	
JUN 0 1 2000	
JUL 1 7 2000	
MAY 1 9 2002	

GAYLORD   PRINTED IN U.S.A.

paid for and no books will be issued to persons in arrears for fines.

Loving Hands
at Home

Also by Diane Johnson

Fair Game

Loving Hands
at Home

Diane Johnson

Harcourt, Brace & World, Inc.
New York

F

70.062

For Fran and Dolph

Loving Hands
at Home

Chapter 1

On a Friday morning I went to apply for a job as a fortuneteller at Pacific Ocean Park. This is a big amusement park in Santa Monica. It looked funny in the rain, deserted, everything stopped, so you saw the rust and peeling paint, and became concerned for the structural soundness of the fun rides, and resolved not to let your children go on them, and intended to write a letter to the Los Angeles *Times* about it.

I knew from the suspicious contraction of his brow that the POP personnel manager did not think I looked like a fortuneteller. I wished I looked like my sister-in-law Patty, who is dark and vivid as a gypsy: I am slight and pale, and I was leading my two-year-old son, Toby, by the hand.

"How old are you, young lady?" the manager asked.

"Twenty-six," I said crisply. I would have liked to embroider upon this, to impress him with my glib loquacity, but it is really a very simple question.

"I would think someone older—more experience of people," he said. "You ever done this kind of thing before? Any carny in the family?"

"No, but I've been unusually good at telling people things about themselves. A kind of second sight—well—not really that, but good intuition." This was untrue. I am dumb about people; they are always surprising me, which is one of the principal points of everything that has happened.

"Tell my fortune," the POP personnel manager said, and stuck out his hand. I looked at it, and at him, and felt bleak, the way you do when your bluff is called. Still, this was the moment I had volunteered myself for. Success and affirmation. I was ashamed to need such little victories.

He was forty-five, pudgy, with derelict old clothes, a large diamond-like ring, and a surprisingly useful-looking hand, as if he did some work with it. I flattened the palm and peered at it with mock concentration. His eyes, when I looked into them, held mine for a hopeful second, betraying, beneath the carnival cynicism, that he really wanted his fortune told. Perhaps everybody does.

"A woman loves you, a much younger woman, but you are not aware of it," I said. It seemed safe enough, since POP is staffed by huge numbers of female high-school dropouts. "Continue taking moderate exercise, but do not overdo. Your shortness of breath is no cause for concern. You will find much happiness in your garden. A moderately large sum of money will come to you when you are fifty, but do not hope to be a millionaire."

I stopped, shrugged, dropped his hand. The convinced, expectant look faded sheepishly from his face, and he grinned.

"Not too bad. Sex, money, and health. That's about the formula. The garden bit was good. How did you know about that? You'll have to dress yourself up a little sharper, though. You could call yourself 'Madame Marietta, Psychic Science Expert from Duke University.' They like the scientific approach nowadays."

I guess I was being hired, and this made me feel brave and relieved. Being hired is like being constantly proved, renewed.

What were the hours to be? I asked him, and it turned out, as it always turned out, that he wanted a fortuneteller more hours than I could be one. So as usual I didn't take the job.

4

After we had agreed on this—it didn't distress him much—I walked around POP with Toby. The sun brightened the clouds and promised to appear. Teen-agers and old men came out to wipe the seats and benches and turn things on. Visitors began to stray in, as if they had been waiting nearby under awnings. We stood by the Ferris wheel, hoping the man would offer to start it up early, but he didn't. Then we walked by the place the handwriting lady used to be. She had been a very old lady six years ago, and was thought to be supernaturally gifted. People came long distances to learn from her about themselves. Of me she had said: "A happy and responsive nature needs freedom for fullest expression of its talents." But as I had no useful talents, this didn't help me much. She had been closer to the mark on Garth, my husband, of whom she said: "The drive toward order and excellence is all-compelling. A meticulous and tense person." A perfect description of Garth's surgeon's personality. He had given her his best, boyish, charming smile, but she was undeceived.

Now above her booth was a sign that said HAVE YOUR HANDWRITING ANALYZED BY IBM MACHINE. I hoped the little old lady was still there, perhaps hidden behind the curtain in deference to the current scientific fad.

We had an hour before it was time to pick up Kate, my four-year-old, from nursery school, so we went to the library. It was here that the strange thing happened to me. As we came out, I was captivated by a strong, pink youth with golden hair who was polishing every speck of dust off every square inch of a beautiful, shining, red motorcycle. What was so attractive was his devotion, his obvious love for his machine; it was this that made me feel I had to stop and admire it. And he did almost expire with pleasure to have a perfectly strange woman walk up and tell him how splendid his Honda was.

He polished away for a few seconds longer, with ears to match the cycle, and then asked me if I'd like to have a ride on it. And I said yes, instantly. I hadn't ever ridden on a

5

motorcycle, and would likely never get the chance again, and it obviously would please this nice young man. I wasn't quite sure what to do with Toby, though, and finally I asked a mother sitting on the bench by the library door if she was going to be there a minute. She said she was, so I asked her to watch him. He howled when I set him on the grass by her feet and he saw I was going to leave. This made me feel guilty, a careless mother, and I tried not to think of the headlines: BABY KIDNAPPED WHILE MOTHER RIDES MOTOR-CYCLE: MOTORCYCLING MOM ABANDONS TOT AT LIBRARY.

But the ride was beautiful, wonderful. You have to put your arms around the driver's waist and lean against his back. I was struck by how nice he felt, solid and warm, more like a friend than a perfect stranger. Riding around Los Angeles on a motorcycle is different from driving in a car. It seems more dangerous, but there is a reckless pleasure in this: it lends the illusion that your life is your own, and not encumbered by the liens upon it of others' affections, your children and husband, your own terrors. The wind blowing is a special exhilarating thing to laugh about and hide from behind the broad warm back of the driver. We roared and blasted and slithered through puddles. People looked at us, thinking, I suppose, that they'd never let their daughters do such things.

I'm not sure how I happened to fall off. I think it was my fault—I think I let go. We hit a little bump, maybe a manhole cover, and at the same time a truck turned left in front of us, throwing up a spray of water and seeming for a second that it would hit us. The next thing I knew, I had simply slid off the back of the motorcycle and landed, skinned and shaking, in the gutter. Something behind me made screeching-brake noises and sent me crawling up onto the curb. This all happened so quickly I had no time to be frightened, and by the time the young man had got off his cycle and run over to me, I knew I wasn't hurt either.

Except in one vital way, the way in which lesser epipha-nies do bruise and shake you. I think it was at the moment I hit the cement that it came to me that people who are happy and good do not ride motorcycles with strangers. Much less fall off them. A pratfall in the middle of Santa Monica Boulevard is too large a symbol to be overlooked.

I suppose, until this time, I had thought myself happy. I was a housewife of the ordinary sort—that is, by circumstance but not by vocation—well-meaning, inept, and normally satisfied, which is to say not greatly satisfied. But I had considered myself more fortunate than many women because I had found, besides my husband, home, and children, an absorbing pursuit, a sort of secret life. It was certainly a secret from Garth and his family. My children rather liked it, and it didn't interfere with ordinary household duties. For two years this secret life had consisted in venturing out on Monday, Wednesday, and Friday mornings to look for jobs, interesting jobs like fortunetelling.

I knew by now I would never actually take a job. It was just a way of seeing new sights, learning about people, preparing myself for an unspecified future something. I suppose I belonged to a whole society of people like me who longingly read want ads. Wish ads. I did it the way other women become hospital volunteers or take courses at night, things I had once done myself. The secret life was better. I thought it emblematic of an attitude toward life that I admired—courageous, eager, and enjoying. And before I came to realize it wasn't any of these things, I had been to some queer corners—laundries and bookshops, alleys, showrooms. How many people besides cleaners have seen the inside of a cleaner's (hot, steaming, stinking)? Of a candy factory? I was once interviewed by a man who wanted help "entertaining visiting business associates." He asked me strange questions like "How do you feel about letting Red China into the United Nations?" But I never found out what kind of business he was in.

At any rate, I had fooled myself for two years that the secret life was really living. It was, for me, a way of being Alma. That was another game I played; it would cross my mind at this or that time to wonder what Alma would do, what she was doing, what had become of her. She had always been for me a symbol of adventurousness, or, perhaps, of license, which was more what I wanted. She was one of those people you consciously label "formative influence" in your mind, and then you manipulate the nature of that influence as circumstances warrant. Of the real nature of Alma I was never sure.

As a child I lived in a small Midwestern town, Bede, Iowa. It was typical of its kind, I suppose, in that it consisted entirely of middle-class people, some richer than others, who had completely uniform values, attitudes, and expectations, so that the meanest farm hand was as moral, Republican, and upwardly mobile as the banker. Financial success was dependent both upon industriousness and upon the length of time you had lived there. Founding families were richest, but for the struggling newcomer there existed a tacit promise for his posterity.

There were, in Bede, two families who represented The Poor. One of them represented the Shiftless Poor. Unfortunately, that wasn't my family; it was Alma's. My family was Deserving Poor, which is much more difficult. When we received charity, the donors were careful of our self-respect. Women my mother sometimes helped with cleaning or sewing were careful to call her Mrs. Coe, respectfully; they might otherwise have been her friends. People expected me to get good grades in school, and I did. My clothes, although shabby, were clean. I was invited to the birthday parties of rich children, by their mothers, for the same reasons that Westwood mothers nowadays try to include a Negro child if they know one. I had a reputation for Character in the community, but secretly I longed with all the passion of my soul to be Alma Phelps instead of me.

Being Alma. It seems a strange obsession now. Until she was eight she was known as Little-Alma-She-Stinks, and she did, but seemed not to mind the derisive name or the smell.

8

At nine or thereabouts she changed from an unwashed, mat-haired, gray-kneed waif to something more positive and more desirable. Then it seemed as if she went unwashed from conviction; she contained an almost adult force of purpose. In her disgust with the social institutions from which she was excluded one sensed principle.

> Karen, Karen, thinks she's smartie
> Lost her pants at the birthday party,

would cause my soul to sink under its self-knowledge. I was a grade-school sycophant.

We were not allowed to play with her. Nobody was. She didn't seem to mind. There were a number of other Phelps children—bigger boys, who eventually were sent to reform schools, and a couple of sisters, who married early—so they had each other for company. I think it was the brothers our mothers worried about, at first, or they worried that Alma would corrupt our principles of hygiene. Later she turned truant, and eventually she was the town bad girl, but by that time she was somehow beyond the reach of the most malicious tongue. For one thing, she grew up beautiful, and people sensed that she was destined to be something truly great—the leader of some spiritual cult or a Hollywood sex goddess. And even the most disapproving adults were loath to criticize the early incarnations of an eventual goddess. Garth's family would really have hated her.

In the eighth grade Alma had no proper coat and so contrived a glorious garment out of a thick old red blanket. Even when the Methodist Auxiliary had given her a real coat, she continued to wear her blanket. She was not afraid to ride strange horses by luring them to pasture fences and jumping on their backs. If Alma had ridden a motorcycle she would not have fallen off.

The young man took me carefully back to the library. I was afraid that Toby wouldn't be there, but he was, toddling happily around on the wet grass. The lady was sitting alertly on the bench, moving her head from side to side to express her impatience. When she saw me, she stood up, as if to say she should have been gone long ago.

"You boy's pants are wet," she said, and strode off across the lawn pushing her baby stroller heavily before her. The young man waited, poised with one foot on the starter pedal, or whatever they are, for me to say again that I wasn't hurt. Then he went off with a roar that took him out of sight around the corner as if he'd been launched. I sat for a long time on the library bench just hugging Toby.

We picked up Katy and went home for lunch. My body, except for a horrendous bruise on my backside, felt better after a hot bath. The rest of me was permanently shaken, scared, although I did not know of what, and I had a new suspicion about things.

And that's how it began—with a suspicion. The way a word you have just learned seems then to be freshly written into every book you read, I seemed from the day I fell off the motorcycle to read upon the everyday faces of everybody else new words. It was rather like a game in which each player wears a label on his back he cannot see, and must guess from what he reads upon the others the badge he wears himself.

Chapter 2

I had fallen off the motorcycle on Friday. On Sunday we went as usual to family dinner at Garth's parents', along with Mahonri and Joan, Sebastian and Patty, and the eleven children. The Mahonris have seven. On the way there I felt wary, alerted by my bruised bottom to the suspicion that, if all was not right in my nice life, things might also be wrong in theirs, but as soon as we got there I lapsed into the mouse disguise I always seemed to wear with them. I could never be the person the family expected—a model Mormon wife for Garth—or myself, which had at least the virtue of coming easy to me, so that I never blamed them for disapproving of me. I just accepted Family Dinner. So did they.

Like most Mormon families, the Fry family is very close. We spent all our Sundays together, and at least one evening during the week, and saw one another during the day to swap baby-sitting and the like. And we were always full of love and co-operation and peace and concord. I had supposed we were happy as well. At least I thought that they were. I was the only non-Mormon, and tended to define myself in their context, like a second-class citizen—denied the vote but happy by association and content with my lot.

Besides my lack of religion, I think my underprivileged background had contributed from the first to their reservations about me. "Underprivileged" was linked in their minds with phrases like "juvenile delinquent," "unwed mother," and, perhaps, "mentally retarded." For a long time they were tense about me at concerts and fancy gatherings. Father Fry would launch into careful explanations of things the rest of them were bound to have known for years.

"Ah, the rondo is an amusing little form," he would say. "But just when you think it's over and are about to begin clapping, there comes the coda. I myself usually wait for everybody else to begin clapping first." Followed by jovial chuckles.

Another thing that has worried them is that my hair is dyed. Mother Fry associates "peroxide blonde" with "chippies," which is what she always calls them. I have never been sure she doesn't think I used to be one, and that Garth was involved, by marrying me, in a heroic rehabilitation effort, like someone in a Russian novel.

Of course she didn't really think that. I tend to make her sound Victorian and prim, when actually she was president of the Relief Society, and felt that after home and church the community is a proper object for woman's concern, and had many other modern attitudes. But about hair dye there remains a lot of superstition in the world.

The Fry family, again as is frequently true of Mormons, is a curious mixture of contemporary sophistication and farmy anachronism. Their house is an example of this. It is of the best all-electric, built-in-kitchen California kind, in which Mother Fry's Duncan Phyfe looks uncomfortable, and she keeps trying to grow tulips and lilacs outside it, like an Englishwoman who refuses to give in to India. The house was built at a time when dining rooms were out of fashion, so the mahogany table, eight chairs, and immense sideboard are squeezed into an L-shaped nook off the living room. It was here that Mother Fry did her best each Sunday to effect a stately, formal meal—damask, silver candlesticks, hand-hemstitched napkins, gracious talk. But it was always

12

marred, because she and Joan and Patty and I were up and down, running to change courses and to supervise the eleven children, whom we put at a picnic table on the patio, or in the kitchen in bad weather.

Every Sunday each daughter-in-law was assigned her share of potluck, and this time I had brought a cake. Although it had fallen on one side, I had evened it up by putting extra frosting between the layers, and although, on the outside, the frosting knife had pulled away the surface of the cake in several places, giving it a littered, mouse-eaten look, I meant well. Cakes, I have heard someplace, are symbolic of love. I put it on the table, and Garth averted his eyes.

"Ah, my favorite, chocolate. With, ah, is it mint frosting?" Father Fry said. He was always tactful, not out of kindness so much as because tact best preserved inviolate his sanctum of private thoughts.

"Just a small piece for me. The waistline," said the oldest brother, Mahonri. He has the heavy, spreading body of the former athlete, and, from his guilty manner, seems always to hear the ghostly voices of old coaches behind him at the table. His wife, Joan, smiled, knowing he had never refused a large piece of *her* cake. She hypocritically praised my lime frosting. From the rest came only a moment of suspicious and embarrassed silence, and finally a stifled sigh from Mother Fry. The sad cake huddled in the center of the festive board, and we all received it silently, the way polite people receive an improper remark. Father Fry, temporizing, brandished the cake knife in reluctant preparation, and I vaguely knew, as always, that their disapproval of me had something to do with cakes. But that seemed silly, like a club which one is not invited to join. Father Fry impassively cut and handed around pieces of cake. The cut pieces revealed great internal holes, as in Swiss cheese. The silence was still strained, but strove for cheerfulness. Suddenly we heard a loud crunch and an exclamation from the middle brother, Sebastian. With an apologetic glance at me, as if to say he hated making this

13

fuss, he took a small brown bottle cap from his mouth, and, in full view of everyone, strove unsuccessfully to secrete it under the edge of his plate. It was the cap off the vanilla bottle. I honestly have never figured out why these things happened to me.

"It would be a great relief, Mother," Garth said, "if Karen and I could just chip in and pay for our share on Sundays, rather than having her make these embarrassing messes every week." His voice aspired to a jocular, affectionate tone, but fell back with a defeated quiver of irritation.

Now the embarrassment, which had been hovering like a fog, capable of dispersion by the bright touch of a tactful remark, descended gloomy and damp. If someone had laughed and said "Poor old Karen," we might have been able to think of my domestic incompetence as a regrettable but endearing fault. Instead it was stonily avoided, the way the truly unforgivable always is. Domestic accomplishments had for the Frys a mystical significance related to femininity and the life force. The hearth, cakes, the cradle are still viable symbols, and lurk like native gods in the breasts of women outwardly converted to the League of Women Voters, and in the breasts of their husbands, the disenfranchised priests of an older worship. Actually the Fry men are not disenfranchised. Mormonism, like all successful creeds, protects and incorporates the old symbols. Although I was no Mormon, I was no apostate about femininity. It was simply that my cakes never turned out.

"Of course, if you'd rather not bring anything," Mother Fry said, looking annoyed, as if she'd been caught exploiting an imbecile child, "there's no need to 'chip in,' as you put it. Joan and Patty and I can take care of things perfectly well. I always supposed that Karen *preferred* to do her share."

I knew I ought to assure them that I did prefer, but truthfully I did not. I had grown discouraged. I could never in the world approach the accomplishments of Mother Fry and my sisters-in-law. They made their own clothing, pies, preserves,

14

rugs, curtains, gifts, hats, greeting cards, dishes (Mother Fry and Patty dabbled in ceramics), soap (just Mother Fry), leather sandals, purses, simple furniture (Patty), and bread.

"There's nothing wrong with this cake," Father Fry said. "Has a fine, chocolatey flavor." A tense lump of resentment and tears in my throat dissolved gratefully. Father Fry was almost the only person in the family I loved, or would have had he not been too remote to inspire love. It seemed to me that he had been badly misled by Mother Fry, and because of her believed that good women not only ought to be but were interested mainly in housekeeping. Homemaking, he termed it, having gathered from somewhere that this was more tactful. There were other anachronistic things about Father Fry, too; he used adjectives like "corny." "Trim" is the word that describes *him* best—trim clothes, shape, manners, words. He is well-dressed, -shaven, -spoken, -thought-of. He is long and long-faced, with pleasant reddish golf-course coloring and white hair, gone at the top of his head but fluffy at the sides. The bare part of his forehead is creased with intellectual wrinkles, and he has square eyebrows. If he has not shaved since morning, his cheeks look as if they were sprinkled with silver dust. All this silver-and-rose color gives him a valuable look.

And he has a valuable air, as subtly befits an economist. His clothes cost money, his stereo costs, his car costs. Father Fry, though not in any way ostentatious, is used to being well-appointed; everything about him is so well-appointed and so effortless, one feels that at his birth his parents must have somehow endowed him with perpetual care, like a California burial plot. In spite of everything, I thought him basically kind and simple, very admiring of Mother Fry's hooked rugs, very enthusiastic about her home-pickled pickles.

"Those holes result from underbeating," Mother Fry said, her essential pedantry conquering her hostility.

"It's such a mystery to me. I think it's clever of you to be able to tell," I heard myself say in an affected, superior voice.

15

I knew I sounded hateful, but I was determined not to sound cowed. Secretly I wondered how you do tell what ails a cake. I longed to know, both because I liked cake and because I believed a person has no right to despise what he cannot do.

Mother Fry, voice sweetened with maternal self-consciousness, began to discourse upon baking. Her husband and sons, regarding her with the rigid smiles of people who are not listening, looked nonetheless pleased at her expertise. Mother Fry has an M.A. in home economics, and it has always been a source of pleasure to her men that her special province is so motherly and suitable. She is a splendid cook, though she runs to molded gelatin salads and the use of marshmallows, and takes perverse pleasure in the concoction of archaic dishes (like head cheese) which require repulsive preparation. Now, about cakes, her deep voice grew richer, with overtones of experience.

Mother Fry is a handsome woman, but aggressively grizzled, as if she cherishes her wrinkles and stiff gray hairs like merit badges of a useful life. She wears no powder or lipstick, does nothing to blur the lineaments of pioneer womanhood one sees in her face. Mother Fry has a genuine pioneer temperament as well, and once enjoyed modest fame as the author of an article in a church magazine to the effect that babies should be born at home because this provides a more natural and thrilling experience for everyone, including the older children, who, I suppose, would derive from the groans and shrieks of their mothers a sense of the miracle of birth. The three Fry boys were, in fact, born in hospitals.

Mother Fry was now describing the principle behind clarifying the butter, and her eyes had brightened fanatically. Her air of indifference to her person and of dedication to some higher endeavor had always made her look to me like an old feminist. She has the sturdy marching body of the Bloomerette, and proudly observes that she can do in a day enough work to kill the average man. It was surprising, in view of this, to hear her voice ring so true on the difference between single- and double-acting baking powder. Mother Fry is of course too young to have been a Bloomerette. I knew from an old photograph that she had in fact been a flapper, very slim and pink-kneed, with smudgy eyes beneath the deep rim of her hat. This photograph, which always made me feel sad, made no prediction of domestic fanaticism. In it one pale hand lay open, limp and dainty, on her lap. Now she is fond of saying, "Look at these hands," and thrusting out, for her sons and daughters-in-law to admire, her knobby, strong, man's hands, proof that she has been equal to the demands of life. And beside the solemnity with which Joan and Patty regarded Mother Fry's hands, and also the demands of life (bake! bear!) I had always felt myself effete and unpleasant, tainted with cynicism and ambition, the incarnation of one of those awful American women Frenchmen are always deploring.

Garth and I had a fascinating French diplomat living across the street from us. At least, I had gathered from his French accent, his Washington D.C. license plate, and his London clothes that he was a diplomat. Now, at the dinner table, I had lapsed into a secret-life fantasy about him—in the real world we had never spoken—and Mother Fry was getting to the important part, the folding of the egg whites into the batter, when she was interrupted by the ringing of the telephone. She got up to answer it in the kitchen. We heard her voice drop, cool and disapproving, and she thrust the receiver around the kitchen door.

"For Sebastian."

Sebastian leaned toward it, and his wife, Patty, shared a conspiratorial grimace with the rest of us. Her expression hardened, the pout deepened, when Sebastian was heard to tell someone he'd leave right away.

"What does she want with you on Sunday? Do you have to go?" Patty asked.

"I guess so. She didn't say why," Sebastian said, and Patty, remembering that a considerate wife doesn't make her

17

husband's job more difficult by complaining, clamped her lips shut and frowned. Sebastian did not appear concerned about either the summons or Patty's displeasure, but composedly finished his cake. Sebastian is the only male Fry who is not a professional man—doctor, lawyer, or teacher. He is a facto-tum, a general secretary-chauffeur, assistant, and companion to a rich heiress art collector named Paris Pratt. It is hard to say whether this job makes him in the eyes of his family a failure or a black sheep, two terms which are not exactly synonymous. None of us had ever determined the exact nature and extent of Sebastian's responsibilities to Mrs. Pratt, and I think it was significant that these were never conjec-tured upon, at least not in front of me, by the rest of the family.

"She thinks she can just snap her fingers and he'll appear from the air any time of day or night," Patty said. Her voice held a whine I had never heard before.

"She's right," Garth said with his usual smile. Garth has a large, angelic face, which seems unable to express an un-pleasant or hostile emotion, but he can be acid. Sebastian glanced at him with irritation and speared a crumb from his empty plate.

"But it's so inconsiderate," Patty continued. "She knows he has a family. Not that she's ever seen us. But what can she possibly want with him this time of day?" She was speaking as if Sebastian were not there, and Sebastian behaved like it. He tossed his napkin on the table and rose.

"Well, Patty, she's an impulsive woman and probably highly neurotic," Father Fry said.

"These rich people pay very little attention to the time schedules of others," Mother Fry added. She was fond of seeming to know about the habits and beliefs of the rich and famous. Patty shrugged her shoulders and tossed her hair, which she was wearing in a single long, thick braid down to her shoulder blades.

"I should be used to it by now," she sighed.

"After all, it is *Sebastian* who has to go to work at all hours," Mother Fry reminded her, gently reproving her dissatisfaction.

"It's lucky that I like it," Sebastian suddenly said, and went out the door.

"You can go to Sacrament with me," Garth told Patty, and she smiled at him in a resigned and grateful, brave way.

Everyone had by now struggled through the cake, and we had arrived at the ceremonious pause, sitting among the litter of forks and crumpled napkins exchanging well-fed observations on the dinner. I emerged from a fantasy about making them an incredible cake, a pink croquembouche nine feet high, to hear Mother Fry saying, "I think cranberry jelly is really the best thing to baste ham with and I always keep coming back to it." But she got no response at all to this, which meant she had exhausted the men's ability to respond with any more compliments. "Well, let's polish off these dishes," she said, and that was the sign that dinner was officially over. Father Fry and Mahonri and Garth bolted to the music room, and we cleared the table to the muffled strains of Bartók. All the Fry men are devoted lovers and patrons of music.

The kitchen after family dinner always had the congratulatory atmosphere of a locker room after a track meet, and I, of course, was always pretty much in the position of a relay man who has dropped a baton. Even Joan and Patty, with whom I was on perfectly good terms the rest of the week, were apt to be unconsciously distant. And I always, always, broke one of Mother Fry's dishes. It was psychologically very suspect, because I never broke dishes at home, but Mother Fry and Joan and Patty could not have helped but think I must shatter whatever I touched, and this certainly lent support to Mother Fry's conviction that I was shattering Garth's life.

Joan and Mother Fry were engaged in a lively discussion about basting ham, and Patty was listening attentively be-

19

cause she considered herself a novice compared with either of them. Joan is the tallest of us, the oldest—thirty-two—and the plainest. She is fleshy and big-breasted, and she has permanents too often; one can almost see, as if by stop-action photography, her metamorphosis into a cartoon dowager. Her size, perpetual pregnancy, placidity, and silence tempt a comparison with some domestic animal, maybe a clever simile involving both cow and rabbit, but any such figure would be unfair, because Joan is intelligent and pleasant. In some ways she was more interesting to me than Patty was. She had that quality referred to by Mother Fry as "inner glow" and attributed by the family to her saintly satisfaction with the role of wife and mother of seven. One did glimpse this glow, through cracks in her serenity, but it burned with something more like the holy light of domestic martyrdom, or even, I had sometimes thought, like a spontaneous combustion of grievances which must have been accumulating like oily paint rags below her docile surface. But nobody had ever heard her complain, and it was perhaps only that I would be resentful if I were in Joan's situation. It is difficult to sort these feelings out.

Patty, Sebastian's wife, is an almost direct opposite of Joan. She is little and slim and dark, given to wearing vivid Capri pants and golden hoop earrings and allowing her eyes to flash. Someone, possibly Sebastian, has told her that she has a gypsy quality, which she now seeks to emphasize, and, possibly unlike Joan, she has an essentially squawlike nature underneath her fiery exterior, in this resembling real gypsies, I suspect. I had always thought it odd of Sebastian not to see that, or perhaps he had.

I dropped and broke a dish. In spite of my protests, Joan helped me sweep up the pieces. Then I cut my finger on a sharp fragment and was retired to a kitchen stool, which made me feel more uncomfortable and useless than ever. But I reassured myself by thinking of Joan, and of how I would not like to be thirty-two and hippy, with seven children and

20

frizzy hair and no light at all in a bleak world of duty and scrub brushes. Mahonri, the junior partner in a busy law firm, makes thirty thousand a year. He has a Buick station wagon and a Corvette. He has a stereo only a few hundred dollars inferior to his father's. He belongs to an expensive golf club and plays two afternoons a week. And Joan, Joan four times a week packed up the accumulated bushels of dirty clothes, including Mahonri's shirts, and carted them off to the laundromat because she hadn't saved enough from her housekeeping money to repair the washer. Joan was to me what the starving people of war-torn Europe were to me as a child; I thought upon her and became thrifty, tidy, and grateful.

It began to grow dark. The dishes were finished, dried, put away. The counters were wiped, the stove was cleaned, the floor was swept, invisible fingerprints were polished off cabinets and refrigerator. Now it was almost time for Sacrament Meeting. Joan and Mahonri went on ahead in the station wagon with their three oldest children. Father Fry took Garth to the study to look at a new camera. Katy was happy watching television, which she was not permitted at home, but Toby was fussy and tired, toddling in complaining circles, shaking his head and wailing. I tried to quiet him with cookies, though this is not approved. Patty, nursing her baby, sat stiffly on a kitchen chair, like those mothers one sees in bus stations, with a blanket tucked lightly over baby and breast. Neither she nor Joan suffers embarrassment over natural functions, and Patty is an active member of La Leche Society, a group dedicated to disseminating information about lactation.

Mother Fry was puttering in the cupboard, saying things like "Ah, what a lovely day," and "I don't see how Joan does it, manages so beautifully, and the children all so well-behaved and neat." Joan's children were well-behaved, but had an overwhelmed air, as if each child could see that there were too many of them, and feared it was perhaps he who was superfluous. But they always had buttons, and both shoes, and she sewed them all dear little dresses and shirts, and this was a triumph in itself.

The family had ceased to talk to me about the quilting and women's study group and Sunday school, and all the other things you do when you are a Mormon. Perhaps they had realized that having one nonchurchgoer is convenient. Father Fry and Garth came in, talking of Pentaflexes. Mother Fry took off her apron, and Patty handed me the baby.

"He hasn't burped yet," she said. I put him over my shoulder.

"I'm a very lucky woman, having all my family so near," Mother Fry said.

"Yes, we all have a lot to be thankful for," Father Fry agreed as he held the kitchen door open. And for the first time I was not convinced; I was aware of too many little clouds—Patty's whine, Garth's outburst, Sebastian speeding off to the mysterious millionairess, Joan's stolid silences. And, above all, all that thankfulness.

"Aunt Karen, will you play with us?" Joan's Sara asked.

"Of course," I said. "Have a nice time," I told the others as they left. It was always a longish three hours for me on Sunday evening. I never seemed to know enough games to last eight children three hours.

Chapter 3

Although he seemed calm when he left family dinner, Sebastian has since told me he was angry, or at least annoyed, at the whole discussion about Paris Pratt. He was annoyed at Garth and Patty for causing the discussion, and at Paris Pratt for putting him for the hundredth time in that absurd position in front of his family, people who couldn't or wouldn't understand why he worked for her at all. Then, because he disliked feeling angry, he tried thinking of something else, and because his tooth hurt where he had bitten down on the bottle cap, he thought of me. He thought only that I was rather sweet and that his family was ungracious. His mind was diverted further, at the top of Mulholland Drive, by a magnificent sight at sea. Far away, tiny but clearly visible against the sky, as if someone had described neat arches with a pen, the spouts of several whales could be seen proceeding down the coast line like the smoke of unseen merry little underwater trains. It looked companionable, as if they were whistling off to a party. He was cheered. It was nice to think that there were such things as whales—ridiculous mammals. He thought of them having whale emotions, perhaps maternal feelings or lust, and was even wondering how it would feel to be a lustful whale before he realized he had fallen into Mrs. Pratt's habit of preposterous empathy.

The reliable destination of his associations, no matter how free, ending him up always at Mrs. Pratt and lust, depressed him again. It was all very well to think of others, of sisters-in-law and whales, but his self, it seemed, was always lurking beneath the surface of his thoughts, ready to jump out in funny clothes and scare him. Sebastian's self had an exotic costume, of which he was perfectly aware, a naked-to-the-waist, crimson-pants, sash-sword-and-one-gold-earring sort of pirate getup in which he hoped one day to ravish away the untouchable Mrs. Pratt.

Now his anger was freshly directed at the predictable feeling of longing as he drove up to the Pratt Foundation gate. It came upon him, curling in his stomach and along his thighs as tangible as a finger stroke, as he opened the gate at the foot of the road, and more intensely as he came in sight of her house, and he was contemptuous of it. Ordinarily, in more self-indulgent moods, he regarded his love for Paris Pratt as no more than a tiresome propensity, like garrulity, something you are aware of and careful not to let interfere with everyday life. He was absolutely aware of it; it formed part of his definition of himself—man, expert on European antiques, husband, father, hopeless lover of Paris Pratt. His love for her was one of the unchangeable things, like going gray and being five foot ten and allergic to pineapple. Pine-apple brought him out in a rash; Mrs. Pratt affected him internally, with a more or less constant intestinal alertness. His love growled around inside him whenever they were together, in a way he was used to, but he resented it when it made audible noises away from her—when he was at home with his children or just driving along on his way somewhere.

She had not come down to the door. Karla, the maid who talked to herself, said she was up in her sitting room. As he climbed the stairs he could hear deep musical groans from behind her closed door. She was evidently at her cello-playing. The memory of the bewildered way she embraced the big instrument charmed him before he had opened the door, and the sight of her, as usual, finished him off. Her back was to him, bent like a willow. She was waving the bow in an excess of frustration at some difficult passage. Strands of pale hair escaped down her back from her neatly tucked bun.

"What was it you wanted?" he said, taking the gruff tone he had resolved upon.

She laid the cello against the table, freeing one hand for gesticulation, and tucked the strand of hair behind her ear. "I was ashamed of myself as soon as I had called you." She smiled. "But there were the police and a lot of people around, and the whole thing was so unsettling, I just said to myself, 'I wish Sebastian were here.' "

"What's happened?" he asked, softened further. She *had* made an admission of need, of sorts.

"Last night, it seems some desperate inverts with a grudge against Emil kidnapped him from his cottage. In terror, Emil escaped them by leaping from the car into a chasm. Breakfast this morning—no Emil. Took a turn by Emil's cottage, and there found great chaos, paint all over, canvases ripped. I sent Alfred and Paul out to hunt. They found him insensible in some leaves."

"Alive?" Sebastian asked.

"Yes, but scared and trembling. Hurt badly, really, with a big bump on his head. So he went to the hospital, we had the police and all, and now I think we must put some death-dealing electrical fence around the whole place. We cannot have our artists being kidnapped, however much they deserve it. And Emil will sue, doubtless. You should have seen his poor skinny little legs. You know what he wears to bed? Nightshirts. Is that a typical homosexual thing? One can see how it could be. Well, poor Emil. So I said I wished Sebastian were here."

Sebastian sat down and laughed.

"Oh, Sebastian, there he was, poor mite, with his face all stubbly and muddy, crying, and you could tell he was crying about being the kind of person people come and hurt and hit. He was so ashamed of that. And all his paintings ruined."

"And the kidnappers?"

"Gone away, of course, and he wouldn't say anything. He told the police he didn't know them, couldn't remember the car. That's almost the worst thing, to think he will need them for friends sometime."

"Will you have him back here?"

"He won't come back. He's furious, too, at me, at this place. He feels we have all violated him in some way. We must never have homosexuals here again, Sebastian. They make me feel so powerless to help them, and they have such sad lives."

"That seems like an unfair prejudice," Sebastian said. Although he believed her sincere about chastity and the life of the mind, he nonetheless preferred her to befriend homosexuals. He reacted like a duped husband to the mere appearance of another normal male around the place. Only, unlike a husband, he could not rage and shout at Mrs. Pratt.

"Homosexuality has no relation to talent, after all," he continued. "Emil would be a hateful little man whatever his affinities."

"It's just me. I don't understand them, and I never know quite how to respond. And I mind not understanding them. Do you think that intrusive? Perhaps it's wrong to try to understand people. But it's better than misunderstanding, at that. And you have to apply the mind to something."

"Intrusiveness is a virtue in the rich," Sebastian said. "Have no fears at all."

"Perhaps I should give up on artists altogether—they're very different from you and me." Mrs. Pratt laughed. "And take up wayward girls or discontented housewives."

"God help them. Stick to artists—you run less danger of damaging the structure of society."

"Oh, stop it. I know I can't change anybody or anything, and that seems too bad, when you consider the unhappy lives . . ."

26

"Idealism is not a virtue in the rich," Sebastian said.

"The Rich. Why do you always characterize me in terms of some tiresome abstraction?"

"It bothers me to think of you too particularly, as you very well know." Now he smiled at her. "Besides, I believe you think of yourself as an abstraction: mind and charity and chastity."

"Ah, no, you impose these things on me. I understand *you,* anyway. You're a Don Juan of the classical sort, fitful and searching for a perfect woman, only you're lazy. So you pretend that I have all the virtues. It saves a lot of trouble and hunting around, and you know I won't disillusion you by giving in."

"How could I find perfection in you?" Sebastian asked. "I was just thinking how too skinny you are. You look like an X ray of yourself."

"We've known each other too long. You see through me, that's all," she said. They laughed and touched hands.

"Why don't you go ahead and play some more?" Sebastian said.

"Oh! A most beautiful Boccherini concerto. I will," she said, and took up the cello again. Sebastian sat near her on the piano bench and watched her play. He had taken to enjoying, almost, the expected desire and longing that welled up in him whenever he watched her do anything. And he was ever newly astonished at the aspects of her that aroused him. Even the pink line of her part, visible as her head bent over the cello, now moved him physically. He suppressed an impulse to reach over and trace it with his finger, and turned to marveling instead at her arms—long thin arms with such minute wrists, bird-boned. He knew if he were closer he could see the tiny blue veins beneath the pale skin of her wrists. Her odor of verbena or lavender or some other archaic thing was appropriate to her dress, one of her customary costumes, flowered, preposterous, something to be worn by a caricature old maid. Perhaps it was this affectation, trying to look like something from an old-fashioned

27

garden, which inspired him to dispel it with forceful demonstrations of his lust. Her thinness made her seem like a bouquet of pressed flowers. He was seized now, as at other times, with an obsessive desire to press her further, to kiss her tiny breasts and narrow throat.

She played a note wrong, looked up at him, recognized his expression, smiled. Then she addressed herself again to her cello.

"The only trouble with this concerto is that the orchestra has most of the melody and the cello just goes ump, oom, ump. Very unsatisfying by itself. You couldn't do the orchestra, could you?"

"I might." Sebastian took the music and turned around on the piano bench. Mrs. Pratt was gazing confidently at him as at a bright child. Sebastian warmed foolishly and found himself able to pick out a rudimentary version of the orchestral line, while she made delighted ump-oom-umps with her cello. The effect was pleasant. In the bottom crevice of his mind, Sebastian arranged what parts of the evening he would report to Patty, leaving out this.

Chapter 4

Ｎone of the rest of us had ever seen Mrs. Pratt, except in newspaper photos, which looked, as all newspaper photos do, like a collection of minute black dots. But then, the next day, I did see her. It is odd how events follow suspicions, as if, by wondering about things, you cause them to happen. Seeing Mrs. Pratt was one of two startling circumstances that Monday, and I have always believed that when two strange things happen in one day it forewarns of a change in life, but the signs are often very hard to interpret. The pattern is usually that something is revealed to you and something is taken away, like the day I lost my wedding ring and learned I was pregnant with Kate.

Mrs. Pratt was revealed to me after the secret-life adventure on Monday morning. I had answered an ad asking for a "woman to read to elderly lady," which sounded like a helpful, pleasant thing to do for someone. By helping people occasionally you can repay the world for giving you other adventures. But this lady, instead of being a sweet, lonely old blind person wanting to hear Proust, was an indolent, disagreeable rich one, recovering from cataracts. She thought she could stand to hear the *Saturday Evening Post,* but you could see she would rather have listened to television.

I wasn't in the mood for strangers anyway. Something—

perhaps the persistent discomfort of the bruise on my back-side—impelled me to investigate lives nearer my own, and the nearest was my friend Sandra, who owned an antique shop on Wilshire, nearby, right in the heart of all those galleries and auction places. Very logical territory for seeing Mrs. Pratt in, actually. At Sandra's, as everywhere, the fragile scent of trouble wafted to my newly aware nose. She complained about her dull life.

As I came out of Sandra's I half glimpsed an authoritative, old, huge Jaguar, the movie kind, and it looked like Sebastian driving. I realized this when it had turned the corner and I couldn't be sure, but it had seemed to be looking for a parking place, so I resolved to wait and find out. I am especially flexible about adventures on secret-life days. I thought myself quite clever, too, to have guessed that they must be coming to the Haverhorn Gallery, which I was standing in front of. I went into it first, delighted with my good fortune, and at the prospect of Patty's pleasure when she got my real-life description, from the female viewpoint, of this lady her husband spent all his time with.

Inside the gallery I was immediately accosted by a plump man looking like the spirit of Christmas, his voice all full of promise and delight, directing me to look around. "They told me, madam, that you were coming," he beamed, "and may I say, frankly, that this gave me great joy, because, as you will see, a person who understands porcelain is bound to recognize that this magnificent collection should not be broken up. Because, I tell you frankly, though these things bring more separately, it would be a shame—well, see for yourself. You just look, and I'll walk quietly along with you in case you have any questions."

"Thank you," I said, feeling deceitful at allowing myself to be mistaken for Paris Pratt, and then the real Paris Pratt came in, and there was no need to tell him which of us was the rich, important woman.

"Good morning, Mrs. Pratt," the gallery man said in a

30

different voice, and backed gently away without saying anything else. Perhaps he hated to repeat his little speech in front of me, but it is more likely that whereas I am an ordinary person ordinarily subject to the unctuous approaches of salesmen, Mrs. Pratt is clearly not, and he sensed it.

At first Mrs. Pratt appeared to be a tall, angular, disappointingly plain woman with pale hair drawn back in a bun, pale lips, low shoes, and an old-fashioned brooch. Her face was mostly concealed by a pair of giant sunglasses, like a pop-art version of a Grant Wood portrait. She walked right at the door of the gallery as if she expected it would open by electric eye, but Sebastian was there a second before she collided, and she came in without ever slackening pace. It occurred to me that she had probably never opened a door for herself in her life. Once inside she drew off her glasses as if they hurt her, and stood blinking in the gallery's gloom. Then I saw what she was really like.

She was like the soul of an elegant and beautiful woman, long dead, which had been uncorked from a bottle and now floated genie-fashion before my eyes. She was fluid, transparent. Since she had no substance, it was her spirit that affected me. This shone out of her eyes, which were huge and perfectly round, the way real eyes never are. Her voice, when I heard it, contributed to her total oddness by being high and ethereal in quality, like the phony spirit voice of a clever medium. I should have known from looking at her that Sebastian loved her, but I didn't.

They saw me, and we had an inevitable conversation full of introductions and explanations. Sebastian felt faintly chagrined, the way people often are when something private of theirs has been found out, but he was pleasant nonetheless. Mrs. Pratt said only the most conventional things, such as "How do you do?" and "Where are your children this morning?" but she said them with compelling graciousness. I can't remember much of what else we said, because, at such times, I am not able to forget myself and concentrate on the

31

details of what is happening. I was too busy thinking about what Mrs. Pratt thought of me.

We walked around together looking at the porcelain, and they made occasional remarks about a shape or glaze. Mrs. Pratt looked at me often, too, and I became convinced that she had something to say to me, though she had never seen me before and knew nothing about me, and could have had no interest in me. It was a curious thing; her face seemed to burn urgently in spite of its pallor. But although I became sure that she had something to say to me alone, that could not be said in front of Sebastian, nothing ever came except, when it was time to leave, she said, "If you care about porcelain, you must get Sebastian to bring you to see ours." And since this was all it came to, it is hard to say why I felt a significant thing had happened, but I did. I have since realized that Mrs. Pratt communicates this urgency whether she means to or not.

But I had not wholly made it up. Sebastian says that after they left, Mrs. Pratt said to him, "I *knew* your sister-in-law the second I saw her. I even knew she was somehow connected with you. Isn't it funny the way you recognize some people and some, like Emil, are forever strangers? Perhaps I should depend more upon this feeling of familiarity. Maybe you can only help people for whom you feel it."

"Fortunately, people like Karen don't need Pratt Foundation. They have families and nice lives, and they aren't artists."

"I wasn't thinking of endowing her." Mrs. Pratt laughed. "I was thinking of sending her secret, silent messages of encouragement." Sebastian gave a disgusted groan and changed the subject to porcelain.

The pattern is that something is revealed to you and something is taken away, but this doubly surprising day differed in that something was revealed to me and something was given. I had always accepted Garth's eccentricities unquestioningly

32

—you don't notice day-to-day madness the way you don't see your children grow—but that afternoon I saw that it had gone too far.

Toby was napping, and Kate and I were in the kitchen getting our usual lunch of peanut-butter sandwiches. I was standing at the sink putting the crusts down the disposer. My mother-in-law and Joan believe in making children eat crusts, but I don't eat them myself, so I don't make Kate. Cutting off crusts was one of the many secrets I kept from Garth's family. But the real point is, I was standing at the sink grinding up crusts and looking out the window when I noticed a mail truck pull up in front of the house. At first I had a pleasant feeling of expectation about a letter or a present. But something was wrong; it took me a minute to notice that the mail truck was green, the way they were a long time ago, instead of the All-American colors they are now. The driver came to the door, gave me papers to sign, argued, reassured, and finally convinced me he had brought us a mail truck, with a purchase order signed "Garth Fry, M.D." I walked out into the front yard to look at it. An old green truck, built like a milk wagon, with an open cab for jumping in and out.

My first reaction was a tepid revulsion, an oh-no-not-again feeling. As long as I'd known him, Garth had been given to coming home with funny things, and until now it had always pleased me to think he had depths of strangeness I couldn't understand. But the eccentric purchases were getting more frequent. Lately a large doghouse, although we had no dog, nine cases of canned chili con carne from a freight yard, and, of course, all those cars—three Citroëns and a Porsche. But until now nothing like this. I felt depleted, outdone; whatever Garth was expressing by buying mail trucks was certainly more compelling than my own mild adventures. Garth's mail truck seemed to tell me that however I might pretend to be a fortuneteller or an Avon lady, I was doomed by my small-ness of spirit to a life of prim convention. Or maybe Garth

33

had gone mad. Anyway, the truck was beyond my under-standing. I let the children play in the rear of it while I figured out how to drive it, though I was really afraid to move it away from the curb.

It grew dark. The mail truck continued enigmatically to sit in front of the house, a large, obtrusive possession that compelled emotion. I began to hate it intensely. I also began to hate how much it had probably cost. Garth and I had accepted between us that I had a problem about money, on account of not having had any most of my life. I was never able to be extravagant, which Garth considered a great virtue and I considered a defect in my character. Thinking about how much Garth must have paid for that mail truck made my stomach churn, as he must have known it would, and I was more miserable because I knew it would have made another person—Alma, say—laugh.

We had spaghetti and stories, and Toby threw his shoes in the toilet because that was the phase he was in. And I, remembering the worst thing—my watch—overreacted and spanked him and put him to bed wailing. His wails made me feel mean and punitive, a bad mother, and the dark shape of the mail truck reproached me from outside.

Finally I heard Garth drive up in the Porsche. I peeked out the living-room window to watch him. Looking pleased, he walked around the mail truck, climbed in the cab, opened the rear doors, slammed them, relishing the solid sound.

"Why can't you remember to get those trikes off the side-walk?" he said as he came in. "We don't need a lawsuit on our hands."

"Sorry. Did you have a good day?" I asked. He never would discuss his work—the Fry men all believe in the sepa-ration of work and home—but I could tell he had. He was wearing a certain expression, pure and swollen, which meant he had saved dozens of lives, or, at least, removed dozens of unaesthetic organs, which was satisfying no matter what happened to the patients. Being a surgeon involves peculiar psychology.

34

"Yes, very," he said, and started for the kitchen. I saw that he wasn't going to say anything about the mail truck. I followed him, trying to think of some way to ask about it without making him mad. He'd been very touchy about the chili.

"Are you hungry?" I asked, hoping he wasn't, because I hadn't saved him any spaghetti. He ate at the hospital often, or came home at funny times, so I had gotten out of the habit of fixing him supper.

"Very hungry," he said.

"There's stuff in the refrigerator," I said.

"Why don't we ever have anything good?" he asked, as he rummaged around in it.

"You keep changing your mind about what's good," I said. He found some Swiss cheese and rye bread. I tried as usual to interest him in a conversation about what kind of a day we'd had; I thought maybe I could cautiously mention how his mail truck had surprised me.

"I didn't do much today. Read, took the kids for a walk," I said. I was used to lying about what I did do on secret-life days, but knew better than to claim I had been cleaning or ironing. I should explain that I didn't do much housekeeping, not because I thought myself too good for it, but because, for reasons I had never figured out, I was terrible at it. Things always went wrong. For example, I was never able to find Kate's shoes when it came time for her to go to nursery school. She took them off in weird places, something I couldn't prevent unless I followed her around all afternoon, and if I did that, nothing else would get done. Other people seem not to have this problem, but it was typical of mine. And how can you enjoy your children, and they you, if you are always allowing shoes to come between you? I know there are mothers who play Beautiful Games about putting away shoes, but I was not one of them.

Garth started to make, and then suppressed, his usual patient but ironic remark about why was I walking and reading instead of cleaning. I guessed his unusual tact had something to do with the mail truck, but all my significant glances out the window failed to elicit a mention of it.

He took his sandwich into the study to watch the Late Show. "Want to watch? You'd enjoy watching more if you had some needlework to do," he said. Neutral enough words, but you knew he meant it as a mean remark.

Television makes me nervous, just as needlework does, so I wandered around the house, turning off lights and wondering, and feeling something restrictive about the darkness, the deep holes of rooms. The house was as stale and oppressive as a known future of infinite tedium. This house *was* the known future. I sat on the edge of the sofa and surveyed it suspiciously. There was my shelf of cookbooks, that I read in secret, a dented pewter pitcher, a few other things, haphazard, insignificant, but mine, standing out from the welter of Garth's various collections—his guns, his paints, his medical volumes, his glass paperweights, his butterflies and coins in neat picture frames, his *National Geographics*. Garth's collections gave me the same helpless drowning sensation his family gave me. I could imagine myself literally drowning in some pathetic way right before their eyes. Falling off a dock, say, and them all watching me and saying that it served me right. A respectable woman knows how to swim. And then, sitting there in my living room, I saw myself swimming for my life through a sea of tribulation, Toby and Kate perched like water wings on my shoulders, bearing aloft between them a box containing biscuits, fresh water, and our few prized possessions—me all greasy like a channel swimmer, them laughing in the spray, making our escape.

I did actually run away once, when I was a child. I remembered this now, how I stuffed a cardboard box with belongings, felt virtuous to have remembered my toothbrush, and stalked off down the sidewalk to Alma's house. Other people's formative childhood experiences have always seemed profounder than mine; I had been unjustly spanked for not picking up some spilled split peas. My father had lost

36

his temper and bruised me sorely, much as I was bruised now from my motorcycle fall.

Alma's house was on a mud road behind the Frosty-Freeze, and she was sitting in the road playing jacks. She was better than anyone at jacks because, playing on the mud road, she had developed great skill at anticipating any erratic bounce of the ball. Thinking of that now, I think of Gilbert's lines about life, which one eventually discovers one is playing "on a cloth untrue / with a twisted cue / and elliptical billiard balls." But Alma learned the game under those conditions, which in some ways gave her an advantage.

She agreed that I should run away, and even offered to come with me to show how it was done.

"I run away a lot," she said, "but then I always come home after. If you're a kid you have to come home again."

"I'm never going home," I said.

We went into Alma's house to gather things. It was a disgusting place, full of dirty upholstered furniture with exposed stuffing, ripped covers, litter of egg cartons, Pepsi bottles, fenders, and hubcaps in the living room, cats, smells, obscenely stained wallpaper. Alma kept her belongings in a lidless cardboard box underneath the sagging bed she shared with a big sister. The sister was still in it, lying there awake but saying nothing. I don't remember what Alma had in her box, except an old T shirt and a phonograph record and a fancy empty bottle on top.

We went into the orchard behind the school and from there out into the field on the other side, where we sat on the bank of the creek and picked the burrs out of our clothes. I was hungry, and my bottom still hurt, but I was very happy. Alma knew about crawfishes, orchards, everything. We ate crab apples—the real apples weren't ripe. Alma said it was all right to eat May apples as well. I had been taught they were poison. The creek was too shallow to bathe in, but Alma wrung out the old T shirt in the water and pressed it against my leg where I had scratched it in brambles. We left the

37

shirt there, and cut across the edge of the golf course to Twenty-third Avenue to the movie theater. Alma was expert at sneaking in.

We sat well down in front. First were three cartoons, and then the main feature, about a mummy who came to life and tracked down people who had disturbed his tomb, and murdered them in ghastly ways or drove them mad. I found it delicious. I don't remember the name of the second feature, but I've never forgotten anything else about it. It had pleasant, normal, real-looking people in it, one of whom turned at night into an evil, hideous panther and tore people to bits. He used to hang around places at evenfall in his friendly, human guise, and then the sky would darken, and you knew he was beginning to change, but the nice people in the movie didn't know until it was too late. Terror infused your blood, so you felt you, too, were changing outward form. Once, he was in the graveyard, and an old woman came there to weep at the grave of someone, and stayed too long, so that the gates were shut after her, and then you saw the sun go down over the hills, and the old woman kneeling in prayer, and then you heard the low growling begin. I remember shaking, and Alma holding my hand. I guess I was having a Significant Trauma. Patty, whom I once told about this, said, "Oedipal castration anxiety," but surely you don't get that if you are female? Whatever it was, I got it from the movie—nothing ever happens to me in the real world. In the movie a brutal father told his daughter to go to the store for a loaf of bread. She was a beautiful girl, with great dark eyes and a kerchief on her head to suggest they were immigrants. She was afraid to go to the store alone, at night, but the father put her out, reviling her, and shut the door of the little house after her. Outside, it was black and raining. She crept up the street. Then she heard something behind her. Human footsteps. She stopped and turned around, but couldn't see anything. She began to walk, walk faster, run. Then the scene changed to inside the mean little house. The girl was pound-ing on the door, pleading to be let in, the father refusing because she could not have gotten the bread so quickly. She was hysterical. "Please! Please!" she was shrieking. The old mother rushed to the door to open it, and the father pushed her away. "Father! Father!" We heard her last screams. Then silence. Then blood began to trickle under the door into the room, soaking the edge of the rug. No sound but the weeping of the mother, the father staring unbelievingly at the growing pool of the girl's blood.

I suddenly felt warm all over, and dizzy, as if I might throw up. I climbed over Alma into the aisle, legs weak, my hands pressed against my mouth. Alma came after me.

"Too much for you, girlie?" a man said in the lobby, laughing. Alma pushed me outside, and I felt better.

"It's just a movie," she said. "He couldn't have really sent her for a loaf of bread anyway. The store wouldn't even be open that time of night."

"It was too scary," I said.

"Do you feel better? They'll let us back in, now they seen us come out."

"I think I better go home," I said. Alma was not at all derisive, though few children would have forgone reminding me that I had said I was never going home.

"All right. But you shouldn't be afraid of things like a movie. I'm going back in. I want to see if they get him."

"All right," I said.

She hesitated, watched me, and then gave me a hug. "You shouldn't be afraid. If things are still bad at home, come back," she said. "If you want, I'll take care of you."

Alma was smaller than I, but I did want her to take care of me. Instead I walked home alone, ashamed of myself, afraid, hurt. Father was not home, but my mother was, and the peas were still all over the kitchen floor. She stepped on them as she fixed supper. I swept them up, of course, and felt my want of courage for a long time. But my sleep was troubled for a long time, too, by visions of blood coming under the door. I made a poor runaway.

And I still would. Besides, from what would I run? My

39

successful husband, my four cars, my seventeen sleeping bags, my mail truck? I wasn't really considering running away. Mostly, as I sat there, I was just wishing the secret life had been better that morning, and thinking how nice it would be to be rich and remarkable, and collect porcelain, and have an amusing man like Sebastian at my side all day.

Chapter 5

Sebastian describes thinking as he drove home Tuesday evening that he had no place in which to be completely himself. He was wondering if anybody ever did, and, if they did, whether it was a good thing. Being yourself perhaps only meant being your worst; still most people had someplace to be it in, while he, it seemed, was always poised for the demands of some pretense. At work he was comfortable, but Paris Pratt was not someone he cared to yawn or sulk or scratch in front of. At home he could sleep or sulk or be stupid when he felt stupid, but there he had to pretend to be loving and husbandly. Sebastian hoped humbly for a devoted or loving or husbandly feeling to overcome him as he pulled into his driveway, but as usual none did. The best he got was a faintly relaxed and expectant rumble, very much connected with wanting dinner and the anticipation of an undemanding silence after it. He pulled a weed out of the geranium bed by the front steps and let himself into the house.

Mark, in his pajamas, came whooping at him and was swept up. Sebastian was reassured by the normality of the paternal pleasure he always felt upon seeing the pink, excited face, and he hugged and kissed his little son. It was always quite a bit better being home than it had seemed it would be a few minutes before he got there.

"Big, big boy," Mark giggled, high in the air.

"What a big boy," Sebastian said, setting him down again.

"Sweetie?" Patty called. Sebastian disentangled Mark, who ran back to the television, and went into the kitchen. Patty looked dashing tonight, like an artist's model, her black hair hanging loose and slightly wavy from having been braided. Over black pants and blouse she wore a vivid orange burlap thing made like a carpenter's apron, with lots of pockets. She was stirring something in the oven, so he kissed her cheek and backed out of the way.

"We're eating in the living room because my stuff isn't dry here," she said. She had been making Christmas trees by pasting shell macaroni on rug cones and then spraying them gold. A number of these were standing on newspapers on the kitchen table, still sticky.

"What are we having?" Sebastian asked.

"Hamburger Stroganoff," Patty said. "Did you see the Christmas trees I made out of the *Reader's Digest?*" She vanished into the laundry and came back with another tree, made from a magazine, each leaf folded triangularly on itself and glued, the whole thing sprayed silver. Sebastian admired it, feebly.

"If we're ready to eat, I'll put Mark down," he said. He took Mark away and read him a chapter of *Wind in the Willows,* knowing, of course, that Mark was too young, and bored by it. When Mark slid off his lap and began to pull his blocks out of the cupboard, Sebastian, a little angry, put him firmly under the covers and kissed him good night.

They took their plates to the living room. Sebastian liked his living room, though it felt less his than Mrs. Pratt's did. This room was just like Patty, and the other was just like Mrs. Pratt, but *he* had chosen almost all the things in that one. Patty sat down in her little Danish chair, and Sebastian sat in his big chair, covered in orange-and-pink flowers, by the fireplace. They had an orange sofa, modern and delicate, on which people seldom sat, and a coffee table made from a

42

cut-down library table, enameled pink, littered with various whimsical objects—pink and yellow paper flowers from Mexico, a red lacquer box, three terra-cotta pots with plants in them, an imitation but interesting wooden idol from Easter Island, a papier-mâché figure Patty had made. People thought it clever of Patty to have trained Mark, still so young, to leave everything alone.

Patty said, "What did you do today?" as she always did, and Sebastian, exaggerating slightly, as he often did, said he had been at UCLA all day in Special Collections, where he had gone after driving Mrs. Pratt to a luncheon conference at noon. He told Patty something about medieval German iconology, which he had been reading about; Patty was fascinated, Sebastian was relaxed.

By this time he had adjusted to the climate of home. What he always experienced upon first coming home was, he supposed, something like cultural shock, or, coming out of Mrs. Pratt's rarefied atmosphere, the faintly stifled feeling of being too rapidly decompressed. At first it was home that seemed not quite real, or, rather, subreal, peopled by beings existing on another, lower plane, whom he visited. But after he had been there awhile, his system and his perceptions always righted themselves. Home was real, Patty and Mark and the baby were his species, flesh and blood, his razor was on the bathroom shelf, the chocolate cake was a particular favorite of his. From this properly reoriented world, Mrs. Pratt's house then seemed to be unnaturally levitated, a supernatural phenomenon. Whenever he thought of her sitting in her house thinking of him—it was a wishful construction—his mind pictured her looking down from above, like a deceased relative. He put his plate on the coffee table and stretched in his comfortable chair.

"There's a meeting we ought to go to, at the nursery school," Patty said. "Karen said she would sit if Garth got home."

"What do they want done now?" At the last parents'

meeting he had gone to, he had been roped into refinishing the schoolroom floors.

"Oh, no, it's a lecture. A man is going to speak on Parent Effectiveness. He's this psychologist who gives a course. Mrs. Hatton took it. She says it's incredible the things that very well-meaning parents do which can be avoided if you are just aware of certain very simple things one is hardly aware of. He teaches you to be aware."

"I think I'd rather be oblivious," Sebastian said.

"It just means things like listening. He apparently gives this lecture on the ego-created automatic hearing censor, or something like that. It's a psychological mechanism that blocks what children say. After she told me about it, I noticed myself. Over and over I caught myself not really listening to Mark, and it's perfectly true that a couple of times I could have avoided a big fuss with him. I know we can't take the course—it costs eighty-five dollars—but I think we should hear what he says tonight."

"All right," Sebastian said, conscientiously eschewing his automatic hearing censor, and charmed with his vision of Patty busy with her innumerable tasks, ears furiously attuned to Mark's prattle, Eric's coos. He added to his imaginary gallery of contemporary iconography a female figure with great trumpet-like ears. Patty's ears were small and brownish, and she had large brown eyes so filled with earnest enthusiasm he would have gotten up to kiss her, but he was comfortable and she had gotten up herself to carry out the plates. Something, either guilt or compassion or altruism, stabbed him. He got up, too.

"I'll do the dishes. You call Karen."

"I'll do them. We have plenty of time."

"No, let me," he said. "You look tired. I just sat around the library all day."

He didn't hear the doorbell, but he heard Patty greet someone, and, sticking his head around the kitchen door, saw Mahonri and his parents. He waved at them, his hand encased in the suds-covered rubber glove he wore because dishwater gave him a rash. He threw the pans into the dishwater to soak and came into the living room. His mother was going on one of her usual subjects, Karen, and his father was as usual trying to ignore the unpleasant.

"We were on our way over to a meeting at Church," Father Fry explained to Sebastian and Patty, "but we had a few minutes beforehand, so we thought we'd call and ask if you were planning to come along."

"Oh, we can't," Patty explained. "We have a nursery school thing."

"I say it's a family problem and a serious one," Mother Fry continued, sitting down next to Mahonri. "I can't sleep at night thinking of Garth. What's happening to him? He often doesn't go to Church, and I know he doesn't wear his garments."

"Well, Mother, for a surgeon, who has to change his clothes in the scrub room, as I believe it's called, garments are inconvenient and can be embarrassing. Remember during the war it was thought better for young Mormon men not to wear their garments in the army, because they got teased and ridiculed. To an outsider, the religious significance of a suit of underwear is likely to seem obscure, even ludicrous. And also, I believe you aren't supposed to wear nylon in an operating room—something about the electricity."

"He just doesn't look *well*," Mother Fry said. "I know he worries. What kind of religious instruction are the children getting, what kind of family attitude when their mother takes her responsibilities so lightly?"

"I think Garth looks pretty good," Mahonri said. "Funny he's never gained any weight. Or maybe that's not surprising, considering Karen's cooking."

"Yes, she doesn't do anything, can't cook, lets Garth manage everything; the children always look shabby . . ." Mother Fry said.

"Karen isn't very well organized, but she has very good

45

intentions, and she does dote on the children, even if she isn't very scientific," Patty said, and Sebastian had a similar impulse to champion an unpopular cause.

"It may be difficult being married to Karen, but I'm sure it's interesting," he said. Now both his mother and Patty fastened him with frowns.

"Yes, I'm sure that's right, quite so," Father Fry said. "We can't always justify our feelings for the woman we love, Mother." His smile for her was gallant and dismissive.

"I think Garth realizes his mistake, all right," she said.

"Karen told me Garth had insured her diamond ring against fire. She thought it was funny, but it seems to me it has sinister unconscious overtones," Patty said.

"Garth never has been practical," Mahonri said. "He just doesn't bother himself with thinking through his insurance program."

"Karen is not a happy person," Mother Fry said. "I doubt she ever will be, until she accepts the duties and responsibilities of being a married woman and a mother."

"That's right; duty isn't always pleasant, but it's the solid thing in life," Mahonri agreed. Sebastian thought this a suitable sentiment for a father of seven.

"Karen could learn a lot from you and Patty and Joan, if she only would," Mahonri continued.

"Well, that's just it." Father Fry's jovial voice indicated that he had found a resolution for the discussion. "You ladies just don't realize what an example you are. You're a tough act to follow, as the saying goes. Very few women come up to your standards, Mother, or could if they tried!"

Sebastian was interested to see whether his mother would buy this. She did, almost. The slightest smile twitched her cheeks, but she routed it.

"Karen must be made to grow up," she said. "It's important to all of us. One rotten apple spoils the barrel. You'll see."

"Look here—it's time to go. Imagine! We have to hustle," Father Fry said, rising. "Meeting starts at seven-thirty."

46

"Well, good night," Mahonri said. "Come over and see Joanie, Patty. She likes to have company. She gets feeling tied down sometimes," he said. He always manifested this rhetorical concern for Joan's plight.

When the family had gone, Patty and Sebastian went back to the kitchen. Sebastian put on his rubber gloves again, and she inspected the way her Christmas trees were drying.

"It's so important to your mother and father that the family be solid," she said. "That's nice, really."

"Mother feels very missionary about Karen, apparently," Sebastian said.

"Why do you think it would be so interesting to be married to Karen?" she asked, with exaggerated petulance, as if she knew she sounded silly, but very much wanted to know underneath.

"She's a lively girl," he began, and stopped, seeing signs of real crossness, which on Patty were a characteristic droop of the chin and faintly asthmatic flair of the nostrils. Sebastian tugged at her hair.

"She'd drive me mad in a day or two," he assured her, "but I hated to hear them talk that way about her cooking." He expected to see the crossness fade from her expression, but it didn't. He began to run fresh hot water in the dishpan.

"They saw you, you know," she said, voice a little higher, crosser.

"What?" Sebastian did not understand, though she was looking at his maneuvers with the pans.

"You might as well have come right out and said it. See, here I am doing dishes for my lazy wife. You couldn't have made it any clearer," she said. Sebastian paused to think. He had never been sure if it was better to humor the irrational notions of women or to ignore them.

"I like to help you, so I was helping you," he said, employing measure and reason.

"It wasn't help. It was a reproach. And what do you think they think?"

"Well, that your sweet disposition and many accomplishments are a disguise. That really you're a shrew who makes me do dishes. And I expect Mahonri'll tell Joan, don't you?" But she was not to be teased.

"You think that's so funny. That's exactly what they'll think, and do." She took a deep breath and lowered her voice. She had had a course on marital relations in college and was very much oriented toward seeing both sides of a question. "I guess it's hard for you to understand a woman's point of view on this, but suppose Father or Mahonri came over and I was out fixing the car?"

"A blow to my masculinity from which I'd never recover," Sebastian said. "No, actually I'd feel bad; because Mahonri would go home and ask Joan why the hell she never fixed the car, and poor Joanie has enough to do."

"Oh, I know you don't care, Sebastian, but please try to understand that I find it embarrassing to have people thinking I'm not good at what I do, and need help with it. A person's role is a very important thing psychologically. That's why people die when they retire. They lose their role identity."

"Sweetheart, are you saying that me doing the dishes will kill you?"

"No, no, of course not. But you *are* trying to take my role. It isn't just the dishes, but that's a good example. It's because you aren't basically very certain about your own, if you want my opinion. I mean, you wouldn't find Honn or Garth doing the dishes. Honn has his role and Joan has hers and they respect each other. You don't respect me. That's why you help me. Just because Mrs. Pratt doesn't ever touch a dish, you think what I do is nasty and degrading, so it's doing me a big favor to help me out with it. Well, how do you think that makes me feel? A person has to feel *important,* Sebastian."

"Oh, come on, this is a bit much, Patty. I think you have a damned hard job, which you do beautifully, and that you deserve a little rest sometimes. If I'm depriving you of your basic satisfactions, I'll quit doing the dishes, okay? I've

48

always thought Honn behaves like a swine to Joan, but I see I was wrong."

"You aren't very insightful," Patty agreed. "I'm sorry. I know I overreacted."

"And how do you mean I'm not sure of my own role?" Sebastian asked, hating himself for being intrigued by Patty's absurd psychologizing.

"I meant that I think it's hard for a man to work for a woman. He's just bound to feel a little emasculated. I know that's a terrible thing to say, and you're probably not even aware of it."

"I certainly am not," Sebastian said.

"And it certainly doesn't show. I didn't mean that. But you're so used to helping women. You help her and then you come home and help me."

"Instead of filling some nice normal male role, you mean," Sebastian said, irritated in spite of himself.

"Oh, Bas," she said, touching his arm, "I'm just silly." She got a dish towel and began drying things out of the rack. "Maybe we shouldn't go to the meeting tonight. I'll call Karen."

In a minute she said, "Well, we'll go, but we'll come right home afterward, and not even stay for refreshments." Her sweet voice was meaningfully soft.

"Yes, dear," Sebastian said, mock meekly. "Where have you put the Ajax?"

Chapter 6

Sebastian and Patty co-operated, but Garth and I had always had a covert struggle about dishes. If I let them accumulate for too many days, he would do them up with a great show of huffy virtue, but if I washed them promptly he would pull out lots of saucers and glasses and plates, and, in the process of fixing his supper, dirty every one, seemingly on purpose. So I never knew whether to do them or let them sit. We had not discussed this, of course. I *had* finally managed to mention the mail truck; I simply asked him please to put it in the garage. He did, but this meant parking two more Citroëns in front of the house, and the sight of them there, expensive and unnecessary, filled me with despair.

"It's crazy, Garth," I told him. "We just don't need four cars and a mail truck. I don't know what's the matter with you."

"Stick to your knitting, cookie," he said, with his most charming smile. Then he walked out the kitchen door muttering "Knitting, ha," and stopped in the front yard to shout, "If you only *could* knit! I could knit better than you!"

And his face, his pretty, boyish face, was contorted with rage, which I thought awfully odd. People don't usually care so much about whether their wives can knit or not. It must be something else, I thought, and put it out of my mind as well as I could, but something cold sat on my spirit.

It was sitting on all of us, like a capricious virus that gives one person fever, another a boil. Its symptoms were various, but in Patty, hardy Patty, it seemed to appear simply as a whine, a quaver, and an intensification of her chronic hatred for her dining-room table. I noticed this on Wednesday morning when I went to her house to baby-sit while she did some last-minute things for Mark's third-birthday party that afternoon.

She was looking well but seemed unhappy and restless, the way I felt myself. I tried to cheer her up by complimenting her on her most recent decorating improvements. Decorating, she often said, fulfilled her. In fact, her house had such a fulfilled look that one longed for a shabby or ugly object in it. Nothing was its original color because everything had been painted to harmonize with the whole. Patty is the type who picks her color scheme first, probably choosing it on the basis of its psychological correspondence to her temperament. Beige, orange, and hot pink conveyed the essence of Patty's modern, ardent, and feminine nature—you saw that she was a sweet girl but so good in bed. Patty is also good at making ugly things into beautiful something elses, as, ugly old trunks into beautiful end tables. Her only difficulty is not knowing when to stop; everything in her rooms seems suddenly to be something else, painted another color, having another use, reminding you of those puzzle drawings of rooms in which you must discover dozens of misplaced objects concealed upside down in the folds of the curtains and the pattern of the carpet.

She sighed. "There's so much I have left to do. I'm repainting the cornices tonight. They just aren't right the way they are now. Do you see what I mean?"

"Mmmm," I mumbled.

"Sebastian doesn't. He thinks I'm silly, but of course men can't really be expected to take an interest in artistic things." A strange remark, considering that the artistic was Sebastian's special province. "At Morris College they're thinking of requiring a course in domestic design, that is, decorating. I think it would be a good thing. Most American homes are atrocious. And then, of course, the men never expect anything better, so the system just perpetuates." Morris College for Women, of which her father is president, still looms large in Patty's life, and one can often detect her father's words there as well. Now her face tightened in a strange, mad way. "Come in here," she said, and led me to the dining room. Toby was already there, sitting under the table and looking up from under his hair as from under a toadstool. I resolved to shear him, but it was so sweet I hated to.

"This dining-room table is driving me out of my mind," she said, with a repressed quiver which made me for a minute think she meant this more than metaphorically. "It just isn't right in here. I try and try. Everything else is so nice, but this, this is so *here* and huge, and Sebastian simply will not hear of getting another one. Anything I want, Sebastian usually gets for me; I don't know why he's so against a new table."

There is never any point in encouraging Patty to talk about her table, so I reminded her of her errands. She found her purse, kissed Mark, and ran. I was not deceived by her complaints, of course. Patty's dining-room table had been a constant irritation to her from the day she saw it, and she had invoked it ever since, mostly on "those days," as the source of all her woes. You simply assumed, when Patty talked about the table, that something else was bothering her.

The table was, she has always said, the only thing about which she and Sebastian have ever disagreed. It was a wedding present, the only dark shadow on an otherwise perfect experience. She must have been thinking about her wedding now; I noticed as I dashed to save her Easter Island figure from Toby that her album of wedding photographs lay open on the coffee table. Patty beautiful in a white veil, handsome Sebastian, the happy faces of her parents and the Frys smiled up at me, flowers all around.

I hate old photographs. What bothers me, I suppose, is the guileless, unsuspecting look the faces wear, not knowing those things will happen to them that you, looking back at them, know have happened. Confidently their faces are recorded, and you know the confidence has mostly been misplaced. Still, not much had happened to suggest that Patty's bridelike radiance was ill-founded. She and Sebastian had been married four years, long enough for two babies and to make all the arrangements of their coexistence—who shall pay bills, who shall paint walls, who shall get up with which baby when he cries at what hour. Four years married is a happy degree, as I remember. The frictions of newness have worn off a four-year marriage, but one is not yet sensible of the number of years that lie ahead, urgent but blank, like canvas stretched over a pit. Or perhaps Patty was beginning to see them ahead. Something, anyway, was the matter.

Patty had met Sebastian when she had been out of college only a few months and had taken a job as an airline stewardess. She liked it; she didn't attach much significance to serving cocktails and dinner, but there were occasionally people who became airsick, and you never knew when someone might have a heart attack or hysterics. Patty's mother worried about crashes, but her father thought it a very suitable occupation for young women and had instigated courses in it at Morris College. He was fond of waggishly quoting her a statistic to the effect that stewardesses always caught desirable husbands.

Patty wasn't looking for one, particularly. Like most people who feel called to things, she had no calculation, and she always assumed, not that marriages are made in heaven, but that the right one would make unmistakable earthly manifestations; one had only to keep one's eyes open and be oneself. Sebastian therefore caught her by surprise.

She met him on an airplane on his way to catalogue a large collection of porcelain he and Mrs. Pratt had bought from an Oak Park estate and subsequently gave to the Art Institute. He was older than anyone she had dated before, had complexities of feature—lines beginning, skin darker, beard harsher, marks of a man nearly thirty. He was handsome and had assurance, was already formed. Patty was captured by her fancy of him seated in his study writing scholarly treatises on old bronze, and felt very callow and humble in the presence of interests that had preceded her and would survive her absence. She listened on tiptoe to him talk about his work, like Dorothea listening to Casaubon. On her days off she went to the Art Institute where he was working and wandered around; he took frequent breaks to show her this and that and kiss her in the little room with the big Rubens in it. Sebastian's kisses were as thrilling as his cultivation.

Sebastian's kisses were thrilling because they promised what they lacked. They were lazy and amused kisses, not because his mind was not on them, but because he, the man of experience, almost thirty, could see no point in the more serious kind of kissing behind a statue with a museum guard peeking, and Patty, used to the desperate embraces of college boys, found much in his self-control to occupy her imagination. Though she hated the idea that he was a divorced man, the realization that he had once been married was physically exciting. He was acquainted with the mysteries, the leisurely, profound experiences of wedded love. Her fancy, which could not supply the details, invested him with the knowledge of innumerable nameless pleasures, and her resulting ardor got her taken to bed soon and satisfactorily. She had had some experience with impatient college boys. Sebastian was a revelation.

Premarital love-making was perhaps the only rebellious thing Patty had ever done. She had been imbued from the earliest age with the wholesome ideals of Morris College, which institution is dedicated to the task of fitting young women for their subsequent roles as homemakers, community leaders, informed voters, and guardians of the young. Basic to this program is the unexceptionable principle that girls should be virgins when they marry, and Patty, whose very father was the leading supporter of this precept, was almost obliged to disregard it. She displeased her family later in the matter of religion, but because religion is not considered as important as virginity in Illinois that didn't really count as a major kick at the traces.

Morris College disapproved of divorce, too, on sociologic rather than religious grounds, and was proud of the fact that Morris girls get them less often than the general population does. Patty's parents were therefore not pleased that Sebastian was a divorced man, though Patty convinced them it had been only a brief, youthful mistake, and at least there were no children involved. Dr. and Mrs. Freed were delighted with Sebastian in other respects. He had charm and good looks, and, in spite of his peculiar profession, could talk sensibly on investments. And he was able to assure Mrs. Freed of the excellence of several pieces of inherited early-American furniture; altogether he seemed to be about as suitable a prospective son-in-law as a person could ask.

Patty was aware and not entirely proud that she set a lot of store by the wedding itself. Sebastian had tried to dissuade her from an elaborate affair, not because he minded going through it, but because it seemed unnecessary. Patty was a little provoked that it seemed less important to him; it reminded her that he had already had the solemn experience, and his realism almost quenched her radiant expectations.

"I know it's just a ritual," she told him, "but I don't think a man can understand how important it is to a woman. It's something she's planned for since she was a tiny girl. It's just practically instinctive. As long as I can remember, I've been changing my mind about silver patterns." She was supported in this by her mother, who said, "You'd always be sorry if you didn't have a lovely wedding to look back on." In spite of the ominous quality of this remark, Patty quoted it; but Sebastian remained disappointingly vague through it all—

would not even discuss the choice of a silver pattern. And he was supposed to know a lot about silver.

He was similarly vague and masculine about the wedding gifts. She supposed it was expecting too much of a man to ask him to join with her in delighted contemplation of an electric coffeepot—and he didn't even drink coffee—or to help her decide which of the toasters to keep, but she would have liked him to seem transported, as she was, with the prospects a toaster implied: a lifetime of breakfasts together. Patty pored over her wedding gifts until she was accused of being acquisitive.

And she began to be afraid of flying. It was a superstitious dread that God would not let her anticipated great happiness come to pass.

She flew into Los Angeles about two weeks before the wedding with an overweight suitcase full of silver and sheets to take to the apartment she and Sebastian had rented and were furnishing. Sebastian wasn't at the airport to meet her, so she took a cab to the apartment, a cute place in Westwood, near the University and not too far from his parents'.

The living room, which had seemed on each previous visit to be so empty—they had bought only one chair—was now incomprehensibly full, occupied almost entirely, it seemed, by a great, black, legged object. She blinked. It was a table. She was dumfounded. It was an old, gigantic, room-swallowing table. Her first thought was that the motherly landlady, always tapping on the door, beaming in and shaking her head over the emptiness, must have brought it up from the basement for them. She walked dubiously around it. Or perhaps Sebastian's mother had lent it. Her house was crowded with furniture. She could not connect it with Sebastian in any other way.

"What *is* it?" she asked, after a minute.

"A wedding present." Sebastian smiled. He walked over to the table and pressed his hand hard against the top, leaving his palm print in the wax. He rubbed at the mark. "It doesn't

56

need to be this big. I put the drop leaves up. I was looking at it."

Patty took a minute to understand that this table was hers. "A wedding present?"

"From Mrs. Pratt. I hadn't even seen it. She must have done some hunting around. It's exceptionally fine."

"Antique," Patty said faintly.

"Seventeen-twenty, seventeen-fifty. A fantastic table, really. She has a similar one, that I bought, but it isn't as fine as this. The legs are perfect, and the feet. Beautiful condition and perfect proportions."

"It's lovely," Patty said, feeling wan. The big black table blighted her indistinct but cozy visions of delicious intimate little suppers. Where on earth would they put it? "It seems so large," she said. Sebastian squatted down and fumbled underneath to release the drop leaves. It was still large.

"It must be very valuable," she said, to say something.

"Fifteen hundred, maybe," Sebastian said. At this Patty was even more affected. She was impressed that Sebastian was so highly thought of at work, and depressed because they obviously couldn't think of disposing of an object so valuable, and humiliated because it still looked like a piece of old, ugly secondhand furniture to her—the kind of thing you think of as having been a good piece in its day.

The table loomed like an interloper, representing the world, intruding upon her conception of private connubial bliss. It had been inflicted upon her, and remained her severest affliction, a convenient scapegoat for her every little woe, from her wedding day until now.

Chapter 7

Now it was afternoon, time for the party, and the table was heaped with presents, presided over by a papier-mâché elephant, his howdah filled with bright favors for the eleven Fry children come to celebrate Mark's being three. I was in the back yard supervising farmer-in-the-dell, which bored the older children and confused the younger ones, but is one of the few games I know. I heard Mother Fry come in the house, heard her rich voice congratulating Patty on the lovely display, heard Patty's sweet voice praising Mother Fry's presents. Mother and Father Fry make something of a production about Giving, are always careful not to let gifts from them be obscured in birthday or Christmas confusion, and make either a separate entrance or a separate occasion to ensure that the children know how generous their grandparents are. Patty, understanding this, was raving enthusiastically about a tricycle Mother Fry had brought. Outside, Joan's Judith, the cheese, began to cry, drowning out the conversation, so I became the cheese, to mollify her, and all the children were delighted. They circled me, shouting, "Aunt Karen's the cheese. The cheese stands alone!"

Then we played statues, and they all got grass stains. Joan, Patty, and Mother Fry sensibly stayed in the house until it was time for the cake and treats. Joan had baked the cake, five layers, each a different color and flavor.

"This is the sort of cake you made for the bake sale, isn't it, Joan?" Mother Fry asked. "I tried to get over to get a piece, but by the time I could leave the Steering Committee Booth, it was completely gone. I believe your cakes sell out as fast as mine used to." In spite of this backhanded reminder that Mother Fry now contributed at a more responsible level, Joan looked pleased. Then, a few minutes later, I went into the kitchen to refill the lemonade pitcher and surprised a tear on Patty's cheek. For an odd instant I thought she was crying because Joan had been praised. But that wasn't it, of course.

"It's the silliest thing," she apologized. "It was something I thought of this morning, and every time I think about it, I just can't help it, there I am crying. It's absolutely silly. . . ." But then we had to go tend to the opening of the presents, and I didn't hear any more.

Only a few incidents marred the children's behavior: Kate spilled her ice cream and orange drink both, and Joan's Peter and Brigham, eleven and twelve, were somewhat impatient with the whole thing, and with Mark, who wouldn't let them carry his presents off to be played with properly by them, and whispered dreadful scatology to each other—"Mark is wee-wee"—and had to be sent from the table. But we got through it all, and made them watch television while we cleaned up.

This was my chance to tell my big story, about seeing the real, live Mrs. Pratt herself. Mother Fry and Joan were interested, a triumph for me, but tears came to Patty's eyes again.

"Sebastian came home last night with terrible bruises," she wailed. Bruises, mentioned in that tone of voice, rightly or wrongly suggest to me badges of carnal sin, though I had not thought of men getting them.

"All over his forearm," she continued disappointingly. "Do you know what from? A bowstring!" Her eyes puckered angrily. "A bowstring. He goes to work every day and spends his time shooting a bow and arrow. Is that what she hires him for, an archery partner?"

59

We murmured sympathetically.

"Don't you see what it must be doing to his self-respect?" Patty continued. "He just says it's part of the job. That's what he always says about everything. But I can't help thinking it must bother him deep down inside. I know it bothers me. I don't care what they say, a woman needs to respect her husband's work. Don't you think?"

"Certainly," Mother Fry said. "A woman is very important in the career of her husband. Goodness knows there were times enough I didn't want to get involved with Father's professional responsibilities. When the boys were little I must have given three parties a week, and that's an exhausting job. But as Father has always said, a man goes no farther than his wife can go with him."

"Well, I can't seem to help Sebastian. He doesn't ask me," Patty said. "Just try to explain to somebody what it is Sebastian does! I can't even explain it to my own parents. I think they think he's some sort of male stenographer."

"Oh, Patty, you can certainly say he's Mrs. Pratt's curator," Mother Fry said, annoyed.

"Just because he goes around to antique shops with her? Sometimes I think I ought to insist on him getting out. For his own sake. And for the kids, too. Katy is so proud of Garth, I heard her in there today saying to Markie, 'My daddy is a doctor,' and she was so proud."

"I don't think a wife ought to interfere in her husband's business," Joan said. "There's women's work and men's work, and they aren't the same thing."

Mother Fry smiled at her. "When you have a good husband, trust him," she said—somewhat inconsistently, it seemed to me—to Patty. "It will all come right in the hereafter, as *my* mother used to say." And that remark, for some reason, was the *coup de grâce*. Patty put down a heap of crumpled wrapping paper and simply howled.

"That's it, that's just it," she cried. "I never thought of it until this morning."

60

"Why, Patty, what is it?" Mother Fry asked.

"The hereafter. Oh, I know it's silly, but maybe a convert takes these things more seriously than other people."

That Patty's sobs had something to do with Mormonism made Joan and Mother Fry edge closer. Patty's faith was both the family pride and the family standard. No born Mormon was willing to let Patty seem more zealous and devout than he; she kept them all up to the mark. For the same reason, they cherished her occasional questions, innocent misinterpretations, reminders that she had freely come to them in the recognition of their truth.

Patty had become a Mormon shortly after she became a Fry. She had taken to marriage with greatest happiness, and to housekeeping in their little apartment, and to the company of her new mother and sisters-in-law. Then, several weeks after the honeymoon, when all her shelf paper was down, and every closet had sachets, she was visited by two ladies who identified themselves as stake missionaries from the Mormon Church. She entertained them, to be cordial, but she was at first a trifle piqued, thinking that Sebastian or his family had caused them to be sent. Sebastian's religion had not seemed an issue between them because it did not seem very important to him, and after she had learned that to marry a Mormon would not compromise any of her vaguely pious Presbyterian principles—it wasn't like marrying a Catholic— she had ceased to think about it. Now it was forced to her attention again, both by these ladies and by the many church activities in which the Fry family seemed to be involved. Patty felt that it would be rude, especially to Mother and Father Fry, to refuse to listen to the missionary ladies, so she did. They began to come weekly and to talk in a modest, sensible, rather impressive way about their religion, and to leave things for her to read. She read them. Gradually, without experiencing any startling spiritual revelations, she began to see that there would be many advantages to becoming a Mormon herself. She would be much more a part of the

61

family activities. More particularly, she was convinced of the advantages of the Mormon Church to children, and of the benefits of a family united in a single religious faith. Sebastian seemed pleased when she finally expressed a desire to join his church, though he assured her she need not do so on his account. His family was simply delighted, of course, except me; I thought it peculiar.

Patty's own family found it more than peculiar, they found it, at first, funny, as if Mormonism were a comic parody of a religion, and finally, when they saw she was serious, they found it appalling. It was clear from their letters that they had always thought of Mormons—Patty could remember that she had done so, too, before meeting Sebastian—as anachronistic bearded bigamists in a quaint colony in the West. Patty realized that her mother was still worried about plural marriages, and wrote long explanatory letters, and finally received a surly message saying they supposed she must do what she must do.

She did. Curiously it was not until she was formally baptized a Mormon that she had any profound religious experience, as if the religion reserved the real illuminations to its initiates. She was baptized by Father Fry, on a Saturday night at the stake house, with the whole family in attendance. Although she had been taught to regard baptism by immersion as vulgar, practiced by ignorant people in the South, her baptism was by immersion and was a thoroughly dignified, though uncomfortable, experience. It was solemn and purifying, and this in spite of the fact that the service was conducted by her relatives, in their ordinary clothes, on a Saturday night. During the ceremony and after, and at the Sacrament service on Sunday, when she was given the Holy Ghost, she was infused with a feeling of joy and conviction quite unlike anything she had ever known. She tried, self-consciously, to describe it to Sebastian, but she found herself unable to express her feeling. It did not seem specifically to involve God or particular points of theology, was more a

62

total sensation of giftedness and goodness, the conviction that however wrong she or other things might seem, their ultimate rightness was assured. Most impressively came a feeling of obligation to herself, to her unborn children, to the community of good people who had accepted her, to be a serene, strong woman. And she now felt more than ever a Fry, sealed to Sebastian and her loved ones for eternity.

It was over this point of Mormon doctrine, sealing, that Patty had been making herself miserable the day of Mark's party.

"It just came to me all of a sudden, something I had never, never thought of before," she said. "I was washing out a load of garments, and for some reason it just popped into my mind to wonder what kind of garments you would wear in the afterlife." The doctrine of an anthropomorphic afterlife, she has often told me, is very pleasant after you get used to it. She had had little trouble accepting it; you just decide to accept it. But she had always been prey to irreverent visions, such as the one that morning, of Sebastian and her strolling down some street in Paradise clad only in their nylon chemises, with the neat appliqués at nipple and crotch. Then her mind endowed them with a whole line of descendants trooping after them in garments.

"And then—I don't know why this never occurred to me before—I suddenly thought, Carola will be there, too." Sebastian's first wife, Carola.

"And I can't tell you how it felt. It just twisted my heart. It was awful. I just began to *bawl*. And every time I think of it, I start all over again. Oh, I know it's silly, but . . ."

Joan and Mother Fry knew a religious crisis when they saw one, and showed their concern. Patty actually looked more hopeful now, as if she expected they could tell her it wasn't true.

"Well, it is true that Carola was sealed to Sebastian in Temple," Mother Fry admitted. "But since everything is perfection in heaven, I know it won't bother you there."

63

"But it bothers me now. I just can't bear the thought of sharing him. I mean, eternity is such a long time, Mother Fry." With this she looked embarrassed. She had never gotten quite used to speaking with complete seriousness of people moving around and having feelings and making love and so on in heaven. Her Protestant upbringing had taught her to regard heaven as sort of a state of disembodied consciousness if it was anything, and it was hard to lose the habit, however much her real beliefs had changed. "Are you sure they weren't unsealed some way when they were divorced?"

"No, it was a civil divorce," Mother Fry said, still at a loss for comfortable words.

"It may be a relief to have someone take him off your hands part of the time," Joan said.

"Presumably everybody gets along in Paradise, don't they?" I asked, but since I am not authorized to speak on Mormon matters, Mother Fry frowned at me.

"No, no," Patty said, "I know, but if you love someone you just don't want to share him."

"Well, I can understand how you feel, Patty," Mother Fry said. "The word of God, naturally, has not always taken evil things like divorce into consideration. You talk to your Bishop about this, and we'll talk to Father, too. I think they can reassure you."

"If it's all true, think what it will be like," Patty said. "Sharing your husband with another woman until the end of time."

Chapter 8

I've never been sure what it was I was sharing *my* husband with. I couldn't understand him at all. He called me from his study Wednesday night to ask if he could have some popcorn to eat while he was watching television.

"Karen, I'm so *hungry*," he called. "Popcorn or a sandwich or *something*." So I made him a peanut-butter sandwich and took it in. As soon as he saw me, he pulled some needles and a ball of yarn out of a sack and began to knit. And he *could* knit better than I. He'd learned, it seems, as a first-year surgical resident, to develop his manual dexterity. This made me uneasy, most uneasy, so I performed propitiative rituals the rest of the week—made the beds early and had dinner on the table when Garth got home—put in order my own little corner of the world. On Thursday afternoon, while Patty and Joan were at quilting, I took the eleven children to the beach, a great energetic gesture of co-operation with life. Usually we just wandered crossly in Joan's back yard.

On Friday morning I went out to apply for a job editing a periodical called *World Rhythm*, dedicated to the philosophy that all natural, social, and cultural phenomena recur at predictable intervals. People from all over wrote in with data proving that there are more salmon in Nova Scotian waters every ninth year, that commodities outperform stocks every fourth year in March, that civilization destroys itself roughly every millennium. But it is difficult to fit yourself into these cosmic plans.

Family dinner, at any rate, recurred at predictable weekly intervals, and I was not prepared for it. I'd been assigned garlic bread and salad—well within my range of competence —but when I did the marketing on Friday afternoon I forgot to buy the necessary lettuce and things. When I realized this on Saturday, I also remembered Garth's criticism of my cake, and how he had said he wished I wouldn't take anything. So I decided not to. Garth either pretended not to or didn't notice.

I lingered in the Fry patio, postponing the moment I would have to walk into the kitchen empty-handed. Toby had learned to walk along the narrow picnic-table bench, tottering precariously. Katy and I watched him and tried to coax him to jump off the end into my arms, but he wasn't quite ready for that. His eyes rolled mistrustfully, as if we were trying to lure him into folly and trouble.

Mahonri's car, sagging like a dachshund in the middle under the great weight of its burden, crept up the hill and lodged in the parking space behind the house. Rivulets of children began trickling down the steps of the patio, as if the beleaguered auto were perspiring them. Through the windshield I could see Joan kneeling on the front seat and rummaging behind it for the maternal paraphernalia that always accompanies her. Joan is one of those people who, if they are going, say, to the beach, take along a hamper of food, a cooler of pop, an umbrella, an army blanket, a radio, sun-tan lotion, changes of clothes for the children, spare bathing suits and caps, inflatable toys, toys for digging, reading matter, toys for building, back rests, a playpen, and the dog. I vaguely admire this, because I am someone who takes only her children and a couple of towels, and always forgets things like money and sun-tan lotion. But the odd thing is that I usually find a dime or a shovel in the sand. I

66

have always thought there was some kind of moral in that, for Joan and for me. For me: can you really count on finding a dime, or does it only work if your luck continues to surprise you? For Joan: if you are prepared for everything, will anything ever happen to you?

Mahonri was standing by the car waiting for her, his hands in his pockets and his expression the usual one he wore around his family, a mask of detachment through which came peeping embarrassment, astonishment, and faint pride, an expression such as he might wear if his trousers had suddenly been torn off to reveal, not only nakedness, but exceptional manliness. His expression tells you he is a man much burdened, but a man equipped to handle trouble, and beget a whole lot more of it.

Suddenly his patriarchal posture crumpled under the demoralizing weight of a diaper bag, an armful of sweaters, and some coloring books. Joan dipped behind the seat again and thrust her arms into something. Then she was out of the car. By Mahonri's expression you now saw that he wouldn't be holding these things if it weren't a special occasion. Their children, jumping all around me, began to shout, "See what Mom has" and "Look at Mom."

Joan was wearing a nice print dress, low shoes, and a stole of mink in one of those odd but lovely colors. It was a beautiful fur, generously cut, long and luxurious, and Joan looked lovely in it, except for a demure, too-pink tint that had come into her face. You could see that although she was trying to be matter-of-fact, she was stunned with pleasure to own a nice thing, all hers.

She kept saying, "Isn't it amazing?" And it was. Patty and Mother Fry rushed into the patio with other exclamations, and we all, with that instinct which makes women appreciate and applaud expensive presents from men, no matter what and no matter who gets them, circled Joan admiringly, and Joan turned on her axis to shine from every angle. Mahonri handed me his armload of sweaters and slipped away, but we

67

continued to demonstrate. It ended when Joan pointed out that it was a hot day. The stole was passed among us, praised, hefted, slipped around each of us, and then deposited in the coolest closet.

"You can wear mink, Joan," Mother Fry said in the kitchen. "You look nice in it. That's the great misfortune of being short like me, as I've explained to Father many's the time. A man likes to see his wife dressed up in mink."

We had not exhausted the topic by the time dinner was served. It was the usual scene. Father Fry sat at the head of the table, beaming rosily. At the opposite end, Mother Fry, after two last-minute trips to the kitchen, settled in and snatched up her napkin.

"Ah, ah," she exclaimed over us, "isn't this fun?" And we agreed, in various murmurs, that it was.

"Mahonri, your bride is quite a vision in mink," Mother Fry said, proud of him for being such a splendid husband, a reflection on his upbringing.

"Isn't she, though? It's a funny thing how I happened to get the ticket," he said. There was a small female hush.

"Ticket?" Mother Fry repeated.

"The ticket to the Market Queen drawing," Joan said quickly, and with a gay laugh, though I think from the look she gave Mahonri that she hadn't wanted him to tell us this. We had been thinking he had bought her the fur, and she had let us think so.

"Actually, I stopped in to buy some cigarettes for my office. I was having clients in that afternoon. This new Market Queen was just opening up, so I stopped there. Often at these openings they have balloons and orchids and whatnot, makes something nice to take back to the family. They were having a drawing, so I filled out a couple of address cards and dropped them in a barrel. Yesterday Joanie got a phone call saying I'd won first prize!"

"Imagine, buying cigarettes, how ironical," Joan said, her face red.

"You didn't have to be there to win," Mahonri said.

"Honn has always been lucky," Mother Fry said. "I remember the time he won the ice skates in the *Children's Way* contest."

"Ice skates in California. I got a lot of good out of them," Mahonri said with a reminiscent smile, pleased at being reminded that he is one of nature's lucky ones.

"About as much good as Joan will . . ." Sebastian began, and instantly subsided. A second of silence reproached him for this accurate but tactless observation.

"Think how cozy one would feel just knowing it was in the closet," I said, hoping to ease things.

"The two of you will have to do a lot of gay things now," Patty said, perhaps with the same motive, but Patty isn't terribly tactful either.

"When Joanie got that phone call, she said she almost fainted. She called me right up. The funny thing is, I wasn't too surprised. I'd had a premonition about the thing. Well, that little trip to the grocery store sure saved me a lot of money," Mahonri said.

"You were considering *buying* a mink stole?" Father Fry asked, in the alert tone he reserves for discussions of money.

"Karen is really going to make *my* life miserable now," Garth said, perhaps meaning to joke, but making it sound as if I would tease him for a mink of my own.

"All women want mink, Father," Sebastian said. "It's both socially determined and innate, like the desire to marry."

"I don't," I said, which was tactless, but I was resenting Garth's remark.

"Well, maybe they do, Sebastian," Father Fry said. "I remember having to do quite a bit of explaining to your mother about—what was it?—a seal coat, I remember. Her sister Rachel had bought herself one. Of course Rachel was still single and teaching school. A family has to be doing pretty well before it can allocate its funds to fur. Of course Mother was a very young girl then."

69

Mother Fry handed around the shrimp bisque, Joan's delicious creation. It was hard to imagine Mother Fry longing for a seal coat. She frowned.

"I certainly had not been teasing Mahonri for a mink stole," Joan said defensively.

"I've always considered fur unbecoming to me," Mother Fry said. "Frankly, a good cloth coat, well styled, is more practical and usually more chic."

"When you get right down to it, what does every fat grocer's wife want? A mink stole. It's so bourgeois—they even have them in the Sears catalogue," Garth said. Joan turned to him, startled, and opened her mouth.

"Garth means it's bourgeois to hanker after a mink stole. It's lovely to have one, of course," I said.

"I'm quite sure Mahonri was not planning to waste money on such a thing," Joan said to Father Fry in a voice that was faint but confident of her husband's wisdom and authority.

"It's natural for a man to want the best for his wife," Mahonri said. Mother Fry beamed at this appropriate sentiment. Father Fry nodded benignly at Mother Fry. Joan turned to Mahonri, mouth still slightly open, and an inscrutable flicker in her eye. Patty turned a radiant and loving smile upon Sebastian, as if to say that she knew there would be closets of mink for her in this world, regardless of what happened in eternity. And then everybody turned sour again.

"Do you think you should buy cigarettes for your clients, Honn?" his mother asked him. "It's one thing to tolerate smoking—you have to, I understand—but providing the cigarettes . . . ?"

Father Fry and Honn smiled indulgently at her without troubling to take the subject up.

"It's just hospitality," Joan said, defending her husband's principles.

"I don't think they should," Patty said, with her convert's ardor. "I don't even offer liquor to my own parents. When they come to my house they just accept that I don't serve it," she said.

"When they come to visit Patty, they sneak off to bars," Sebastian said.

"Oh, Bas!" Mother Fry laughed. She considers everything he says hilarious. This is because she thinks of him as her witty son. I think it wrong of mothers to analyze the characters of their children. It can't be done, and the danger is that the children may come to believe what their mothers have constructed. To Mother Fry, Mahonri is the strong, sturdy one, and Garth, God help him, is sensitive. Mother Fry is careful not to injure his feelings, and is a regular vigilante to insure that nobody else does. She routinely asks everyone in the family what they are giving him for Christmas, and if she fears he won't like your present, she makes you take it back, or else offers to buy something else herself and put your name on it, to spare you the trouble. Her idea is that if Garth doesn't like your present, he will feel that you don't like *him,* and that would be more than his sensitive soul could bear. I suppose he has gone through life being protected in this way, so it's surprising, really, that he has turned out bearable. Poor Garth.

In the mink commotion it was not noticed that I had come without salad and bread, but now the moment was at hand. We were clearing away the remains of Joan's delicious shrimp bisque, and it was time for salad and bread. At first I had intended to sit defiantly in my chair, but now I hoped to confess to Mother Fry contritely and privately in the kitchen. It was too late though; she had noticed. She brought in the vegetables and lamb and silently put them on the table.

"I had forgotten that Karen wasn't to bring anything, so we're a little short of food today," she said. "I wish she had reminded me."

Nothing more was said. Nobody looked at me, frowned, did anything. Father Fry carved blandly. Everybody avoided my eye. But within me welled a most profound feeling of shame and failure, the most intense sensation of humiliation I have ever had. It is odd that by such a small thing, garlic bread, you can be made to see the awful, childish things you are. Or perhaps this misery was a warning to me that the wrong things were becoming important. I did not know which.

Sebastian, as if to draw off the disapproving pause, told a wonderful story about finding a small, minor, but definitely genuine Rodin bust in the downtown Salvation Army.

"It just happened to catch my eye from the midst of a clutter of useless objects in the window. It simply looked important. I wasn't sure what it was, and was confused at first by the Japanese characters cast into the base. But I paid the guy his quarter and bore it off to the library, where I confirmed it as Rodin and explained the Japanese writing. Around the turn of the century, the Japanese bought a lot of art in Paris, or had things cast and painted to suit them. This little bust—a study for a large work—probably was brought to this country by a consul or ambassador, and then when the embassies were dismantled at the beginning of the war, it ended up in someone's cellar. Whence to the Salvation Army."

There is something splendid about the idea of bargain treasures. They suggest possibilities, hope, and we all responded to the suggestion except Patty, who left the table abruptly, with an agitated flip of hair and a cast-down napkin. No one paid much attention—she had perhaps heard the baby cry.

"So Sebastian's had his bit of luck, too, this week," Father Fry said.

"We're a lucky, lucky family," Mother Fry agreed.

In my shame and chagrin, I dawdled, finding excuses for postponing going into the kitchen to help with the dishes. I hovered over the children outside for a while, and then went to the bathroom. I met Sebastian in the hall. He did a funny double-take, as if he was surprised to see me there, but his expression was friendly.

"It was odd to see you in that auction place," he said finally. "It was like getting my worlds mixed up. Like coming home to find Mrs. Pratt cooking my supper."

72

"I have several worlds myself," I said.

"And one of them is porcelain?"

"No, I just happened to be in there. I didn't realize what an expert *you* are."

"Has it escaped you that no one ever asks me what I am," He smiled.

"It's assumed to be something slightly sinister."

"Yeah, I suppose so. Can you ever get out in the afternoons?"

I don't know what I thought he was going to suggest, but my mind went through that sequence of being startled, as if someone had said something improper, and then realizing that they hadn't, and then being chagrined at my own mind for supposing they had. I opened my mouth to say something or other.

"I have to drive up to Santa Barbara on Tuesday to a big estate auction that supposedly will offer some fine pieces. I thought maybe you'd like to come along."

"I'd love to," I said. It began to dawn on me that Sebastian was an ally, a Fry who liked me. He started to say something, but broke off when Patty came down the hall. She smiled at us both in a sweet, conspiratorial way, which made me realize that they probably had agreed that he should take me out and give me nice, brotherly advice. The hall suddenly seemed hot with the moist climate of compassion, and I walked past them into the dining room wondering if I did really want to go to Santa Barbara with compassionate Sebastian after all.

But the thought of an ally was sustaining. I felt up to helping with the dishes. Then, as I approached the kitchen, I could hear Mother Fry lecturing on something and quoting Mormon scripture: "Behold, the ax is laid at the root of the tree; therefore every tree that bringeth not forth good fruit shall be hewn down and cast into the fire." I looked it up later: Chapter Five, verse fifty-two of the Book of Alma. I supposed she was talking of me.

Chapter 9

Sebastian has since told me he was not quite sure why he invited me to drive with him to the auction in Santa Barbara. It had been a vague gesture of kindness and support, born from his sense that I was beleaguered and confused. In any case, the prospect of company on the drive was pleasant to him, and he liked me.

"Garth has made me promise not to buy anything," I heard myself saying, though I had not mentioned it to Garth. I suppose I was saying that I knew it was all a family, aboveboard expedition. In retrospect I can see that the fact that I had to say this probably meant I hoped it wasn't.

"Ah, well, there may not be anything to buy," he said. "They put out a small and very incomplete catalogue. I'm just gambling that the whole lot may be dark; that is, that the catalogue descriptions are inaccurate, and that things may be mistaken or undervalued. Bargain-hunting, in other words."

"You and Garth," I said. "But what kinds of things do you buy?"

"Anything. Not too much little stuff, though I will go for porcelain and silver. Furniture, mostly."

"And then what do you do with it?"

"She has a big house—make room for it somewhere. Add it to the collection, as we say."

"Do you ever keep anything for yourself?" I asked. This seemed to amuse him.

"I try not to poach on Patty's province. If I brought home old furniture, she would think she was being rejected. And it would become one of those appalling family anecdotes, to be recounted on Sundays. The Day Sebastian Bought the Chair. Like The Day Sebastian Rode the Unicycle."

"I wish you boys *would* do some new things. I'm getting tired of the same old stories," I said. "Anyway, furniture and art are your profession. I should think Patty would want your advice. At home you must feel a little as if you were renting furnished." From his frown I could see that he thought I was criticizing Patty, or becoming too personal.

"It feels a little like that, at times," he granted. He remembered I had seen him smoke, so he pulled out a new pack of cigarettes and offered me one. I took it.

"I quit smoking when I married Garth. I guess there's something a little absurd about two adults sneaking off to smoke—childish—but here we are." I coughed, quite spontaneously, which was strange, because actually I had never quit smoking. I had been smoking secretly since I married Garth. "Is it a gesture of defiance with you, Sebastian, or do you just like to smoke?"

"Both," he said. "Mostly I just like to smoke."

"Do you still consider yourself a Mormon?"

"A Jack Mormon, I guess. I do smoke, I do drink, I seldom wear garments. . . ."

I could not contain an impulsive question. "Does Patty wear garments?"

"Yes," he said. "On the other hand, I don't drink coffee, I do go to meeting, and I tithe. What am I?"

"A creature of habit?" I suggested.

"No, a wistful, part-time Mormon, a nostalgic Mormon," he said. I was thinking of something else I had always wanted to know.

"Mother Fry feels it's more religious to wear the garments under the brassière, next to the skin, but most younger women wear them over, like slips," I said. "Does Patty, do you mind . . . ?" I had never been able to talk to Patty about this.

"Over, like a slip," Sebastian said, but not as if he wished to discuss it. I was quiet after this, reprimanded, and just sat there giving the kind of luxurious sigh which means simultaneously that you are glad to be there and can't think of anything to say. Sebastian told me some amusing auction stories.

We found the estate, after a few false starts, by turning down a palm-lined, gravel road leading to a flat parking area. Beyond, up a hill, stood a great, flat-roofed ranch house. Many cars and small pickup trucks and vans had already arrived, and patches of people moved up the path toward the house. The largest number of these appeared to be dealers, balding, stooped, plump little men with pale skins and long fingers, like caricatures of dealers, or small, bobbing homosexuals calling to each other along the drive. In this company Sebastian himself looked strange, like a cowboy or a rock-'n'-roll singer—straight, no tie, open shirt, no acquisitive smolder in a squinty eye. He seemed to have a special feigned expression of disinterest as he strolled along up to the house.

The house and its furnishings, Sebastian said, had been put together with more money than either taste or judgment. He was struck immediately by the wrongness of its arrangement, and pointed out flashy fake highboys and inferior large paintings prominently displayed in specially constructed niches, while some fine small pieces were stuck in obscure corners. The effect of rich ignorance made him hopeful of finding a few small treasures cheap, something he greatly enjoyed. The house was clogged with furniture, and every table top was covered with bits of china and figurines dragged from cupboards. Sebastian began at the front door, and worked his way clockwise around each room, writing in his notebook, opening drawers, touching things. I followed him, as full of questions as Katy would have been, and he seemed to enjoy imparting his lore.

"Lacquer grows harder with age. Old lacquer can't be pierced with a pin, which is why I'm poking this cabinet with this pin."

"Old pieces will have old dust at the bottom of the worm holes. If you put a little resin or wax on a pin and stick it into the holes, you can tell by the dust something about the authenticity of a thing. This doesn't have any dust. There are more fakes around than you could imagine."

"Old veneer is of uneven thickness, and thicker than modern veneer."

"Mostly you just go by the look of a thing, and whether it feels right to you."

We ended on the back porch looking at some rolled-up rugs. Sebastian suggested lemonade. "They always have it somewhere at these sales." We found card tables set up with coffee, tea, and lemonade on the side porch.

"Are you going to bid on anything?" I asked.

"Yeah, a couple of things."

"I'd be afraid to. I know other people do it—maybe even quite timid people do it—but I never could. It's the same thing as never mentioning the things you really want for fear that fortune will then deny you. If I were to commit myself boldly and bid for something at an auction, the furies themselves would come down and outbid me."

"You're like the Chinese mothers who cover the faces of their beautiful babies and loudly say, so the gods may overhear, 'Ah, ugly, poor, pitiful, wretched, despicable object, who would want you?' You mistrust fate, I mean."

"I have no reason to mistrust it, or trust it either," I said, but I think Sebastian was right. I mistrusted it, and some people, like Alma, trust it perfectly. I am still not sure which is right.

Sebastian, trusting in fate, bid calmly and bought two items only. One was a bed, an "interesting early combination of Adam and Hepplewhite," which he discoursed upon to me, pointing out reeded posts and a carved urn on the headboard; he said it was Revolutionary or a little later, and seemed very pleased with it. The other was a large blue-and-white Chinese porcelain ginger jar.

"It's an exceptional one. The design is an allegory of spring," he explained. "The blue represents the cracking of the ice, and the Prunus blossoms represent, well, blossoms—the resurgence of life."

"Whatever Prunus blossoms are," I said. "But it is a lovely thing."

"I thought of it for her bathroom, just to stand in the corner. It has the right colors and shape."

I stood around watching things while Sebastian arranged to have the bed delivered and the jar packed to take with us. Then we walked back to the parking lot. Sebastian was clearly satisfied with his purchases and with the whole afternoon. On the homeward drive, however, I became conscious that we had fulfilled only half our purpose, that something more was needed to explain my presence there. Our being together had as yet a slightly unconsummated feeling. So I was not really surprised when Sebastian pulled off the road, producing a surprising scrunch of gravel and scaring me.

"It's okay. I just want to talk to you for a minute," he said. "I worry about you, frankly. You seem to have such a hard time with the family, quite needlessly. Every Sunday for six years I've watched them pecking away at you, and you resent it, but you also act like you deserve it. You have a chastised air, vaguely *déclassée,* like someone from a home for wayward girls. You're really better than that. That's mostly what I wanted to say."

"If only they could accept that I'm not a great cake baker," I said.

"They can't accept that. That's why I'm talking to *you.* You have to learn to accept them, and not care what they think of you. Learn not to care. Quit being hostile or sorry or apologetic. Don't care, that's all. You have to spend the rest of your life with these people, remember."

I cannot explain or justify the effect this remark had on me. I heard myself give something like a sneeze, and then large tears began to spill uncontrollably out of my eyes. It was very unlike me. I mopped at them with my fingers, and Sebastian looked at me with compassion and something resembling satisfaction, like an emotion-dowser who felt a certain pride in sensing, locating, and bringing forth running water. He hesitated delicately behind the wheel and then slid closer in case I wanted to sob on his breast or anything.

"I'm sorry. There seems to be an epidemic of tears lately," I said, thinking of Patty. But he didn't understand what I meant.

"Was it the idea of spending your life with us?" This possibility made him feel fond of me. One ought not to like a prospect of thousands of family dinners.

"Yes," I said, "it was, I don't know—the idea of spending the rest of my life doing anything I'm doing now. What if this is all there is? What if it's just going to turn out like this?"

He looked sympathetic and said nothing.

"It sounds stupid, but, Sebastian, do you ever think to yourself about what you want to be when you grow up? I find myself thinking, when I grow up I'll—and then I think, Oh, God, you *are* grown up, idiot. Up is now. But I can never find a way to make it count for anything."

"I like what I do," Sebastian said. "I'm ahead of you there, maybe. That isn't my problem. What *do* you want to be when you grow up?"

"Well, nothing. That's the trouble. Nothing you can name, like computer programer or Greek scholar. I want to *do* things, and be the product of all that I do. Great big things and little stupid ones, like going into the music room after dinner with a drink of whisky—I bet it never occurred to any of you that we might like to come out of the kitchen once in awhile. Oh, Sebastian, you have no idea what I want to do—the things I want to do."

He smiled. "Suppose you tell me."

"I want to go in the music room. I want to stay home on Sundays and not even go to family dinner. What I really want to do is go many places far away—not to escape, but just to go there. I want to learn all foreign languages and everything else besides. I want to make things, but not hostess aprons. I want to work on some monument, to myself, or to life, or to something."

"So does everybody," Sebastian said.

"That's not all, not nearly. I want to have beautiful friends with fine minds, and forty lovers, and a dozen children—maybe all with different fathers, because I want them all to be different and wonderful. And a splendid sunshiny place to play with them in. I want everything—I feel so greedy and hungry. The thing is, Sebastian, that I feel strong, very strong sometimes, but it's like being a strong, powerful wrestler locked up in a cage with no opponent. No, it's like being Antaeus, you know? I feel like that. As if some Hercules of boring, useless duty was holding me away from earth, and my strength just ebbs. It's as if I had in me some kernel of desire and life, and it keeps swelling and pressing until I have to burst or else grow to accommodate it. But there's no soil to grow in. God, what a mess of metaphor. I'm sorry. . . ."

"You have to learn to live on air," Sebastian said, with an unaccountable note of bitterness. "Everybody does."

"And I keep thinking that the life kernel must lie in some people like a shriveled pea. In Mahonri and Joan, your mother and father, maybe in Garth. Maybe in you."

"Not in me, my dear," Sebastian said.

"But what if everyone, plodding along, has this pain in his insides of wanting to grow? Maybe mine is no worse than anybody else's? Maybe I have no more business than anybody else to do Awful, Splendid things. Maybe the lesson of life, miserable life, is that you just have to lie passively in the arms of Hercules until the strength passes out altogether, and then you can bear things as they are. But I cannot bear that, Sebastian, and I cannot bear to think of others doing it. I think if your life kernel doesn't grow, it eventually turns to cancer, I think, oh, hell . . ."

Then suddenly Sebastian was kissing me, in an unbrotherly way, real kisses, and the two of us went slipping, arms entwined, down into an efficient horizontal position on the car seat. I had put my arms tightly around his neck.

"Oh, God, you have such beautiful honey skin," he said. I remember in a minute or two I twisted around somehow so that he could touch my breasts. This startled him and he pulled away, caressed me once, lightly and carefully, with a connoisseur's touch, as if I were Chippendale or Ming, and then sat up. He took my hand and pulled me vertical again.

"Hmmm, sorry," he said, looking both aghast and pleased, the latter perhaps at his strength of character in ending the embraces: I was embarrassed. I could feel my hot cheeks; my hands were doing involuntary ritual smoothings, hair-pattings.

"It's all right," I assured him.

"You have a weird power, you know," he said. "I'm sorry to have interrupted."

"I ranted a little, I'm afraid. Like a Housewife Whitman."

Sebastian was silent. He had figured himself out very easily. For a minute I had taken on some of the distracted, intense quality of Mrs. Pratt.

"Well, live your secret life, Karen, don't just daydream," he said finally.

"I will. I do." I considered for one second telling him about my real secret life, but I could see that it would only seem ineffectual and unrealistic to him, as it did to me, just now, after I had been vaunting my strength so. "Do you have a secret life, Sebastian?"

He hesitated. "I have a secret fantasy life, anyway." For an instant he considered telling me about Mrs. Pratt, but he didn't, partly because he remembered my friendship with Patty, and partly from some conventional sense that it would be rude to kiss a woman and then tell her you'd been thinking

81

of someone else. I suppose if Sebastian had told me about Mrs. Pratt then, in the car, things would have turned out very differently.

"Maybe they all do," I said.

"Who? What?"

"Have secret lives. Garth must have one, all those funny things he buys. He never talks about it, though. Mahonri, Joan, Patty. Does Patty have a secret life?"

"Not such an urgent one, anyway. Mostly she thinks life would clear up if the bathroom were a better shade of green."

"She wants a new dining-room table," I said.

"Oh, yes, that, too."

"It wouldn't clear up, though. I don't think you can expect life to clear up," I said. "But you mustn't get immune to it, either. You want to be constantly afflicted."

"Your theories are disarming, but what are you *doing* about life, Karen?" Sebastian asked.

"Nothing," I had to admit. That was true, at least in essence. "Making plans. Like people who manage to endure life in prison by devising ingenious but impracticable schemes to escape. Maybe that's what all people do, all their lives."

"It strikes me," Sebastian said, starting the car, "that you worry too much about how life must be for others. Too much empathy is simply ruinous."

"Too much empathy is simply the ultimate egoism," I said.

We had a good drive home, and no more mention of life or kissing. I walked into my kitchen feeling fantastically strong, like a hallucination of myself, glowing with excitement of emotional rhetoric and friendship. But the untidy sameness of home, Kate playing with doll dishes and bits of hibiscus blossom on the steps, and Toby's squeaks of welcome, did much to reassert the claims of normal life. As I paid the baby sitter, I could feel the euphoria ebb away like party gaiety, leaving, nonetheless, a little residue of determination not to be ordinarily satisfied or dumbly anxious or bland and unaware, or any of those wicked wastings of a life.

One matter needed to be considered separately—Sebastian's kisses. The more I thought of them, the more I saw it was possible that I wouldn't have minded making love to Sebastian—would have liked to, in a way. My thoughts went on a bit in protest at this, trying to feel shocked and horrified, but it didn't work. Instead, I kept wondering how it felt to commit adultery, and whether it would be especially satisfying to commit it in Mother Fry's kitchen. Then I was overcome with gratitude and pleasure at the extent of my own depravity. If I could do that, I thought, I could do anything. A sense of power is heady to the timid and inert.

Chapter 10

So love, or, to make the conventional distinction, sex, entered the picture and from then on took over. No, it had been there all the time, like another new word, and I had just been my usual slow self.

Of course everybody knows that sex is everywhere, and reads books about it, and deplores its debasement on billboards, and is in possession of the relevant facts about prevailing mores. And though I suppose your interpretation of the facts is always modified by your personal habits, it is difficult not to know in a general way all there is to be known on the subject. Only, I have a tendency to think myself representative—to believe others capable of no more than I am. I was soon proved wrong about that, too.

I had considered myself sensible, literate, liberal, and normal about sex. Garth and I had a Healthy Marital Adjustment and made love regularly to our mutual satisfaction; there was nothing about which we could not have spoken; only, of course, we had nothing to discuss. I had considered this felicity the natural consequence of having had, both by accident and conviction, the healthiest possible sexual history; I was exposed at the correct psychological moments to the correct information, adhered without any trouble to the best Midwestern traditions of premarital virginity, and the experience that made the greatest impression on me—that which Patty calls the "sexual awareness trauma"—was not very lurid, in retrospect. Bede, Ohio, was no last outpost of Victorian prudery. In the seventh grade we were given lectures on reproduction by an elderly doctor who employed, so far as I remember, delicate metaphors about fish and the bittersweet vine. In the ninth grade we were prepared with specific information—we learned, for instance, that certain parts of the male anatomy, though peculiar, were perfectly clean and need not be shrunk from. The straight facts were accompanied by a number of moral strictures, but for the unbelieving there were even vague allusions to contraception.

The first suggestion that love-making, besides being beautiful, might be fun, came of course from Alma Phelps. Neither I nor my friends believed it at the time—there has always been a predictable ten-year interval, like cultural lag, between me and Alma. At the time, I found the idea appalling.

Alma had come to a birthday party in her honor, the whim of my girl friends in our sophomore year of high school, following exposure to some uplifting lecture or spiritual experience. Girls of fifteen are given to fits of religiosity and social conscience, and my friends, perhaps I, too, suddenly felt conscientious about Alma. We also felt responsible. Ignored so long, looked down upon—no wonder she was a bad girl, and only needed a feeling of acceptance and the example of nice girls, to reform. It was February, so we made nut cups decorated with hatchets and paper cherries; there was about George Washington, model of virtue and rectitude, a suitability that pleased us. The party was at my house, where things were shabby enough to make Alma feel at home. It is odd that she came, but she did, and seemed to have a nice time. We had paper plates for the ice cream and cake, and sat on the dingy flowered rug in our living room in an intimate cluster, glowing with Alma's pleasure.

"Gee, this cake is great," Alma said. "You guys are very

good. I mean it." We warmed further, hoping that her recognition of an abstract principle of goodness marked, as we had planned, the first step in her conversion to it. We denied being good, of course, in modest murmurs.

"Helping others and finishing your homework and not Doing It with boys," Alma went on, sweetly. I swallowed and thought of my mother, who must have been somewhere in the kitchen within earshot. We looked at each other. It was not a subject any of us had ever discussed, except to express routine disapproval.

Charlotte French, the most articulate proselyte of goodness among us, seized immediately upon this allusion. Alma had played right into our hands.

"It would be very silly to do it with a boy," Charlotte said in an austere, authoritative voice. We saw that she was clever in not suggesting that it was *wrong* to sleep with boys.

"Depends on how you look at it, I guess, like most things," Alma said.

"The way everyone would talk about you, and you'd never get invited anywhere nice. You'd never go to any of the dances or anything." This, I thought, was a most telling argument, daring and clever of Charlotte to pretend she didn't realize that Alma was never invited to proms or parties; Alma would get the point, and think on all those proms and parties, and reform.

"Oh, for gosh sakes," Alma said, very disgustedly. "You don't even know what it's like, I bet." She twisted her truly golden hair and smiled at us. Her legs, stretched out on the floor, were bare and golden, too. They were somehow very aware legs. The thin legs of the rest of us were encased in baggy, newly acquired nylons.

"Would you want to know what it's like?" she asked. My face felt funny. I shot to my feet and went to the kitchen door to see where Mother was. I saw her out the back door hanging up clothes, and when I sat down again nobody had yet spoken. I suppose we were all, separately, considering

86

whether we actually *would* like to know. It might be awful and disappointing. Or stimulating and corrupting. I was conscious of cherishing my delicate neutrality of attitude toward what sex might be like, and of fearing to have it unbalanced on the side of either nastiness or sublimity.

"First you have to decide if you want to do it. You wouldn't want a boy who wasn't nice or not cute. Or too young," she began in a practical voice.

"Oh, dear, I have to be home. I'm sorry. By four, I mean," Janet Pearson said confusedly, and ran from the room. None of the rest of us even looked at her. I was sitting so still that I was conscious of swaying. We waited tensely for what would come next. Ice cream melted in drips onto the rug from the side of Charlotte French's crooked paper plate. Her acne looked purple. Alma was satisfied with our immobile silence. She had always been fond of mischief.

"You can tell a lot from the way a boy kisses. It can't be soft and sloppy." We had all had kisses like that, at least. I now see that Alma was teasing us, but loftily. She was liking us, too.

"If you think you will, you let them put their hands on your bust. There's no point doing that if you don't think you will, because it makes you feel aroused, and the boy, too, for no reason." This much had happened to me, but it had not made me feel aroused. I knew myself inferior to Alma. The long pause was stifling.

"The same with touching you between the legs," she said. At this, she seemed to my dazed faculties to have grown larger than life and impossibly fair, like an angel speaking on the divine order of unmentionable things. Her face was, as it always was, serene and laughing. I heard my mother come back into the kitchen, but I lacked the power to get up and shut the door.

"Then you find a place to go, and make sure you have plenty of time. Hurrying is bad. You find a soft place, grass, or a bed if nobody's home. Remember it's you on the

87

bottom." She paused, as if about to qualify this, but continued. "Then you let the boy do what he wants until everything is nice and ready." This mystified us, but no one called for clarification.

"Then—" she lowered her voice—"he puts it in. That's almost the best time, the first feeling of being filled with this thing inside you. But pretty soon you get another feeling—whoops, it just comes over you in waves, your toes curl up, your insides are opening and closing like wings. Sometimes it gets you right away, and sometimes after a long time. Either way is fine. Then the boy comes. That's nice, too, the way they twitch and groan. Then he can't do it any more for a while, so you just talk about things." Her voice trailed off. "Any questions?" she added, in an imitation teacher voice. We all, I suppose, could think of a million, but nobody asked them. Her account, with wings in it, differed strongly—in character though not in technicalities—from the hygiene-class version.

"Suppose you have a baby," Charlotte said in her flat voice.

"Well, you take precautions," she said, "or the boy does." But she didn't explain them. We sat.

"So what is a dance, when you can make love?" she said. But that still seemed an unnatural attitude. We had not been convinced by her, but we were fascinated.

"What do you do when all the boys are taking other girls to dances?" Marilyn Nordstrom asked.

"I have a lot of things I like to do," Alma said. "The whole world is full of things I like to do." To most of us, at that age, the world seemed to be a collection of things we did not like to do. But we were in no mood to discuss Alma's philosophy of simple pleasures.

"It is just wrong to give yourself to anybody unless you love them and they love you," Charlotte said. It was the hygiene-class position.

"Oh, you wouldn't unless you loved them, in a way,"

88

Alma said. "It doesn't matter if they love you. What are you trying to get, anyway? Just fun, and you get to know someone that way. That's pretty interesting. Well, sometimes it isn't, and that's the end of that. But you never know until you find out. That's the trouble with most people. People are scared. They try to keep you from finding out things. They try to keep themselves from finding out."

"*What* does the boy put in you?" Norma Cooper suddenly whispered. We had forgotten that she was more ignorant than the rest of us. Her family was prudish, and she had no brothers.

"His thing," Alma said.

"Oh," Norma said, but I had a feeling she still had no idea what was meant. There were a few other questions, which I don't remember. I chiefly remember my excitement, and Alma's grown-up poise, and the way she stood and smoothed her skirt over her round bottom and said she had a date. As she intended, we could imagine, envision.

Everyone else went home, too. I stood in the living room looking at the leftover party, flat Coke in paper cups, puddles of ice cream, crumbs, crumpled napkins, everything limp, melted, and lukewarm. It was then the horror filled me to think of love. The pleasant revelations of hygiene class had never held terrors, but now I saw it clearly, as Alma had intended—a different picture, hands on me, violation. The notion of pleasure itself chilled and frightened me—perhaps it was the vision of pleasure in another aspect, flat, stale, melted, afterward. Or a fear of being too defective and too frightened ever to make a present of myself. Too miserly. When I became too scared, I carried out the plates and cups and helped my mother peel potatoes in the kitchen. I am aware that most people learn about sex in more direct ways, but this was the closest I came for years. Eventually my revulsion dissolved into mere apprehension, and was disguised beneath collegiate sophistication, and finally was dispelled, as promptly as it was acquired, by a good, honorable Mormon man.

Garth's honor was the reason we got married the way we did. We were passionately in love, but he had a strange scruple about sleeping with me; he was one of those men who would not dream of dishonoring the girl he wanted to marry. This seemed at the time a charming and noble attitude, but I see it now as suspect, implying a lurking prudery I was not then wise enough to understand. I wonder now if I would have married Garth if my sexual curiosity had been satisfied beforehand.

But we got married. Garth was a considerate and patient lover, I proved a successful and enthusiastic initiate, and that was almost all there was to it. Physical love ceased to be, for me, and I supposed for other married women I knew, a subject of much concern. It was a given, a universal proposition, from which could be derived, time after time, the same dependable conclusion, for others in the same manner as myself.

And that, about love, had been that, until the day after Sebastian and I went to the auction. It was on Friday that I lost my innocence, or my unnatural naïveté, and learned of the relation of sex to dissatisfaction. There are not too many other things a respectable person can do, it seems, to enliven his lot. The great, glorious gestures are mostly denied us.

The first demonstration of this relation was in the morning, and it was mild. I answered a secret-life ad for an "animal lover for important work," thinking perhaps I would meet some antivivisectionists, or a mad old person with beloved pets. The address was in Venice, a section of Los Angeles I particularly like and feel at home in. Nothing is expected of you there.

But I was startled when I saw where I was headed. It appeared to be a hotel, one of the old-fashioned, store-fronted frame kind, with the words "Venice Hotel" painted in gay-nineties lettering on the glass window. Through the window you could see the inevitable potted palms in the lobby. The inhabitants, in various attitudes of boredom and

90

drowsiness, lay motionless or asleep, or stared out at the street. Only, they were not old lonely men; they were cats. All the old men were cats instead. Then you saw that the lettering said "Venice Hotel for Cats." A big ginger tabby stretched and yawned at me through the window. I rang a bell marked "Ring for Service," and in a moment someone came.

She was a girl of about twenty, in Levi's and man's shirt. She simply stood and looked at me, and dragged on a cigarette that was already short enough to burn her fingers. Her fingernails had been bitten, but otherwise she had an air of serenity and innocence. She had no make-up, sandy hair, a slightly dark tooth in front. I wondered if anything had ever happened in her life, and decided not. She seemed to have been born into odd charities; her parents might have met in Salvation Army work. Behind her, several cats circled like suspicious mastiffs. When I explained that I had come about the ad, she opened the door wider and stepped back.

"Kitty, kitty, kitty!" Toby cried, flinging out his arms. Old cats raised their heads and then went back to napping. An old, fat man in a torn maroon sweater appeared at the back of the room. We all stood just looking. The air held a thick animal-cage smell.

When the girl spoke, it was with a dismissive air, as if she had determined already that I had the wrong sort of look, of optimism or indolence, to suit her purposes. She must have seen that I was someone who didn't love cats in the right way. "We hoped to have volunteer help, actually," she said. Her high, sweet, nasal voice had a faint Oklahoma or Kansas accent. "We'll be able to appeal for volunteers when our nonprofit-organization charter is approved in Sacramento. Until then we just need help with the feeding and care." She stopped to throw a cigarette past me out the door. The old man came forward, buttoning the sweater over his slack stomach. He picked up a cat and fondled it with long fingers as he walked. The cat purred and writhed against his sleeve. I

91

became aware then of a subliminal hum in the room, and saw how truly many cats there were, a roomful, hundreds, banks of cats lying on chairs, under chairs, against the walls, stalking around, all quiet except for the electronic purring or humming that made me feel I was in a room with a great machine.

"Our founder, Mrs. Mason, is so sick I'm afraid she'll never be able to work again," the girl said with a quaver, and shared a sorrowing glance with the old man. "You've got no idea how much work we do here. We work nearly around the clock as it is. Fifty-two pounds of food a day, these cats alone eat, and keeping the place clean . . . Without more donations we won't be able to take any more cats in here, ever. We need a bigger place. We turn cats down; people bring cats in every day that we just can't keep."

"Do you try to find homes for your cats?" I asked, holding Toby tightly by the collar as he strained after a calico tom that brushed against his legs. "I have two cats," I said. "We love cats. . . ."

"We try," she said. "It'll be better when we can get some publicity. And we need someplace to keep kittens. You can't raise kittens in a kennel; they just don't make it, not even with shots. An adult cat, no problem. This is the only place you can bring your cat and be sure she'll live out her natural life. Not like some of these agencies who claim one thing, do the other."

"I hope your cats are fixed, young lady," the old man said. "That's what we keep telling people. The only solution in the long run is to fix them all."

The girl lighted another cigarette and asked me if I would like to donate my time. I almost wanted to—not, I think, for the sake of the cats, but for her sake. It was a vague wish that she could have some time off, make herself look pretty, maybe meet some nice young man, somebody besides nutty cat-fanciers. Perhaps she had no other home than this.

"We have to turn down cats every day," she said, her

92

voice rising a note. "You can imagine how awful—back on the street, and the pound gets them. Did you know that not one cat has ever been adopted from the West Side pound? It's a death house. And people desert cats; they go away and leave them. Cats can get along on their own; that's the feeling. But you should see the wretched cats that come in here, starving, thin, and we just have no room. . . ."

Now the old man came closer and put one arm consolingly around her shoulders. The cat smell was stronger on him than on her. I suddenly began to be suffocated and depressed by all those empty cat eyes everywhere; it was horrifying, the way a mass of people suddenly sometimes becomes. This seemed now an asylum of staring idiot children. I stammered and wished the girl well, and dragged Toby toward the door and out into the street. We looked back through the glass front to see the girl, thin shoulders drooping forlornly at the responsibilities facing her, at the evil in the world, at the sad fate of cats.

But there was something in the world for her, too, I guess. It made me shudder, but there it was. As I turned for a last look at them, I saw the old man stroking a dusty black cat which nestled between him and the girl. Now he stroked its back and head, now the shabby shoulder of the girl, now the cat, now the girl's neck; now, as I watched, he stroked her left breast with his old dirty hand, and she stood still, as if she were holding her breath.

Chapter 11

And so the relation of sex and desperation as revealed in the afternoon by Joan. I had always thought of Joan as practical, too, in a masochistic way, but I was mistaking her undemonstrative and methodical manner for practicality. What Joan did in the afternoons was awfully impractical, when you come to think about it.

Joan has omelette pans and every other sort of cooking thing, so I went to her house to borrow her large fish-shaped mold. I was going to make a salmon mousse for Sunday dinner. This resolution sprang to my mind—garnished, parsleyed, and complete—as a way of atoning for not having made salad the week before. I had even resolved, just to show how absolute my contrition was, to use fresh salmon from a fish market instead of salmon from a can, and to make salmon mousse over and over again, as many times as it took to make it come out right, even if it took all day Saturday and cost a lot of money.

I picked Kate up from school and got to Joan's about twelve-thirty, intending to leave the children in the car and just run in for a second. One never visits with Joan very long, because she gets so restless and begins edging nervously toward the sink after ten minutes of conversation; one feels that to delay Joan fifteen minutes from her appointed duties would create such an appalling backlog that she wouldn't recover until the next leap year. But when Toby saw that I was going to leave him in the car, he began to cry. I was anxious to shut him up lest he wake Joan's William, who sleeps from noon until two, the only quiet hours in her day, so I allowed him and Kate to get out of the car, and took them directly to the back-yard swings. Then I knocked, stuck my head in the family room, called, and went into the kitchen. Joan was not there, but I did not yet suppose anything was wrong. Instead I tiptoed through the dining room to the living room, trying to be quiet on account of William, and hoping, but not believing, that Joan might herself be resting.

In point of fact, nothing was wrong, in the sense of injury or illness. Joan was in the living room, lying on the couch. The only odd thing was that a man was also lying on the couch, on Joan. He was somebody I had never seen before, and was wearing an olive-green shirt, suggesting employment in some uniformed capacity, perhaps the fluoridated water man, or someone come to look at the telephone. His olive-green trousers and Joan's red pedal-pushers were hung neatly over the coffee table. They had taken their shoes off. Of Joan I could see only her bare legs, one arm slung tightly around the man's neck, and her frizzy hair spreading upon the sofa pillow.

I registered these details in a second—one scarcely stands and watches. Then I stepped into the dining room, where I couldn't be seen, and began, dazedly, to tiptoe back to the kitchen. Although I had often participated in primal scenes, I had never beheld one before, and it shocked me, first of all, to see how silly it looked. Beholding Joan and some strange man was of course beyond belief. My only thought was to sneak away quietly; none of the really satisfying aspects of this discovery occurred to me until later. I got to the kitchen all right, but then Katy came into the family room, shouting loudly.

"Hurry up, Mommie, you're taking too long. I'm hungry," she called.

I heard dim, horrified squeaks and rustlings from the living room. I thought of several courses of action: I could run outside into the yard and pretend I was just getting there, or I could pretend to be doing something in an absorbed way in the kitchen—perhaps looking at a book or fixing a bra strap. I cast around desperately for something to pretend to do, but I couldn't see a single thing. At the same time I was aware that it was Joan who must be thinking wildly; I had only to act as if I hadn't noticed anything, and nothing need be said. I stood distractedly in the middle of the floor.

"Hush, darling, you'll wake William. I'll go find Auntie Joan," I managed to say, in a loud, blithe voice, as a warning of my presence. Joan, barefoot and wearing the red pedal-pushers, came into the kitchen from the dining room. Her eyes were bright, and the rosy color of her cheeks was very becoming. Her expression, under a shallow smile, was wary.

"Hello, Karen," she said in a calm voice. "I wasn't expecting you." At this truthful and unnerving accusation my voice wobbled.

"Hello, Joan," it said. My face turned some unaccustomed color, and my hands went wet. "I just stopped by to borrow your fish mold." She had only to look at me, of course.

"I suppose you're pretty surprised," she said, in a voice of the type usually described as flat. Not knowing how to reply to this understatement, I nodded and said nothing. Kate tugged at me and began to remind me how hungry she was. This, a hungry child, seemed to stimulate a reflex in Joan.

"I'll make you a sandwich, Katy," she said, and did so in what must have been thirty seconds. "Take it outside so I can talk to Mommie." She led Kate out and returned to me.

"Naturally you must be wondering," she said. Her face had a purposeful, embarrassed expression, a grownup obliged to discuss sex with a too-curious child.

"No! No, of course not. I mean, I'm not Mother Fry, after all—you don't have to explain to me," I protested, anxious to make clear that I wasn't indignant or disgusted. I *was*

96

curious, and, by now, gently elated, the way you are when the teacher's pet is finally exposed as a cheat. The analogy is exact.

"Will you have some Seven-Up? Have you had lunch? Sit down," she said. Joan is one of those compulsively hospitable people who cannot even confess adultery without feeding you first.

"I'm going to make a mousse," I said. "But I needed your fish mold."

"I suppose you think I'm terrible," she said, still standing. A defensive tremor crept into her voice for the first time.

"Somebody else might, but I don't," I said, liking her better for her astounding behavior. I try not to make moral judgments about people, and, these apart, it is hard not to admire a person who surprises you vastly when you have supposed yourself to understand her perfectly. Besides, it's a pleasure to act charitably toward people who have upon occasion acted uncharitably toward you.

"Maybe I'd better tell you about it," Joan said, sitting down opposite me. I think she was glad to talk about it to somebody at last, and she told her story wonderingly, as if she were just now hearing it herself for the first time.

The first time it happened, it happened because she thought she was going to die, she said. She may not have allowed herself to think out loud about death, but the oppressive sickness of fear quickened her stomach whenever she put her hand to her breast hoping the lump had gone away. It remained, hard and sinister, in her right breast in spite of her frequent touches. She remembered having read that if you get cancer while you are young you are more likely to die of it fast. She remembered having read that you can catch cancer from old houses or trees.

But one blessing of a large family is that you don't have much time to brood about your own cares, even mortal ones. Joan's fears were drummed out of her mind by the insistent breakfast clamor of the seven children and Mahonri. They had bacon, dry cereal, and orange juice, all except Judy, who was allergic to orange juice and had apple juice instead, and Mahonri, who hated dry cereal and so had eggs and toast instead, and Petey, a big eater, who had two eggs besides his dry cereal. Because only four of the children stayed to lunch at school—Sara, Judy, and William were too young—she had only four lunches to pack. She fixed egg-salad sandwiches, carrot sticks, raisin cookies, an apple, and a half-pint of milk apiece. Joan was conscientious about giving them a balanced diet, because she had attended a series of lectures on nutrition at the church some years before.

By ten minutes after eight, all the children were gone except William, the youngest, then three. He was just getting over the measles, which he had caught two weeks after Margaret, Sara, Brigham, Nephi, and Judy had had them. Petey was expected to come down with them momentarily. William, convalescent, was fussy and whining, complaining on a note that seemed to pain Joan physically. She scrubbed the kitchen floor, an excuse to put him out in the back yard, but he sat on the doorstep and cried until she became afraid the neighbors would complain or think she was mistreating him. All the while, the lump stayed there, silent and mocking. As she was scrubbing she thought she could feel pains radiating into her chest and a numbness in her upper arm betraying the damage already done by the malignant mass. Her hand relaxed involuntarily, so that she dropped the scrub brush, and this frightened her so much that she trembled.

It was by now nearly nine o'clock, and she saw plainly that she could not stay the remaining three quietest hours of her day doing housework and listening to the querulous William without precipitating herself into a real state of panic and, worse, lassitude. Her life was so busy that she had formed few friendships outside the church, had no girl friends or neighbors she felt like visiting. The only social, distracting thing she could think of was to do her mission visits, calling on people to try to interest them in Mormonism. It was a funny time to do mission visits—these were ordinarily done in the evening—but daytime was better for finding elderly people and housewives at home. Joan often did her mission visits during the day, and alone, although the rules said you were to go in pairs. She had always told herself she didn't ever have enough notice to be able to arrange a convenient time with her visiting partner. And, by herself, she had been very successful—had two converts to her credit.

She went upstairs and put on a nice polka-dot silk dress, a pair of stockings of which the runs were above the knees and didn't show, medium heels, and some lipstick. Then she got her literature together and took William next door to Mrs. Snow, a little old lady who loved him and now and then enjoyed having Joan bring him over. This she almost never did for fear of finding herself with a free morning on her hands. My theory is that Joan feared idleness because if she had any leisure time at all she could no longer claim to have none, and since a little leisure would scarcely make a difference to her overworked existence, it was better not to lose the moral advantage of having none at all. This is probably why she kept on doing her laundry at the laundromat, too.

Mrs. Snow was a Catholic. Joan began a few sentences of her mission-visit speech on her, just for practice, but was kindly shooed away.

"Go on, go on. Me and William are going to have a cookie," she said. Joan tried to leave a pamphlet, because this is also the rule, but Mrs. Snow wouldn't have any pamphlets either.

Joan's district was more than twelve blocks away, so she took the car. At the first house she found no one home. At the second, she found a Mormon woman who invited her in for a little chat. At the third, a pale woman in curlers and breakfast coat told her she wasn't interested in hearing about Mormonism, and disapproved of people coming around bothering her about it. This embarrassed Joan, who was quite well aware what her own reaction would be if Episcopalians or Baptists came seeking to convert her. She was also aware that most well-established religions, with the exception of her own, do not come after you; the ones that do are, with the exception of her own, a bit weird and fanatic, like Jehovah's Witnesses. She smiled apologetically at the woman and turned to walk away, catching her heel in the doormat and nearly falling as she did so. Her breast began to hurt again.

The door of the fourth house, a big, well-tended Colonial, was opened by a young man, perhaps twenty-five years old, wearing jeans, baggy sweater, and a cast on one foot. He told her to come in and stumped back to a sofa on which he had evidently been lying. A blanket had slid off. Pillows were piled on the arm of the sofa. He sat down again and elevated his foot on the pillows. Joan followed hesitantly, convinced that this young man was not a likely convert but mindful of the rule that says to speak to all who will listen. He pointed at a chair and asked her to sit down.

"Are you familiar with the LDS Church?" she asked, at the same time beginning to feel sick fear again, brought on, she thought, by the sight of the invalid couch, the pillows, the crumpled blanket, a pitcher of water and some pills on a nearby table. In spite of the manifest robustness of the patient, the accoutrements of illness reminded her of her lump. She caught herself almost putting up her hand to touch it again. When she had mastered this impulse, she found she did not know whether he had replied to her question or not. She was afraid to repeat it for fear he had, and if he had it was now up to her to say something. She wondered how long she had been distracted and what he must think of her silence.

"Let me tell you something about it," she set off briskly. "The founder of the Church was, as you may know, Joseph Smith, born in New York State in 1805."

The young man listened quietly, with the faintest suggestion of mock earnestness. It struck her in the middle of a

100

sentence that he was probably just glad for distraction after the boredom of being laid up, but she wasn't sure what effect the sincerity of your listener ought to have upon your discourse, or even if you ought to question his sincerity as long as he listened.

"These golden tablets . . ." she was saying.

"You know something?" he said. "Forgive me for interrupting, but you have the most beautiful big breasts."

Joan shut her mouth and stared, but the words, because of their wild improbability, had no effect except to halt her speech.

"Forgive me," he said, leaning over and extending his hand, "but really, I . . ." He put his hand squarely upon her breast, the one with the sore lump in it.

Joan stiffened, shocked and surprised so profoundly that she could say or do nothing. At the same time, the young man's hand seemed, through her clothes, to warm her poor sick breast with a healing and soothing heat. For a second she had the reassuring sense of being at the doctor's, but when she fully understood his action, she gasped and tried to rise. He dropped his hand and himself rose, grasped her elbow as if he were escorting her to a theater seat, and guided her firmly onto the sofa next to him. Immediately, while Joan was frozen with confusion, he began to unbutton the top of her polka-dot silk dress and put his fingers around her breast next to the skin. The effect was galvanic. His touch felt, now, both erotic and restorative. At the same time the slight pain reminded her of the awful probability of cancer. She gave a moan of dread and despair. The young man, mistaking this for desire, pressed her back against the pillows with delighted and enthusiastic kisses and caresses, until Joan's mortal fear and outraged dignity dissolved into real desire. It was not five minutes until her thighs yielded to the urging of the young man's hand, parted, and she felt his weight come solidly down upon her. This reassuring feeling, followed by an even more exquisite sensation, caused her to abandon completely

101

the nagging reservations that had occurred to her between kisses and to enjoy whatever it was she was doing—she was not at that moment even sure—to the utmost. At the climax she burst into tears of relief and pleasure, which startled the young man so much that he had to stop and stare and compose himself before he could continue. She lay quietly, feeling pleasantly relaxed and used, while he performed the last several convulsions, withdrew, and neatly zipped up his jeans.

"My God, are you great, are you beautiful!" he said, wonderingly. Joan, not being able to think of a condemnatory or indignant remark, and not wanting to, stood up, rearranged her clothes, and patted her hair.

"If you'd like to tell me more about your religion, I think I could concentrate better now," the young man said, with sincerity, courtesy, and no trace of facetiousness. This struck Joan, who is generally humorless, as being funny. She laughed, gathered up her purse and literature, patted him fondly on his cheek, and told him she thought she'd be going. Something had opened, or closed, or shifted, in her mind.

"This mission visiting is rather tiring," she said, which is the closest thing to a joke I have ever heard Joan make. She firmly and wisely resisted all the young man's questions about her name and circumstances, and left without looking back. I think this was strong-minded of Joan; a lot of women would have tried to be emotional.

I believe it is characteristic of women who have deceived their husbands, at least the first time, to feel guilt, consternation, and remorse. Joan felt none of these, at first because she was too busy. She drove back, got William, talked to Mrs. Snow, and dashed into her own kitchen just in time to greet Sara and Judy as they came home for lunch. By the time these were fed and made to rest, Margaret and Nephi, who got out at two, came home, and she had to make snacks. At three-fifteen, Brigham and Peter came home. During all this activity she had had very little time to consider her remarka-

102

ble transgression, and by the time she did have a minute to think it over, while she was ironing—between four, after the last of the snacks, and four-thirty, when it was time to start making supper for the younger children—she had begun to notice something even more remarkable. This was that since twelve o'clock she had fed seven children in three shifts, done lunch and breakfast and snack dishes, made Jell-O for supper, mixed some bread dough, ironed three shirts, answered four phone calls from salesmen and pollsters, read two stories to William and Judith, who napped, and never once during all this had she felt tense or cross or unhappy. Moreover, she had not once thought of her lump. She put her hand up to it now, half expecting it to be gone, fled before the radiant satisfaction of her body. It was still there, but it failed to stir the same panic in her. She was forced to conclude, when she finally did have a minute wonderingly to go over the whole thing in her mind, that it had done her a lot of good. She knew she would not get pregnant, because her period was due the next day. She hoped she wouldn't feel too upset when she saw Mahonri. Except for these fears she felt exceedingly well, and when Mahonri came home she felt even better. She cooked him a lovely dinner, and was gay and gracious to him, not out of guilt, but because she was in such genuine high spirits. That was all. Joanie Fry, respectable mother of seven, member of the P.-T.A., Sunday-school teacher, mission visitor, cook, seamstress, handyman around the house, president of the young married group at church, and Heart Sunday Volunteer, had taken up illicit sex as a way of making herself feel better, with no more compunction than about taking aspirin. I suppose she was lucky to have a tractable nature. If she had rationalizations, she didn't tell them to me, except that she did say she didn't believe in denying your nature.

The lump had gone away after her menstrual period.

I listened to her account with an accepting and impassive face, I hoped. That was how she told it, with no trace of guilt and little of self-consciousness. As I listened and after I left her, my feelings wavered wildly between affection and contempt. It made me fonder of her to think that behind the denmother disguise her hostility had found this incredible means of expression, but I despised her unawareness, her inability to provide herself with a theoretical justification. Or perhaps that was the most magnificent thing of all? I wavered. Joan and the soft-water man. All afternoon I kept bursting out laughing, and half wishing that Mother Fry had been with me. It's nice that you can't ever guess which people will surprise you.

I would have liked to have a lover, a real one, not just someone come to fix the furnace. But where do you meet lovers, anyway? Perhaps I should pursue the fascinating French diplomat across the street, I thought, though I knew he was not real. In the real world, as everyone is aware, there are no fascinating French diplomats; no dark stranger knocks at your kitchen door, invests you with beauty both physical and spiritual, enthralls your soul in perfect communion with his own powerful, sensitive soul, performs sonatas on your Steinway, takes you several times on every visit—always with great tenderness, astonishing artistry, and simultaneous orgasm—sends presents, and forever after, even when he is far away, remembers your birthday with an anonymous bouquet of your favorite flowers. He makes you see you never had it so good. You never did, and, of course, you never will. You never will.

I thought about it, though. I strove to imagine certain feelings, physical sensations, and the condition of wild loving. But these things thoughts cannot supply. The imagination aspires, flags, and fails the tense body. It is better, really, not to think about love at all.

Chapter 12

Sebastian had gone that same Friday to the County Museum. He was thinking, as usual, about love, and he was disgusted at it, or at himself for being someone who thought his life would come right if only he could get to bed with the right woman. There was nothing wrong with his life, as he knew. He was happy in his work, a thing denied to many. He had a nice family—lovely wife and children. Still, he was more than usually oppressed by his disorderly emotional life. His fondness for Patty, his childish, impotent attachment to Paris Pratt, his irritation with his parents, his ambivalence about religion—these were always feelings he had before kept tightly compartmentalized, as if in so many sealed drums in his mind. And now all this emotional gasoline seemed to be leaking, streaming together into an uncomfortable and smelly puddle in his mind, and he was apprehensive, as if someone were approaching him with a match.

He had gone to the museum to look over its collection of assorted curious early California objects—tableware and mining pans and camp gear—because he had in mind to give it more. He had been buying such things when they turned up, without being very interested in them, and by now had an assemblage neither he nor Mrs. Pratt cared about spending any time or money on. He decided to give it to the museum.

Then, because he was depressed, he wandered around the galleries awhile looking at pictures. Ordinarily Sebastian was able to repose himself, order his spirit, in the simple process of aesthetic experience. His response was by now both profound and reflex; he was able to put himself into the proper frame of mind the way someone does who practices self-hypnosis and can at the click of his fingers entrance himself. And, though he had ceased to admit it to himself, Sebastian's judgment of a work of art began with this simple subjectivity; he relied on it, and bolstered by his critical faculties the dictates of his taste. But now he stared blankly at canvas after canvas and felt like a broken electronic device; the message—waves of color, line, spatial relationships, content, and form—was being sent, but he was not receiving. His mind for art was as stony and chill as the shining marble thigh of the Monacelli Venus, whose curves, proportion, mass, usually so warmed him.

He left painting and tried looking at his favorite objects—the quarter-ton jade rock, the Chinese crystal ball, and, his special passion, the fossil Aepyornis egg, an immense, perfectly shaped and perfectly textured natural wonder. He could never see it without longing to touch it, but it, like everything he wanted, it seemed, was locked in a glass cage. He did touch and stroke the surface of the jade boulder, polished smooth by the sea, warm, reassuring. It reminded him of a time he had seen "tranquillity stones" in a store—little smooth pebbles you could buy for a dollar and be tranquilized by if you held them in your hand. He had examined one and it hadn't worked, but the sensation of exquisite smoothness had been pleasing. He thought now of the many stones, in cathedrals, on fountains, which were worn smooth by the pressure of human fingers and lips. He wondered about the special affinity of people and stones. He wondered why he was standing there stroking a rock and hadn't bothered to look at the porcelain or silver. A surfeit of art, he supposed.

106

As he was leaving he was spotted by Chisholm, one of the directors, and, astonishingly, instead of wanting to chat with Sebastian about the Pratt collection, Chisholm drew him into his office, said they had heard he might leave Pratt, that they were hiring an additional curator, that they were wondering if they might approach him. Sebastian, from his muddle, had not felt able to say yes or no about anything, had expressed his pleasure, and had escaped after giving the impression, he supposed, that he might indeed be approached.

Considerably agitated, he took a turn in the rose garden outside the museum, and then, because it was hot, sat in the lattice gazebo. He supposed he should go back and confess to Chisholm that he wasn't considering leaving Pratt, but then he decided not to. It was pleasant to be wooed, and he told himself he should not refuse to think about another job, should not stifle possibilities before he had had any time to think about them. He felt unable to trust his feelings on any matter. He had a fantasy interview with Paris Pratt in which he told her that he was leaving, and she told him that she, and the Pratt Foundation, couldn't live without him. He rehearsed the interview a couple of times over, despite his perfect knowledge that it was absurd.

"Give me one good reason why I should stay," he heard himself saying. She was standing by the window—no, they were in the garden. She, plucking a rose and toying with the petals, dared not meet his eyes. She stared into the heart of the rose. She was wearing her absurd antique blue velvet robe with the train, something he had found in an attic.

"Well, then, this is it, I guess," he said, in a harsh voice, watching her. She raised her eyes.

"Oh, Sebastian, I could not live without you." Faltering voice, blush, swoop, tears, kisses.

"Shit," Sebastian said aloud, earning a startled glare from an elderly lady enjoying the gazebo with him. He wondered why his fantasies always came out like sentimental nine-teenth-century novels. He never read sentimental nineteenth-century novels. He wondered if mawkishness was the inevitable consequence of long, hopeless attachments, such as his for Paris. Or perhaps only the constitutionally mawkish ever had long, hopeless attachments. He didn't think of himself as naturally foolish and sentimental, but his relationship with her was suspiciously so. Perhaps her function in his life was to provide an outlet for that which was romantic in his nature, the way other people read thrillers or travel folders. One ought, everyone deserved, to have something to yearn toward. Possessing Mrs. Pratt would probably spoil things at that, he told himself, as he had told himself before.

Still, what a joy to contemplate it. The act of possessing her, entering her frail body, would involve tempering his consuming lust with a certain physical moderation, and compensating for the requisite restraint with immoderate emotional outpourings of speech. Not that she would really break, but she would bruise, crush. What he really wanted was to bruise and crush her, and to tell her everything in his heart. He meditated upon this. But all his mind could contain was the beginnings of the fancy, the embraces of Paris Pratt, and anticipation so intense that the mind could only discard in disgust the pale platonic form of what the reality would be. He picked the thought up and cast it down, picked it up and cast it down, exhausted with the effort of trying to translate his wish into physical sensation, and sent his distracted gaze around the gazebo as if it were prison.

The little old lady appeared uneasy with him now, and looked as though she wanted to leave but feared to try, as if he might detain her. He supposed he did look confused—deranged, even. He got into his car and drove back to the Foundation. A small truck had backed into the first drive behind the cottage that had belonged to Emil and now belonged to some new artist moving in. The wife, wearing a striped something—pillowcase, apparently—was directing the men in an imperious, insecure voice and a New York accent. She was little, dark, young, and full of being a painter's wife.

108

A man, presumably the painter, hulked nearby on a rock, watching. Sebastian went closer to ask them if they needed anything, to meet them, to have a better look at this new man around the place.

"Ah, Prince Charming!" the painter said to him.

"I beg your pardon?" said the startled Sebastian.

"I was just sitting here thinking that it was all like a scene from *Snow White*. Little Snow White—my wife there—and her dwarves fetching and toting things into the quaint cottage, and you walking up looking like Prince Charming. No offense." He laughed.

Sebastian was irritated, by this and by the fact that the painter was big and ornamental, which Paris was sure to like.

"That's the Queen's castle up there?" the painter asked.

"Uh?" Sebastian had lost the thread of all this.

"The wicked stepmother."

"Mrs. Pratt," Sebastian said. "Yes, that's her house. She'll probably be along soon to welcome you, if she hasn't come yet."

"There really is such a person then? I had been thinking she must be a trademark, like Elsie the Cow. Betty Crocker. Paris Pratt."

"She's real, all right," Sebastian began. At the same moment, he saw the painter's face suddenly transfigured by an expression of mystical transport, as if he were seeing the ghost of his angel mother, and, looking farther, saw Mrs. Pratt floating toward them in an unearthly old flowing chiffon gown which streamed behind her in the breeze. So did her thin gold hair, and the effect was that of a slightly mature Blessed Damozel. The painter's handsome, dour face brightened up no end, and by the door of the cottage, the little New York wife, now carrying a toddler, had paused and was watching the apparition with an expression of apprehension.

"My dear man," Mrs. Pratt said, "I have seen your paintings, and they are most impressive, but why *do* you confine yourself within the limits of nonobjectivism? You'll

109

never say anything there—I immediately wanted to tell you this. One sees you are a fine draftsman, and something of a romantic, though you apparently feel uncomfortable about that, which you needn't, for you have considerable vigor, and . . ."

"Excuse me, I'll see you later," Sebastian said, and walked away crossly toward the main house. On top of his existing depression he now felt a new premonition superimposed, that he was in for one of those futile, miserable periods of watching her become fascinated with someone. What he hated was that this always affected him when it had no business doing so. He had headaches and became impatient with everyone, overate with a stiff sense of self-justification, read trash, hated the Pratt money and made a few unwise purchases with it, stayed inside libraries and museums until he felt pale, and generally behaved like the surly nephew in a Chekhovian play. The past couple of years he had disguised his feelings when he could, because he also found it intolerable when she fussed over him soothingly and dragged him off for wholesome outdoor sports, and reminded him of her disdain for the physical. He knew it would be odd if an independent, lovely, rich woman didn't have interests, however chaste, in men, but nothing ever made him feel better when she had them. Her relationships may have been spiritual, but his jealousy was physical, and it hurt.

He went into the library and sulked in the big leather chair. His head hurt, and he was irritated to hear Mrs. Pratt's voice in the hallway talking of inspiration and Redon, and the painter's responses, full of dates and names. Sebastian remembered from the application form that the painter was a Harvard man, and that by itself was annoying to a graduate of Brigham Young University. He read awhile and finally fell asleep.

He awoke because he felt a presence. It was Mrs. Pratt, standing by the ottoman at his feet, smiling with the patronizing tenderness of someone who has caught another adult

110

asleep in the middle of the day. For a moment his mind, lulled by sleep, stirred with the comfortable concupiscence of the newly awakened. She smelled of lemon and leaves. Then he remembered his irritation and frowned up at her.

"You're an intelligent-looking sleeper," she said. "Most people have such a vacuous expression."

"Vacuous is what I felt," he said, "with that painter. No, I felt like your eunuch, following at three paces to protect you. A eunuch is what you need around here, somebody who wouldn't mind when two-bit painters take over the place."

"Silly, the man has been here an hour!" she said. "Are you going to act like a jealous husband already?"

"No. No, in fact I'm thinking of leaving," he said. "I've been offered a job at the County Museum." He straightened up for a discussion.

She blinked. "Are you going to take it?"

"Maybe."

"Oh." He could tell nothing from her expression.

"Well, do you think I should?"

"I suppose it would have certain advantages for you."

"Yes, I'd been thinking it would."

"Oh."

"Is that all? 'Oh?' " Why in hell wouldn't she say something about how she felt?

"Do you want a raise?" she asked.

"No, God damn it, I do not want a raise," he snarled. "What *do* you want?"

"I guess I want you to plead with me to stay."

"I know that, of course. But of course I can't. Of course I don't want you to go."

"May I consider that you have said you don't want me to go?"

"Yes."

"So why in hell can't you just say it? Somebody works for you, you wish them to continue, you say so. Is that so hard?"

"Oh, Sebastian, I just don't want you to think I'm prom-

111

ising anything. You make our relationship so difficult, your imagined *tendresse* for me does . . ."

"Oh, I'm not going to quit, God damn it."

"I didn't think you would, actually. There is too much of you here. More of you than of me," she said.

"Of both of us, perhaps? I like to think we are in accord on some level at least."

"Of us, certainly, but I didn't want to imply . . ."

"Never mind. The first person plural implies nothing around here. You and I have a beautiful bond about old chairs. Someday I'm going to smash one over your head, too."

"Violence is always pointless," she said with a smile. "Drive me into the village, would you please?"

"Yes, madam," Sebastian said, like the chauffeur he felt himself to be.

For the first time in a long time he was glad to get home, but as soon as he remembered that Patty had had her wisdom tooth out, he was less glad, because things were bound to be in a mess. In fact, they weren't. While I was baby-sitting I had been so entirely absorbed in thoughts of Joan that I'd done all kinds of things—started dinner and bathed Mark and Eric—and scarcely noticed it. Sebastian thanked me and said he could take over. Patty had gotten home about five. Now her Novocain had worn off, and she was in pain, and followed Sebastian around with ice cubes tied in a rag pressed against her jaw. She seemed to be hoping he could do something to make her feel better. He didn't feel entertaining, but he did read to Mark and put the baby to bed, and then finished getting dinner for himself and Patty—soup and ground meat, things that she could eat all right.

At the table, to make her happy, even though he realized while he was doing it that he was making a mistake, he told her about the job offer. It did please her. She took her hand away from her jaw and smiled with the side of her mouth that still worked.

112

"See, you *are* an expert in your own right. You don't have to depend on Mrs. Pratt at all," she said. Odd that she supposed he did.

"I don't depend on Mrs. Pratt," he said.

"Well, it must be nice to be recognized as a professional, I mean. You should be very pleased."

"I've been recognized as a professional for some time, I trust," he said touchily. "But I am pleased, I guess."

"How much does it pay?"

"I didn't ask about the details. The whole thing took me by surprise."

"I should have warned you. I might have known they had something like that in mind. Mr. Chisholm asked me at Art Council Juniors whether you ever thought of leaving Pratt."

That was how it had come about, of course. "You shouldn't have told them I was," he said, hurt that she had had any part in it.

"I didn't, but we have talked about it, and that's what I said. That you had talked about it. It never does to nip these things in the bud."

"It was unfair to lead them on. But so did I. I was too surprised to say no."

"Are you going to say no?" She pressed her hand to her jaw again. Ice water dribbled down her wrist and off her elbow onto the table.

"I'm perfectly content where I am. I have more money, more independence, more authority, at Pratt."

"Catering to the whims of a rich, neurotic woman?"

"Directing her collections. I'd hardly be the director of the museum."

"Of course if you're *status* conscious," she said, ambiguously. "Don't give them a final answer yet. I think we ought to find out all about it before we make up our minds." Probably she didn't feel strong enough to argue her point right now, but Sebastian could see he was in for a scene about it some time or other. He, like Patty, preferred some other time. He was sorry he had mentioned it at all. He ate his soup and said nothing. Then his eye fell on a deep, new, pale wide scratch on the surface of the table to the left of his plate. All the raw feelings of the day concentrated themselves into one chill of rage at this desecration.

"How did *that* happen?"

"What? Oh. That's awful, isn't it? Mark and his truck."

"What the hell was he doing with his truck in here?"

"I didn't realize it. I was in the kitchen."

"I've asked and asked you to keep him out of here."

"Well, Sebastian, he's a three-year-old child and this is his house. He has to come through the dining room to get to the kitchen."

"Not with trucks."

"We shouldn't have furniture we have to be so careful of. I've told you that. Children are just hard on furniture."

"This table is the only decent thing we've got. You could at least be careful of it." He was sorry he had said this. Her eyes widened with hurt.

"I thought you liked our house. I've tried very hard to make an attractive home, I . . ."

"I'm sorry. The house is charming, of course. I didn't mean that. This is the most valuable thing in it, though, and you could keep Mark away from it. You manage to keep him away from all the crap on the coffee table. You never have liked this table, and you just won't be bothered with it, isn't that it?"

"I suppose my role in life is to protect it? My mission? I have other things to do besides hover over a table, suppressing my children and having to account to you for every little scratch," she said, voice now thoroughly angry.

Sebastian saw how he had sounded. He apologized, assured her. But she was not soothed.

"You like that table because the divine Mrs. Pratt gave it to you, isn't that it? Darling Mrs. Pratt, who can afford a thousand dollars for a table, and I'm sure there are no sordid scratches on her tables, either, which must be very nice, only . . ."

"For God's sake, Carola," Sebastian said. They were silent while horror suffused him, moving upward from his toes. He had never believed in slips like this happening. Patty stared at him, angry tears crowding her eyes. She pushed her soup away, spilling it, and stood up with a dramatic gesture of rage.

"Darling Mrs. Pratt. So!" she said. She gulped. The tears spilled. She gave an anguished hiss and ran to the bedroom. Sebastian, shaken, and wondering what he was in for now, mopped up the soup with paper napkins before it could damage the surface of the table.

Chapter 13

I had barely seen Garth for several days. He had a new project, outfitting his mail truck for his annual fishing trip with Mahonri in the Sierras. I didn't know how he figured his truck would get up those mountains, but its performance wasn't really the point. He enjoyed the woodworking, nailing things in, hanging little cabinets and racks for fishing tackle. Like a good general, he always provided himself with numerous alternate routes of retreat from Kate and Toby and me—his woodwork, the hospital, listening to string quartets with his father, roaming, buying things. It did make me sad, a little, to think that maybe he had to make himself a cozy house in a mail truck because he felt so homeless in the real house with me.

But he was happily occupied. For the first time ever I had to remind him that we were due at family dinner. I hadn't gotten around to the salmon mousse, of course, but I had thought of something better, and felt confident, even eager, to go.

At the market I had had a great inspiration, a simple, beautiful plan—it was so simple and beautiful that I couldn't believe that I'd never thought of it before. But that does tell you something about the domestic climate of the Fry household. Cake mix. I had never thought of it before.

I took the cake to family dinner in my electric frying pan.

"Dessert," I said, but Mother Fry was not curious enough to look inside. She was involved in telling Patty and Joan about a lecture by Mrs. F. R. Frembling, "one of the great women of our time," and an expert on weaving. Mother Fry, whether or not she had ever aspired to fame in her chosen field of home economics, seemed to achieve a measure of it vicariously, by attributing fame and greatness to all those with whom she was associated, however tangentially—to the lecturer she had heard, to the book she had read, to the movie she had seen.

Joan seemed unsettled by my newly knowing presence. Rather than encounter my eye with significant sisterly glances, she avoided it, but she made attempts to include me in the conversation, and once, when Mother Fry praised her because her children were being so perfect out on the patio—"You can always tell a good mother by her children"—Joan blushed, a genuine Victorian empurpling of the face and ears. I knew the blush was meant for me, although in fact I couldn't see any reason why Joan could not be an adulteress and a good mother at the same time. Just as Joan's children were being praised, my own children came inside wailing about something, and their noses were running. Colds, Mother Fry has always made quite clear, have something to do with maternal negligence.

We sat down to dinner promptly at six, and the men talked about Vietnam. They were interrupted at intervals by Mother Fry talking about Mrs. Frembling. Her *non sequiturs* were more startling than usual, I thought. The note of anxiety I always sensed in her self-satisfied discourse was shriller. She was insistent, as a child is, for attention.

"Now, Mother," Father Fry finally said, "the rest of us didn't hear Mrs. Frembling." She was quiet a second, then tried something else.

"If you ask me, they should send all women over fifty to Vietnam," she said. We looked up.

"Why not? A woman over fifty is as strong as she ever

117

was, and has a lot more endurance than a man, too. And most of them haven't got anything else to do. You take young men, you have to interrupt their schooling, and later on their careers, and they have families to support, but a woman over fifty, after her children are grown, might just as well be defending her country. This prejudice against women is impractical, if only people would think sensibly."

Of course it was too appalling an idea to be debated seriously. Her sons assured her they did not want her to go to Vietnam, and Mahonri changed the subject to the revival of double-breasted suits. I—and perhaps Joan and Patty, too—was simply sad. Mother Fry is a highly capable woman, intelligent and vigorous, but she had gone wrong—poured out upon insubstantial things talents that must once have been like molten steel and now, hardened and cold at sixty, were formless and valueless, lead nickels she tried desperately to pass off everywhere as real.

"Let me get you some ketchup, Dad," she said. "No, no, I'll get it." Neither Father Fry nor anyone else had in fact offered to get it. She ran to the kitchen, returned, and sat down breathing heavily. "Oh, my old feet hurt today," she said with coy, mock grandmotherliness. But the heavy breathing was real. Her sons, observing this, turned imperceptibly to Garth. Was she developing heart trouble? Father Fry's expression was merely cross, as if he feared she would require a new pair of shoes for her hurting old feet.

"Woman's work is never done," she remarked with a cheerful smile. "I remember the days when that was literally true, when you boys were little and one of you would always be having the chicken pox or a bad cold and would need sitting up with all night. Many's the night we saw the sun rise, remember, Dad?"

Father Fry smiled reminiscently, but we all knew, and he knew we knew, that he had never stayed up all night with a sick child in his life. She had scored off him, but he didn't feel it much. The boys must have felt guilty about all those sleepless nights she spent, though. Even Garth looked un-

118

comfortable. She was scoring off them, and they did feel it. Mahonri blew his nose.

"It was funny. The nights I had been up, I'd get the washing done before breakfast and have it on the line by sunrise. You can imagine how popular I was with the other ladies in the neighborhood. Well, we get spoiled, with our modern conveniences. These days I think I'd rather have nine children and an automatic washer than four children and none. My back hurts just thinking of that old washboard."

Was she always like this, or was she getting worse, or was I just noticing for the first time? I was drawn in and puzzled. Now she seemed to be scoring off Joan, and that was too petty for words. Even Patty couldn't stand that.

"Didn't you even have one of those old wringer washers, Mother Fry?" she asked.

"Oh, they had them, but I preferred a tub and board. Things do get much cleaner that way. But we get lazy in our old age."

"The day Mother gets lazy, it'll be because she's broken her leg," Sebastian said, in an easily recognizable attempt to reassure himself that she would live forever, would not topple into an early grave because of overwork.

"Interestingly enough, people who keep on the job live longest by far. Hard work goes with long life," Garth said, perhaps with the same motive. This remark, however, created another awkward moment, during which we all considered Father Fry, retired for four years and thriving on it. He helped himself to potato salad and ignored us.

"Really, though, Mother, if you are having trouble with your back and feet, I think you should have somebody in to help you with the heavy work," Sebastian said.

"I keep trying to get Joanie to get some of those orthopedic shoes. She has a little foot trouble. They say most of it can be corrected with proper shoes," Mahonri said. "But she thinks they're too ugly."

"They *are* ugly," Joan insisted. "They look like old ladies' shoes." Joan is the reverse of chic, but she must have drawn the line at stout shoes.

"Women always hate to recognize that they're over sixteen," Mahonri said, as if it had been his task all his life to assure them of the melancholy truth. "After all, Joanie, you're over thirty and a mother of seven—what's more important, your health or your looks?" He was solicitous.

"There's nothing wrong with my feet," Joan said pitifully. It was odd that Joan, in family discussions, was always having to defend herself against charges of frivolity—mink stoles and flimsy shoes—when it was only me whom any of them actually considered frivolous. I suppose the reason was that Joan was an extreme example of Woman's Lot, and therefore made them feel uneasy. They thought they admired her, but she was really a living reproach.

"There's always something pathetic about a woman who clings to the vain, girlish things, having the hair dyed, all that eye goo," Mother Fry said. "On the other hand, there's no reason she should wear shoes she thinks are ugly. I don't mind them myself—they're very practical—but you just can't generalize about feet."

Mahonri stretched and moved his chair back. "Yup," he said, "those of us who are getting a little—ahem—heavy— we'd be worried if our wives were young and trim." Everyone but Mother Fry felt insulted for Joan again.

The awkward moment took the edge off my triumph, but I still savored every precious word of it. When the dinner was cleared I uncovered my cake, put it on a plate, bore it proudly, with modest blankness of face, into the presence. Mother Fry's eyes, I fancy, opened a trifle.

"That looks very nice, Karen," Father Fry said. He confidently cut the cake and handed it around. Light, smooth-textured. Patty beamed at me. Mahonri said, "Ah."

The silence clearly demanded a comment from Mother Fry. Her smile was genuine, lit by hopes, perhaps. The inspiring teacher is finally rewarded.

"Now this is a good cake," she said. "You got the egg white stiff enough. It just takes time and practice."

"Interesting flavor," Joan said.

"I'd love the recipe," Patty said, which was perhaps going too far in the direction of kindness. I held my breath for someone to guess the secret—deceit is both sweet and alarming. But I needn't have worried. None of them probably had ever, that they knew of, tasted a cake-mix cake.

My moment of favor was unfortunately short, because after dinner I had to tell them I had to go somewhere and couldn't baby-sit. They looked so bewildered I almost changed my mind. But I had something rather special to do. Mother Fry looked at Garth, as if she expected him to order me to stay, but he, feeling guilty that he had told me I'd have to go by myself, simply said we had a "long-standing engagement." So they took the children with them to church. Garth and I went home, he to his garage, and I to get ready for Mrs. Pratt's party.

Chapter 14

Sebastian's part in what happened after the party is probably explained by his problems with Patty and Mrs. Pratt. For me it was, I suppose you could say, an existential experience. I can account for it in several ways. First, Garth wasn't there. And then, I think I had been asking for a long time for something of this sort to happen to me. And there were all those voices—Sebastian's and Alma's, and my own inner one—forever urging me to do things instead of watching other people do them. And there was my own timidity, as tangible as a physical defect, needing to be overcome. Besides, I had the example of Joan. When I went to the party I had no notion, of course, that anything extraordinary would happen there.

I was excited, to begin with, to be invited. I felt especially singled out and remembered. And when Sebastian showed no knowledge that we were invited, I felt extra sure that it was Mrs. Pratt asking particularly for me, even though the card was addressed to Garth, too, and described a rather public and evidently routine Open House. Garth, of course, did not want to go. That is a game we had played for a long time—not liking each other's parties.

"I think I'll work out in the garage if it's not too hot," he said. "Do you think it's too hot?"

You got to Mrs. Pratt's by driving up Bel-Air Road and

122

turning off on Cimarron Way—a street of mansions, electric fences, gardeners' trucks, and *cave canem* signs. The pavement ended as you climbed higher into the hills, and a mud road, ordinarily closed by a farm gate which now stood open, twisted off out of sight around a curve. You passed by this and onto the road, which, even after you had rounded the curve, did not seem to lead anywhere in particular, except, if you were careless, into a frightening ravine at the left.

I saw that I was driving along the wall of a canyon, and after I had gone a quarter mile I could see, ahead and below in the canyon bottom, the roof of a large house and the smaller roofs of cottages planted among twisted California live oaks and taller, greener eucalyptus. The road descended steeply into the canyon at the end, but it was so thickly planted on either side that I could see little of the actual grounds until I came abruptly into a clearing, past two tennis courts and a pool, and onto a wide paved area in front of a row of garages. I found that I was at the back of a gigantic house, built on a slope, two stories where we were, but probably three in front. It was stucco, rather square, a California version of English architecture, crossed with brown-painted exterior beams and a peaked, improbable cottage roof on the whole immense thing.

It was clearly not a party just for me. An empty bus parked outside had brought deserving Negro high-school students. There were imperious women in saris with red marks between their eyes—Brahmanesses?—and old friends, and the artists from her colony of cottages, all wearing artist beards or handmade clothes, as if she required that they dress up like stereotypes when they came to live there.

Mrs. Pratt's house is an assault upon the senses, a place where everything is beautiful, even the things that aren't old or rare. Everywhere great furniture and paintings and rugs live beside things that are unstylish and old and comfortable-looking. A photograph stands on the piano by a Rodin bust, a carpet in the hall is worn. These things give elegance, a

123

feeling of evolution, warm emanations of beauty from every corner. And then the shameless, overpoweringly rare and splendid things give you more of a lump in your throat than they would in a museum. They make you remember how they had been made for the powerful and dead of the world.

"Imagine *living* here," people whispered. The Negroes and Indians looked almost disapproving. There is something humiliating about so much beauty. I felt this, too, and kept wishing I were larger or more special. Somebody asked me what I did, and I said, "I keep a hospital for cats."

When a great number of people had arrived, a door at the end of the long gallery opened, and we all felt a hot, gusty wind whip in, and then, as if that had been an elemental forewarning of her person, Mrs. Pratt strode across the threshold. The clock struck nine at this moment, and people seemed to come awake, as in one of those stories about magic toymakers. Voices became loud and varied in pitch, everyone seeking an individual frequency on which he alone could be heard, and because everyone could not speak to Mrs. Pratt at once, they now spoke to each other, where before they had wandered silent and awe-struck.

Mrs. Pratt invited us all into a dining room, where a table was laid with sandwiches and cookies and coffee and a sweet brandy-and-fruit punch, which the high-school students looked longingly at and didn't dare drink in front of their teachers, and everybody else had a lot of. I had a couple of cups, and hovered near where Mrs. Pratt was standing, like a candle in the corner of the room, tall and pale, shedding light. She made no attempt to mingle with her guests, but neither did she seem to be standing aloof from them. She was a fixed and gracious point. Groups of people came tentatively to her and were spoken to, and came away whispering. She had a special way of looking at people, as if examining them under the luminosity of her gaze for qualities invisible under ordinary light. It is hard to say how much of Mrs. Pratt's peculiar power radiates from her soul and how much is just that which naturally accrues to someone incredibly rich. You cannot always remember her actual words, and when you can they sound plain enough, so you cannot explain why it is they have struck you so exactly right.

At about nine-thirty, Sebastian appeared, which surprised me. He got sandwiches and punch for Mrs. Pratt, and was very solicitous. His solicitude, together with his good looks and graying hair, made him appear unfortunately gigolo-like. He was surprised to see me, too, and took me around the living room to hear about the most beloved of his treasures. That was the first time I realized that Sebastian thought of this as his place, his own monument.

A little later, when he had been beckoned away by some important men from another museum, and I had wandered back to the punch bowl—drink has a special fascination for me, because I come by it so rarely in my Mormon milieu— Mrs. Pratt began to say things that struck me exactly right. I remember them.

She drew me to her corner by some unexpressed command. "You look like someone who has left her self at home, Mrs. Fry," she said to me in her spirit voice. "Or is it just negative capability?"

"I've always thought that was just a rationalization of Keats's for not being clever at parties," I said, and felt praised when she laughed.

"You look like someone, in fact—do you mind personal remarks? I make them always, but I mean them quite impersonally, of course. I mean them as truths, and of course truth is utterly impersonal. You look like someone who has not made the important decision yet."

She paused so that I would have to ask what decision. I asked. It is delicious to hear significant truths about yourself.

"Ah. Whether or not it is possible to be happy in this world. Is it or is it not possible? You have to look at the facts and decide about that, before you can begin anything. One's most essential principles must rest on that."

"Surely that's not the kind of thing that can be decided on principle?" I said.

"Well, perhaps no one principle obtains. Perhaps it's a matter of archetypes. Some people march through life, and some stumble, but it seems to me that no matter how they go, sailing or stumbling, every life is bound to end up conforming to some archetype, some well-known organizing motif; it's as if all variations of human existence could be collected in a book of master plots, so perhaps it's only a matter of finding a good one."

It was this remark that struck me, perhaps because I had been wondering about my life in almost those same terms. Until I fell off the motorcycle I had conceived of my life as conforming to one of the great favorite master plots—rags to riches. The poor and timid girl who manages, because of the triumphant collusion of personal merit and circumstance, to marry a prosperous and handsome man. And to sustain this image of myself, I had tended, perhaps, to exaggerate the rags part of my personal history. Actually we were poor only by local Midwestern standards. My childhood was bleak to me, but not so bad that I can blame things on it. There were few true horrors; little cruelty or sickness. It was mostly shades of gray, the whole of it comprehended in a general feeling of deprivation and dismay—unpleasant feelings but not urgent ones—and that is really not the proper sort of a beginning for a rags-to-riches story.

"It's hard to guess your own archetype," I said.

"You don't guess it, you *choose* it. You learn the choices from the lives of others, just as it is from them you learn whether or not it is possible to be happy. Possible for *you*. Well, you squirm at these oversimplifications. You are just like your brother-in-law."

In fact, I prefer oversimplifications, but you have to make sure you have them right, and I was never sure what conclusions to draw from the lives of others.

"It is the principal thing one learns from parents," Mrs. Pratt added. But it was my parents who had confused me.

My father, though an alcoholic, was a charming man. It's true that he didn't introduce me to poetry and the Great Russians at an early age, but at least he did make sure that I looked up every word I didn't know in the dictionary. That is an optimistic trait, but alcoholism is a pessimistic one, and because he was drunk three-quarters of the time, I have to suppose that his real feelings about life were too despairing to be overborne by simple lexicographic curiosity.

My mother despised him, but she was a college graduate and had read books on child rearing which told her never to reveal this to her children. Mother's master plot—the reverse, I hope, of mine—was that of the gentlewoman in reduced circumstances, poor but genteel, suffering her lot in proud silence. She seemed to exemplify the most horrible philosophy of which I could conceive: that it is *not* possible to be happy in this world. She felt it wrong to make demands of life, and even disapproved of religion. The consistency of her refusal to take solace terrified me. I used to try to catch her being happy—would surprise her at her sewing or bring her a present—but she was always the same, implacable, sweet, sad. I would have been reassured by complaining, bitterness, some sign that she knew an idea of joy, some absolute to which life should attain and of which she had been cheated.

With all this she was not a grim or sour woman. She even had a reputation for gaiety, and at her death people said to me that "she always had a smile for everyone." In fact she had an incongruous giggle for petty catastrophe which might have passed for lightheartedness if one did not see that the things which amused her—a torn stocking or fallen cake— did so only because they confirmed her opinion of existence: life thwarts the best of bakers; snags await the most circumspect step.

"I'd rather not learn that lesson," I told Mrs. Pratt.

"I think it is one's duty to be happy, as an example to others," she said.

I expect it is never possible to talk to Mrs. Pratt very long

127

without other people crowding around her, which they began to do now, and she abruptly switched to making sensible remarks about Vuillard. Sebastian reappeared and beckoned me away.

"Come on. Get another drink and I'll give you the rest of the art tour." I didn't need any more to drink, but I wanted to see the house, so I walked with him through the kitchen, which was giant and nearly empty, like a failed restaurant, and into an adjacent pantry where Sebastian made us drinks of whisky—we confessed to hating fruit punch. I asked him what he did about having been drinking when he went home to Patty.

"What husbands have done immemorially. Chew gum or eat mints."

Now we had come out into some sort of library. I had to stop and stare all over again. Sebastian watched me, smiling. It was his house, of course. You wanted to roll in it like a cat. Above me on the library wall a great antelope head, incongruous but somehow magnificent, leered down at us.

"There is no beauty without wit, she says," Sebastian said. "So we keep them. All these beasts were shot by the late Mr. Pratt."

"What happened to Mr. Pratt?"

"He came to a bad end, like Francis MacComber."

"She shot him?"

"No, some other woman did, I think. On a safari. She never talks about it. He was a fortune hunter as well as a big-game hunter, it is said."

"I don't blame her for not marrying again. If I weren't married, I wouldn't marry again. I think you outgrow it," I said.

Sebastian smiled. "That'd be a shame," he said. "This is a Reginald Marsh. I particularly like it. That is an inferior Rousseau. The greatest thing in here is the Dutch secretary, fourteenth century, almost Florentine in design. There is an insipid Degas, and there's the famous Rodin bust you've heard me tell about."

128

Sebastian's love for the place was manifest and touching. He lingered over little bits of things on mantelpieces. He glowed. The tour was a painstaking one. We inspected, tile by tile, the decorated wall he had literally dug up himself out of a ruined hacienda in Mazatlán; he tried to convey to me his astonishment over the condition and workmanship of an ancient Chinese rug, and explained why a certain pretty chest was really vulgar. Sometimes he absent-mindedly dusted things as we walked by them.

"I wish all this were yours, Sebastian. It should be, you love it so," I said.

"No, it doesn't matter. I don't think it matters who it belongs to. We rescue these things for a little while and then someday somebody will rescue them from us."

"The thing is having them, isn't it? Otherwise you would look at them in a museum."

"No, not having, it's finding them. It's making a whole, making it all add up, an expression, love, whatever. I think about it quite a bit, and that's the best explanation I can give. It's harder to justify than some men's work."

"I think you're lucky," I said, and put my hand on his arm. He touched my hair.

"Things aren't so bad, really, are they?" he said.

"Sometimes they seem not so bad," I said, and smiled, and they did not. He hugged me and kissed the top of my head in a brotherly way. "I think I'm learning not to let the big dragon frighten me," I said.

"Good. A dragon is a mythical beast."

"Today at family dinner I could see that. A poor old woman who is disappointed with her life and thinks she's only fit to be sent to Vietnam."

He looked at me. "The big dragon is my *father*," he said. "Surely you see that?"

This confused me. "No, Father Fry is all right. A kind and intelligent man."

"And thoroughly self-involved. His career, his comfort, his

129

concerts—we have all, always, been a great nuisance to him."

"Well, he's passive and vague, sometimes, but . . ."

"Half of what Mother does she does to try to get some reaction from him, even now. Look at my new apron, look at my poor old feet. It's always been that way. When we were little he always worked on Saturday and Sunday, and she would say, 'Poor Father, three little boys just make too much noise for him to concentrate around here.' She believed it. And then once Garth and I walked up to the office to see him, and he was listening to the Philharmonic on his portable radio. And he never bought her anything, so she's made a virtue of necessity, and says she wouldn't respect a woman who is interested in clothes. I may be a lousy husband and father in many ways, but I give Patty as much money as I can. Father doesn't relate to anyone, really, but Father. And he's always had such socially acceptable reasons for doing just what he wants to do—you know—'a man in his position just has to be well-dressed,' 'he just hates being away three weeks in Washington, but . . .' "

"You make him sound like Garth," I said.

"Well, Garth is just like him, only more so," Sebastian said. "Father is guilty of a lot of crimes. He's simply sold poor old Mother on how valuable she is around the house."

"That's what I think. That she's been sold," I said.

He nodded. "Don't you be."

"That's my problem. I'm not. And you have to be sold on something," I said.

He smiled and nodded again, and we went on to see the upstairs. It occurred to me that my children and Sebastian were the only people in the world I felt close to. I didn't even think of Garth to exclude him from the list.

Mrs. Pratt's bedroom was curiously austere, like the cell of a rich medieval nun. It had a funny silver bed and a dresser, that was all. Her bath was simple, too—white tub and tile, blue towels, in one corner the Prunus-blossom vase. Across

130

the hall from the bath was a long moonlit glass porch, from which we could look down upon the lawn, the road, the peaks of the cottages. Mrs. Pratt's canyon wilderness looked formal and tidy at night, the trees trimmed by darkness into neat shapes and the lawn smoothed. I could see the lights in the cottages, could hear the crunch of tires on rock, a car leaving. Where we were, it smelled of turpentine and paint. I waded into a heap of rags, which Sebastian picked up and put on a chair. His arm was around my waist, affecting that whole side of my body with a strange alertness. I was aware that if he moved his fingertips a little they would touch my left breast, and found myself for an instant hoping they would. It was curious, the way my skin went painfully touchy, as if I had been singed.

On the floor in the moonlight a tapestry was spread, the pale figures visible—a unicorn, naked nymphs, hunters in the background, a long-armed lady extending a garland, her gauzy dress exposing dimples and curves. She was woven to look very rosy and three-dimensional, and made me feel flat and shadowy by comparison. Sebastian squeezed my waist and said something in a normal voice about how the open house would go on for hours. We watched an artist return to his cottage.

"Mrs. Pratt is sitting for her new painter. She sits on the tapestry, I guess. She used to do her yoga exercises out here—that's her yoga mat under the tapestry." He let me go, walked over to an easel, and turned it around to face the window. "And this is the picture, evidently."

It was clearly a picture of Mrs. Pratt. The moon shone on her very brightly: Mrs. Pratt naked, sitting primly on the tapestry, a pot of old-fashioned ferns, very realistically painted, behind her left shoulder, her hair done in its most severe knot. It was a beautiful picture, beige thin lady on the rose-and-buff background, ferns, the nude itself a mere thin shape, square-shouldered and bent forward slightly to look out of the picture with big round eyes. Sebastian held up a

131

match and illumined her briefly, bringing up the beiges of her body and the tapestry. Then he shook out the match and looked at her still longer in the moonlight.

"You are more beautiful and real," he said.

"Simply painted in another fashion," I said, attempting a cheery bantering tone. But the note faltered. I was swept by a feeling of tired dependency, not really very different from the tense sexual awareness of a few moments before. In Sebastian's arms they blended nicely, and carried me off before them on a crest of excitement, trusting and eager. Sebastian was kissing me and saying things into my ear. This is it, I remember thinking. It was, too. It isn't that I didn't know what I was doing, but that I said to hell with it. It isn't often you can say that and really mean it; it's a great gift. The discarded shreds of anxious and self-protective morality lay around me in heaps, with my dress, stockings, growing pile of clothing and qualms tossed off to one side. I had a brief objective vision of how we must look, a handsome naked couple on the tapestry in the moonlight, but this vision was obliterated by the feel of it, insanely hopeful, important. What was important? I wasn't sure. Something to do with loving Sebastian, maybe. Passion, communion, and pleasure. For one instant I caught the lunar eyes of Mrs. Pratt's portrait, which seemed, like the eyes of pictures in gothic novels, to live and to watch me, but their intention was not malign. They glowed, enjoining us to passion, communion, and pleasure. Then Sebastian's shoulder above me blotted her out, and my mind forgot itself in the embraces.

It was, in fact, hard to sustain utter abandonment, because nothing happened in the expected way. Things waned. Sebastian writhed in anguish and apology. Things waxed hopeful and waned again. My body and hopes fluctuated in a tidal, female way awhile, and then, as my mind suddenly grasped why all this was important, it forgot my body altogether. My arms were around Sebastian's chest, my lips were against his neck, but my thoughts departed on significant flight. Here, in this

132

unseemly and surprising way, I was finally participating in my own adventure. A modest *acte gratuit*, but mine own. Where before in my small adventures, looking at people, I had been as uncomprehending as Joan, I was for a few moments now as fully conscious, as purposeful as Alma, whom I seemed to see in Mrs. Pratt's picture, watching us. This love-making was for me something very brave, momentous. When I realized that, I think I rendered some mechanical assistance, worried that it might otherwise not count as an *acte gratuit* after all. Finally it did count, technically. I returned to it as if I were rematerializing out of another dimension, slowly becoming aware of my own length and density, my horizontal position, my cold knees, and of the man lying on my breast in an attitude of depletion, to whom I was still temporarily conjoined. This was the actuality, the significant thing. I hugged Sebastian and kissed him in an ecstasy of gratitude and delight.

Suddenly we were cold, awkward, exposed. Fondly we kissed and drew apart and dressed. Sebastian wavered between apology, assurances of his love, and a dazed silence. Clearly he was staggered by our wickedness. I felt it necessary to disguise my exultancy a little, and was careful not to say anything about the future, for fear that would startle and upset him. But I suppose I conceived of myself as being now under his special care.

He walked me downstairs, with an arm around my shoulder. There were still a lot of people there.

"Want to stay awhile?" he asked.

"No, I'll go home. I'm still—I've had plenty to drink," I said. We went out through a back hallway. After the brightness of the past moments the world outside seemed dark and fresh.

He helped me into my car, leaned in, and kissed me through the open window.

"I'm not sure whether to be sorry or glad," he said, smiling. "I'm both, I guess."

"I know. Me, too," I said, though I was only glad.

"Take care," he said, and stepped back into the shadows. I waved and went home. It is odd how one must convey oneself to and from great adventures in the most everyday manner, and even the most exalted transport of spirit cannot disguise that one is stopping, starting, shifting gears, watching out. When I got home it was nearly one o'clock. I had to concentrate on being quiet and on doing things naturally, with that extra degree of precision that proves one is not drunk. The hand that holds the toothbrush mustn't shake, and buttonholes are dealt with swiftly and surely. I stood over Garth's bed, looking down and half hoping he would wake and want to make love to me. Making love to two men in one night would compound my wickedness in an interesting way, take me as far as I could imagine along the road to depravity. Also, I was tense and unsatisfied. That I wished only to use Garth in this way struck me as monstrous but pleasant. I fell asleep in a whirling bed, swollen with the satisfying megalomania of sin.

Chapter 15

For Sebastian it had not been a meaningful existential experience, of course, but an embarrassing, tawdry, and drunken adulterous act with his brother's wife. The memory sank upon him after his first perceptions of the day and the room; before he was any better oriented than that the whole thing came over him with a horrid cramp in his intestines, causing him to sit up and look around in the hope of finding he was wrong about who and where he was and was therefore wrong about last night and hadn't done it. He knew he had, though. The particulars crowded his memory, which was damned strange, he thought, considering how drunk he had been. He clearly saw the familiar sisterly face lying beneath him on the tapestry, with a unicorn under her right ear. No, his right, her left ear. An unfortunate symbol, the unicorn, as it turned out. And the way her eyes kept opening in astonishment and then closing courteously, as if nothing were wrong. His stupid apologies. He shivered with horror as the full significance of the thing became clearer. Pretty little body, straightforward married way of pressing her thighs against him, arms around his chest. Panic seized him. This had to be undone somehow. Garth's wife!

Now he identified a terrible pain in his head—a separate pain from that produced by his anxious emotion. The head was a hangover. It could be fixed with aspirin. He went to the bathroom for aspirin, and Patty called to him about breakfast.

"Just juice," he croaked. He could at least get away from here. "I'm late." Patty was always so acute about seeing when he was upset.

"Watch Daddy," she said crossly, and put Mark in at the bathroom door. "I keep hoping he'll get the idea." Mark, the front of his overalls wet, obediently watched while Sebastian, knowing what was expected, obediently urinated. Then he went back to the bedroom for his clothes. Almost without thinking about it, he reached in his top drawer, pulled out a suit of garments, began to put them on. When he realized what he was doing, seeking this protective fetish, he smiled with chagrin, but he kept them on. Who is God for if not for the wicked?

It could be undone. He thought of calling from Mrs. Pratt's and apologizing, but could you just apologize something like that away? A slip; I love and respect you, but let's pretend it didn't happen. Not very gallant. He tried, as he drove to the Foundation, to correct his spineless sense of personal injury, tried thinking of his innocent prey, that poor beleaguered child, ready to fall a victim to kindness and sympathy. Kindly, loving, sympathetic Sebastian, her only ally and admirer. What could he tell her now? He could feel, physically, the burden of her trust and affection pressing at the back of his head. The head still hurt him. The muscle at the back of his neck was tight as a fist. That was anxiety, not alcohol. He could imagine her at home right now, feeling guilty but happy, loved by someone. He tried not to, but he could not help wishing her in oblivion, and that made him feel doubly guilty. He kept seeing her breasts and the little smile with which she kept reassuring him. If only, damn her, she had not been quite so patient and encouraging. It was funny that he had never liked her better than he did now, exasperated as he was.

136

He went straight to his workroom, avoiding any place Mrs. Pratt might be. She was the last—the second to last—person he wanted to see right now. He composed himself for work, assembling little pots of varnish and paint, glue, wax, the tiny brushes and knives. He fiddled with lights over the canvas he was repairing, fluorescent, ultraviolet, and settled on the strong light from the window. He sat down at the table. He put his glass in his eye. He barricaded himself with all this paraphernalia from thoughts of reality. But his hand wasn't steady. That was drink, not anxiety. The turmoil of his thoughts continued. He absently scraped at a peeling patch of gold leaf on the frame, and constructed, rejected, constructed frenzied plots to undo it all. And rejected them. And overturned a pot of turpentine onto a sheet of leaf, making a golden mess. A golden mess was it, all right. A new horror shot him to his feet. The sunroom. Rumpled tapestry, signs, stains maybe, perhaps an article of clothing left behind. He bolted from the room and up the back stairway.

The room was orderly. Either a maid had been in or we had left it orderly. This was the first thing that had given him any relief, and he savored it, feeling that because this was right, the rest might come right, too.

He stood where we had lain, the remembrance of it more peculiar and unreal in this real room than it had been in his thoughts. Where he had expected an indelible presence to linger over the place like a ghost, there was only the smooth tapestry, the bright morning light, the canvas on the easel, the bare wall. It was as if he had done nothing, as if he had been convicted of a crime on evidence furnished from spying on his dreams. It was impossible to think of any woman but Paris Pratt being in this house.

His gaze, which had been avoiding it, now encountered the painting in progress, from which Mrs. Pratt, naked and severe, stared out at him. Her painted eyes must have surveyed the spectacle, and this struck him as funny, Mrs. Pratt watching his bungling and despicable deed. Mrs. Pratt watching probably accounted for his bungling—Mrs. Pratt and guilt and thoughts of Garth. Had he even thought of Garth? Probably, and with some satisfaction. This is for you, Garth the doctor. There was, apparently, no bottom to his malice and irresponsibility. With Mrs. Pratt looking on. If only it had been she upon the tapestry.

The transparency of his psychology embarrassed him. He would have thought that upon reaching middle age he had become tolerably complex; instead he was constantly being appalled to discover behind his deeds, thoughts even, some silly, simple, always primitive and mostly ignoble wish or motive. Now, sleeping with Karen because he loved Paris, or hated Garth, and/or was lustful and drunk, and jealous that Mrs. Pratt took off her clothes for her new painter. For whatever reason. There was no one simple explanation, of course, but the complexities eluded his mind. Perception of the intricacies of his situation seemed to depend, as in chess, on the sophistication of the intelligence involved, and his mind now was as blank as a board upon which stood one pawn, himself, hapless and culpable. He couldn't even figure out the next move.

He was startled by the opening of the door behind him, and Mrs. Pratt's voice. She walked in, looking very awake and fresh, her hair in its knot, and a book—Montaigne—in her hand. She wore an old flowered bathrobe, knee-length, and was barefoot. She might have been going for a swim.

"My God, love, what's the matter?" she said, seeing his face.

Sebastian now realized that he was holding his head in a histrionic gesture of despair. He dropped his hands and managed a phony smile, intending to say something about his hangover.

"I've returned to the scene of the crime. I seem to have seduced my sister-in-law in here last night," he said instead. There was probably a simple reason for having told her this, but it only seemed inscrutably stupid. She padded toward him on her long, delicate feet. It was then he realized that she must have come in to sit for her painter, and therefore probably had nothing on under the bathrobe.

She looked at him with a strange, alert, surprised expression, as if she was thinking back.

"Oh, did you really? What a funny thing to do. Or perhaps she seduced you?"

"Leave me my sense of villainy, at least. It was a thoroughly rotten thing to do."

Her expression changed now; she looked icy and peevish. "Well, why are you telling me? I suppose you think it's my fault?"

Sabastian did not follow this new train of thought, whatever it was, and her sudden belligerence confused him.

"I meant, why are you telling me about your sordid deeds?" she said.

"But why should I think it's your fault?"

"Isn't it just a way of telling me you have other interests besides me? You are gloating, Sebastian."

"For God's sake, you asked me!"

"I'm not interested. Physical seduction is very uninteresting."

"Yeah, you've been making that plain for years."

"I *am* sorry you've taken advantage of your sister-in-law," she said, "poor little thing."

"Well, so am I. That's what I was telling you," Sebastian said.

"She will become emotionally involved, and she's a nice little girl. She doesn't deserve that. I suppose I could have saved her from it," she said.

"You mean sort of diverted my brutish lust into a harmless channel?" Sebastian said maliciously. "You're a philanthropist to the core."

"It *would* be the ultimate in self-sacrificing charitable acts, believe me," she said. "But that's not what I meant; I . . ."

"Look, you really believe I made a pass at poor Karen

139

because I couldn't have you, don't you?" Sebastian said, enraged at her conceit, and more particularly because he could see the truth in this.

"Yes, of course I do," she said. "I've been listening to you moan of frustration for years."

"Karen is a pretty girl, a very desirable girl," he pointed out.

"Karen is younger and prettier, but I am a challenge," Paris sniffed. "The male ego wants most what it can't have."

"And you've been holding out for six years as a lesson to my pride?" He grasped her arm.

"No, idiot, *my* pride. Rich ladies don't sleep with their young, handsome chauffeurs, not if they have any pride." Then she stopped, and put her hand over her mouth, and smiled nervously.

"I am not your God-damned chauffeur," Sebastian shouted.

"I know it. Sorry," she said.

"That doesn't sound as if you'd think it such an act of charity, anyhow," Sebastian said.

"And I'm not such a harmless channel, either, friend," she said, freeing her arm. "What a rude thing for you to say, anyway."

"You're so God-damned afraid I'll grow a handlebar mustache and steal your fortune," Sebastian said.

"What? What?"

"What I said. You think if I have designs on your so-called most priceless possession, it must be because I want your money. You have such a stingy little soul. It keeps you from doing what you really want to do."

"I do not! There are other, much more important aspects of life, which I prefer to keep uncomplicated by . . ."

"Do you really think all men are after your money?" Sebastian attempted a pitying laugh.

"They *are* always after my money," she said.

"Aah," Sebastian said in disgust, "you poor dumb little woman, you wouldn't know the difference. I guess you think

140

I've been driving you to your cello lessons for six years so you'll remember me in your will, eh?"

"Oh, no, not you. *You* are in love with my Matisses, that's all," she said. "You revel in my Renoirs."

"See? I'm in love with you, and you don't know the difference. Big philanthropist, big lady philosopher, big truthteller, you don't even know love if it hits you over the head."

"Oh, yes, you're in love with me, so you make love to Karen. Ah, well, that's what I said, isn't it?" She sounded surprised.

"All right. Maybe that's right," Sebastian said calmly. "That's probably right. But the thing is, I love you. Two wives, two kids, a mountain of resolutions, and I still keep on loving you in this moronic way—oh yes, and your Matisses and your Renoirs. This place belongs to you, but I've put it together, remember, and I love it. It and you. Look, don't you even know me? You won't let me love you because I'm the chauffeur, is that it? Or you think I'm after your money? Or you worry about my wives, is that it? Or that I'm a little younger."

"I'm just too old to play Lady Chatterley, that's all," she said.

"You are not too old," Sebastian said, hearing himself shout again.

"And I don't like playing home-wrecker either."

"What's the difference? You've been playing that whether you want to or not. You can't help it. *I* can't help it. Look, don't you want to sleep with me? So say so."

"I've said it before."

"So say it again," he said, reaching for her shoulder.

"Oh, Sebastian," she said, evading him, "of course I do. You're a handsome man. You have beautiful shoulders and beautiful hands—I don't need to, that's all."

"I have a beautiful urge to kill you," Sebastian said, "but you're so stupid I feel sorry for you."

"I am not, not, stupid. I'm right about this."

141

"No, you're really stupid. And sore. You're sore, aren't you? Jealous."

"Oh, don't be silly. I'm perfectly used to your having other women—all those pretty little wives. I like thinking of you in your sweet cottage having a happy life."

Sebastian laughed. He was angry but he was beginning to be aware, his blood began to sense, a note of possibility in all this. Mrs. Pratt was getting angry, too. Her body seemed to tremble inside the bathrobe.

"I mean, I'm happy that you're adjusted, Sebastian."

"I'm not adjusted, Paris. I'll never be adjusted, since you put it in that ridiculous way, to not having you." He was surprised and somewhat embarrassed at the tremulous sound of his voice. She looked at him a long time, and then her head drooped like a sad lily.

"Oh, Sebastian, perhaps I have been very stupid about you. Have I ruined your life?"

"Only a very poor-spirited man would consider his life ruined for such a reason. You've made me unhappy, or you have not made me happy."

"I see the thing perfectly well—I suppose I've really been tormenting you. And for no very good reason, only I have thought—my thinking isn't clear to me now. Look, I'm just a very ordinary woman."

She quickly unbuttoned the bathrobe and held it open, showing him her naked body, thin and pale and bony, ordinary enough in truth, but seeming a bright ray of beauty to Sebastian. The suggestiveness of her gesture struck them both at once. She closed the robe and shivered.

"Sleeping with someone is nothing so much. I don't know why I've made a big thing of it. Vanity. Oh, I'm ashamed of that, I . . ." She stopped. Sebastian couldn't think of anything to say either. They stood. The moment bleached out between them.

"Oh, come on, Paris," Sebastian said finally, not knowing quite what he meant. He was conscious that his headache was much, much worse, had seemed to change the shape of

142

his head, was affecting his hearing as if he were standing in a tunnel, and that his blood seemed to circulate through his chest in a discernible network of icy vessels, like a drawing by Vesalius. He had taken her arm again.

"I can't account for it. I feel as if I had been punctured, and all my theories drained away. I can't remember them," she said, her voice little.

"I know them all. The life of the mind. The Platonic ladder without the first rung—because we were so advanced in sensibility."

"Gone. I suspect them suddenly. Do you think all that was needed all along was for you to shout horrid things at me?"

"I've tried that," Sebastian said.

"Have you? I don't remember," she said. He drew her with him away from the sun porch and down the hall.

"I've been afraid," he said. She frowned but suffered herself to be led. Now Sebastian's pain seemed to be drowned in the violence of his other emotions—jubilation, hope. Her eyes held a trance of revelation. Sebastian stopped at the door of her bedroom.

"Are you afraid now?" he asked.

She took a deep breath and smiled. "Are you such a lion? Dear me. But I *am,* probably. For such an ignoble reason, it occurs to me." She faced him in the doorway. "Maybe I've just been afraid of losing you. I am afraid. A spell breaking. It seems so simple, and shameful and selfish. Afraid that once you make love to me you will no longer want to. It's so humiliating to realize . . ."

"If the spell is broken, that's probably just as well." He smiled. "We'll see."

She still hadn't run away, but she curved dejectedly from him and seemed to shrink inside the robe. "I feel as though I were telling you good-bye, instead of being about to—oh, Sebastian, I feel like crying," she said, but she *was* smiling. Sebastian pulled her inside her room and closed the door behind them. They contemplated the bed.

"I love you," he said.

143

"Please, Sebastian, don't be sentimental. I simply couldn't bear it," she said with a quaver. Sebastian took her in his arms and thought for an instant of Patty, a blandly guilty stab, the way one suddenly thinks of a distant neglected relative and resolves to write him. He thought, too, of Karen and of facing her again, but this was only a flicker, like phantom-limb pain, in a part of him quite discarded. He had in his arms the fragile repository of his hopes for as long as he could remember. His emotions, powerful ones formed of impulses only, like electric charges, flowed around her. He felt a galvanic sense of completeness, as if he and she had been arc-welded. They kissed longer. At last she slipped out of the bathrobe and came into his arms naked. Sebastian was racked with ambivalence between his desire to press her to him and to hold her away to look as long as he liked upon the sweet body his heart had so often contemplated. He pressed her to him and at length, clumsily, one-handed, began to take off his shirt and trousers.

Her eyes, which had been ecstatically closed, now opened. A faint inquisitive and alarmed crease appeared on her brow. She drew her head back to look at him.

Suddenly he knew why. The realization struck him even before she said, "What on earth have you got on, Sebastian?"

He had his garments on, of course. There he stood before the object of his passion, the beautiful pale naked lady trembling ardently in his arms, she who had filled his thoughts, informed his every erotic impulse for six years, in a baggy nylon union suit with appliqués on nipple and crotch. It was just. He recognized that.

"I, oh, Christ, garments," he said. "Mormon underwear."

Mrs. Pratt was nonplused, but only for a second before she was possessed again of the unfailing poise of the true lady.

"How exciting," she whispered into his ear, pressing to him again. "It adds something, brings out the Salome in a woman. It's like seducing John the Baptist."

They lay together naked on her bed. When he thought about it afterward, Sebastian was surprised at how nearly

144

their love-making had approached the ecstatic revelations he had always imagined. He sat up to look at her, and to stroke her damp breasts and stomach, and to wonder at the way his eye, sated with curves—Rubens, Renoir, Botticelli bottoms —reposed itself in Paris's angles. There was something exciting about sharpness, the direct erotic appeal that the languorous inertia of roundness lacked. Even at this moment, his own body warm and weak with pleasure, he responded to the delicious, fragile set of her shoulder, the right angle at the intersection of collarbone and a tendon of her neck, the angle of the jawbone beneath the ear, the level line of the eyebrows, the straight nose. Her round eyes, which looked at him now with, he hoped, affection, satisfaction, were her only deviation from the rectilinear.

"My rectilinear love," he said, and kissed her small round navel.

"Maybe I'll have a baby," she observed in a loving voice. "We should have used something."

"That would be nice. You could pass him off as an orphan from somewhere, one of your numberless good works." He liked the idea of a love-child, suddenly.

"I'm too old, though."

"No, you're not. Ah, and my child would inherit your vast fortune, just as I've always planned."

"Sebastian Fitz-Pratt," she said. "I like that."

"Oh! I love you," Sebastian cried, overjoyed about equally with her presence and his own returning powers. He took her in his arms again.

Later they lay a long time on the bed talking. She wanted to hear about Karen. Sebastian could just bear, now, to think about it.

"But what is she *like?*" Paris insisted. "I don't have any sense of her, beyond a pair of big curious eyes."

"Well, I don't know. She's on the other side, someone who has crossed over with the rest of us. She's one of us, whoever we are."

"We are lovers," Paris said.

145

"Yes, that's what she is. But she is just realizing it."

"Perhaps she loves you?"

"No. Oh, no. We've spent each Sunday for six years together, and only in the past few weeks have I begun to see this glimmer, a camaraderie. After six years she seems to be saying, 'Here I am.' But it isn't love of me."

"Ah, yes, she is just realizing things," Paris said. "We care about her, I think."

"Yes," Sebastian said. "We do care about her. We love her. I wonder how I can tell her that? I was trying to, I guess, by making love to her, though that was unhelpful, wrong. Or maybe not. Karen is someone you want things to happen to, for her. It seems distant, as if it had not been me with her last night. Can a person be both timid and brave?"

"You can't be brave unless you are afraid," Paris said. "Nothing counts unless you are. Why *are* we talking in this vein?"

"The grandeur of the occasion. Karen is the brave child at the foot of the dark stair, then. There are other things, too. Her body is new and lovely. I want good things to happen to her, but she will have to do such hard things first. I don't know what, exactly."

"Nobody knows what they have to do. It *is* a dark stair."

"The image promises a bright light at the top of it," Sebastian said. "I don't know about that either."

"If you could depend on a bright light, you wouldn't be brave," Paris said. "I suppose we could help Karen up the first step."

"Oh, no, she'll get there."

"We are philanthropists," Paris said, and rolled over closer to her night table to reach for the telephone. Sebastian thought at first she was going to summon some minion to come fix up Karen's life. Then, horrified, he realized it would be more like Paris to be calling up Karen herself. She was such a believer in directness, confrontation.

"For God's sake, put that down," he said, reaching over

146

her. She held the phone away. A male voice hummed in the receiver. She smiled.

"Dr. Fry? Doctor Garth Fry? Let me tell you something. Tell your wife to stop seeing my husband. Just tell her to leave him alone or there'll be trouble." There were sputters in the receiver. She replaced it.

"Are you out of your mind?" Sebastian was sitting up staring. Paris lay back against her pillows and tucked her arms beneath her head. She was laughing at his face.

"What the hell were you doing? Now Garth will be all over her. My God! She's got enough trouble. If you think that's going to get *me* out of it . . ."

"That wasn't her husband; it was your father," Paris said, face serene with delight. Sebastian put his feet on the floor and looked around for his pants, as if he had to go put out fires somewhere.

"You are . . . you're out of your mind," he said.

"And you're very dull, love," she said. "Stay, I'll tell you." Sebastian looked at her, but he was seeing a variety of horrible scenes involving various combinations of his relatives.

"What are you afraid of, anyway?" Paris said. "Karen will be all right. We are making things easy for her, really. It's always easier when life forces you to do what you want to do anyway. Forces you to examine the choices, and consider what you've done."

"But it's so peremptory—I'm sure she's considering what she's done as it is. I don't see that it was necessary to raise suspicions in the minds of my family."

"Oh, you're just in the grip of a very ordinary scruple about not tattling, that's all. Ordinary scruples are so limiting, Sebastian."

"Ordinary small scruples are all I seem to have left," he said, and smiled.

For an unscrupulous man, he felt very happy. The best metaphor he could find for the feeling was the one about the

147

load off the mind. He could now at least count on his love for Paris, and everything else would be bound to fall in line. He would be a better husband and father now, his own man, at ease inside, a model husband and father, generous and loving, a devoted husband, the kindest of providers. He even felt able to cope with the Karen situation, though he still had not the slightest notion what would happen. He was, as he came up the walk at home, for a man who had left after breakfast in the most desperate misery, the very picture of someone who had had a good day.

He was late for dinner, and the boys were already in bed. With Patty, this usually meant she wanted to discuss something with him. He withered with fear that she wanted to start in on the subject of his employment, an obsession with her, it seemed. Patty had been taught in her course on marital relations at Morris not to nag; instead, when she wanted to bring something up, she provided softeners and sweeteners. Tonight she had a good dinner—fresh salmon roasted on the charcoal grill in the back yard, and she had done the roasting, though this was locally a man's province and one which Sebastian accepted but disliked. Sebastian read the paper, or pretended to—his mind was busy—while she put the food on the table and arranged flowers in the middle. He wondered what was on her mind.

"Well, out with it," he said finally, feeling fond of her, as he would of a pretty and helpful secretary.

"Out? Oh." She laughed. "How was your day?"

"Part good, part bad," Sebastian said truthfully. "How about yours?"

"Fine," she said.

"What's on your mind, honey?"

She saw that he was looking at the elaborate supper, and laughed again. "Nothing, honestly. I just want to have everything nice for you, Bas, that's all. I really do try. . . ." A wistful note crept in under her laughter.

"Everything is just the way I like it," he said. She hovered for additional assurances—perhaps that was all that was on her mind—but Sebastian did not feel effusive. Finally she began to carry off the plates, looking disconsolate.

He made up for this by reading to her, a pastime which she found companionable and he found mercifully the reverse. She curled up at his feet, leaning against his knees with the rug she was hooking drawn up over her lap, and listened to several chapters of *Lord Jim*. At nearly ten she pushed back the rug and laid her face against his knees.

"I'm sleepy," she said, in a tone he recognized. She had learned in her course on marital relations at Morris that it was proper to take the initiative in these matters and therefore had never felt embarrassment at doing so. Sebastian broke off in the middle of the paragraph and felt every ounce of energy leave his body. He could see they would have to get on some kind of schedule at home.

"You're sleepy but I'm tired," he said, sounding, he supposed, like a housewife.

"All that tennis and archery," Patty said, with an edge in her voice. For a change he didn't feel annoyed.

He felt, in fact, pleased at his own good-natured adaptability to the demands of life. "Oh, come on, then, Mama," he said, patting her hair.

"Patty," he said later, "are you asleep?"

"No," she said.

He was silent, attending a struggle that raged within him; one part of his consciousness observed, powerless and horrified, while the sleepy, guilty, loving, and tired man that constituted most of him wrestled weakly with an impulse that the loving but guilty have always had, resisted, argued, and, at length, the resistance overcome, yielded to. Over the silent protests of his more prudent self, he spoke, in a drowsy, affable voice.

"Do you still want a new table?"

She rustled and lifted her head. "Yes! I'm dying to get rid of that old thing. We can sell it."

149

"No, but we can buy a new one. It's okay with me."

Now she sat upright, amazed. "I want a good one, you know, maybe three hundred dollars."

"Yeah, I know."

"Well, but can we afford it?"

"Yes, dear, that's why I'm telling you to buy it." She toppled rapturously onto his chest and kissed him.

"Sebastian, did you get a raise today?" she whispered.

"I got a bonus," he said, after a second's pause.

Chapter 16

Sebastian had waked up that morning miserable, but I was exhilarated. Life on the other side. It's pleasant waking up to find yourself painlessly passed over into a new state. I half wanted to spring out of bed, but Garth was up clattering in the kitchen, so I lay considering things. Garth, with his uncanny sense of what would discomfort me, came back upstairs with a glass of orange juice for me—a nearly unprecedented kindness. So I was stricken a moment with guilt, controlled it, and listened with extra amiability to his monologue, mostly addressed to himself, about an operation he was going off to do. When he had washed his hands again and left, my thoughts drifted once more to Sebastian's caresses.

I reviewed my crimes and counted them up: I had trespassed against married love, conjugal vows, friendship, tribal incest taboos (maybe; I wasn't sure what they were in our tribe), motherhood, and common sense. And then I did bound out of bed with a great spurt of energy and enthusiasm, took a bath, fed the children breakfast, cleaned the kitchen drawers. Kate's cold was worse, so she had to stay home from nursery school, but I didn't mind. My real secret life had taken such an interesting turn that I didn't even look at the paper to see what I was missing. Instead, the children and I made taffy apples, which actually didn't turn out well because for no apparent reason the goo wouldn't stick to the apples. I tried everything—dipping them in vinegar, scouring them with Ajax—all the time worrying about what kind of horribly goo-resistant carcinogen they had been sprayed with. Finally I called Mother Fry. Perhaps I just wanted to hear her voice, or it may have been an unworthy attempt to bring my domesticity to her notice. She seemed impressed that I was making my children taffy apples, but had no remedy for the problem, which, her tone implied, would not have arisen for normally competent people. In the end I let Kate and Toby eat the taffy separately from the apples, which pleased them just as well. In the afternoon we went to the beach. The world was passive and challenging, like a beautiful but enigmatic poem whose interpretation depends upon the erudition of the reader.

By next day I was qualmish and self-critical, wanting to understand just what it was I had done and why. Was I a Joan or an Alma? Finally I went to visit Joan, to see if there was now a mystical bond between us, and whether I now understood her better.

I had learned a lot since the day I fell off the motorcycle, but Joan, I thought again as soon as I saw her, had so far learned nothing. She was depressed, she said. She was a couple of days late with her period, and this always made her feel clogged and wretched. She seemed distracted, too, by something that had happened that morning, though she wasn't sure what it was. It was fuzzy and confusing to her then, though she has since recalled the experience in detail. It was an important experience; I think it was the first loose rock in the subsequent landslide.

It had started about eight-thirty that morning. The door slammed, and the house was abruptly soundless. She stood silently at the stove for a minute, letting the fact of solitude register. William could be heard outside scraping a toy against the sandbox, but that was mercifully outside. She was alone. She continued to rub the Brillo pad against the burner,

152

brightening the metal where the breakfast egg had burned on. Then she scoured the frying pans in the sink. She had learned that letting them soak while she did the rest of the kitchen was more efficient than attacking them straight off. She swept the linoleum, mopped the scuffed parts, covered the toaster, crumbed the table a final time, and went upstairs to do beds. She remembered hearing a woman in Primary say that her daughter spent an hour every morning doing the bathroom, and she felt guilty, because she took only a half hour. Wondering what extra things the daughter did, she dropped a handful of crumpled paper napkins off the kitchen table into the bathroom sink, and used them one by one to wipe the mirror, tub, top and underside of the toilet seat, and around the base of it. Then she flushed the napkins away and scrubbed the floor very thoroughly, and disinfected with pine-smelling solutions. She made beds, seven children's beds, including three high bunk beds. Several children had remembered to hang up their pajamas. This ought to be noted for commendation later, but she suddenly felt herself unequal to the task of determining who was dutiful, who was erring. It was about time they were hanging up their pajamas.

She turned back the covers on her and Mahonri's bed and began to tighten the bottom sheet. They had a king-size bed, which was only natural considering her height and Mahonri's general bulk. She brushed the sheet, startled at how littered it was. Specks, smudges, hairs. She had just put this sheet on. She peered closer at the debris. Was it possible that they were such dirty people? The dirt was mostly on Mahonri's side, too. She looked to see if there were any signs on the sheet of the conjugal act. There were not. It was strange that there never were. She would have let another woman change her sheets any day, except for this sediment left by Mahonri. She picked a hair off the pillow and quickly tossed the blankets up again. She was uneasy at her own revulsion. To shake it off, she started briskly down to the service porch to iron. She felt that it was better to do a little ironing every day than to save it for all at once. She scorned the school that told you to turn on the TV and enjoy yourself while you ironed.

"Ironing is ironing," she had said to Mother Fry, "and you might as well face facts." Mother Fry had agreed.

She started in by picking up Mahonri's shirt and noting immediately that the jam stain had not come out, so it would have to be hand-spotted. That peculiar nagging center of irritation became more acute. Well, natural enough; when you wash something you like it to come clean. She put the shirt aside and picked up a child's blouse. It was not unstained itself, but this did not feel so exasperating. It was not so important if a child's blouse was stained. A man's white shirt has to be immaculate.

William came in and went out again. Joan, her heart beating strangely, got up and turned on the television. This was quite unlike her, but she felt the need of noise. She was not ordinarily one of those women who have time to watch TV during the day. A scene grew upon the screen, showing a woman with her head buried in her hands, her shoulders shaking, behind her a man in a white doctor's jacket, looking grave, and at the door behind him, a woman in an elegant coat, watching the crying woman with an expression of malice and hatred on her face. For a reason she could not understand, Joan felt a prickle of horror, and left the ironing board again to change the station. It had been a premonitory twinge, a sensation brief but unpleasant, that such emotions as grief and malice do contort human faces and alter human lives. Those stricken faces had seemed to have a pertinence, a relevence to her own life, and yet she could not say why. She turned the television off and then turned the iron off and went to look in the back yard. William, more than three years old, stood in the sandbox without his pants on. He had soiled himself; his buttocks and thighs were smeared. Joan stamped out the door and across the grass, and dragged him inside to the bathroom. She could not say a word to him; she was, she could not understand why, suffocating with anger.

William, sensing it, began to howl and wrestle with her. His face grew red with indignation, he reeked foully, he made horrible noises. She shook him and stood him in the empty bathtub while she got a rag to clean him with. She barely allowed herself to look at his red, wet, contorted face, but when she did, she was struck with his resemblance to Mahonri. It was an instant in which she saw the man in the child; William was Mahonri, plump, reeking, red, and screaming, with smeared and stinking loins. Joan, unable to endure this, dispelled the moment by smacking William's face, thrusting the rag at him, telling him to clean himself, and running from the bathroom.

She would never be the same again. She sat on a kitchen chair, weary and violated, exhausted by the effort of not seeing for one moment what she had seen. What had she seen? This was not so clear. She had always known that William looked like Mahonri; that was nothing. Did she hate William? Was it not exasperation over his toilet lapse, but real hatred of her own child she had glimpsed? Not quite. She groped. Her brain was steadily on the track of some firm, verifiable, verbalizable truth, something you could tell people or embroider on a sampler, and she was going to discover it. That red, child's face, the fat stomach, the dangling penis, the howls. The howls. It was Mahonri. She had felt a pure sensation of hatred for Mahonri. She hated Mahonri.

She rose immediately from the chair, sorrowful that she had been vouchsafed this knowledge, and went into the bathroom, where she gently cleaned and kissed poor sobbing William, who had never before been struck by his mother. She sent him back outside with cookies, and then, in her usual methodical fashion, began to make sure that she had interpreted herself correctly.

She went upstairs and looked at Mahonri's clothes, standing quite patiently before them as one does before a wonder of nature, waiting to be suffused with the appropriate emotion. It was, in this case, hatred. She stood smelling the characteristic odor of shaving cream and hair dressing that came off his clothes, and shivered with disgust. She looked at his hairbrush, encrusted between the bristles with oil and dandruff, and her stomach churned. His toothbrush was vile with a deposit of unrinsed toothpaste. The insides of his slippers were stained with sweat from his feet. Horrible, horrible. She began a kind of distracted orgy of emotion, feeding her revulsion on any detail. Their wedding picture— see the signs of incipient coarseness, his selfish eyes—a stick of gum left on the dresser, the size of his suits. She missed nothing—the peeling place in the bathroom where he should repaint, the space where the washing machine ought to be and was not, his stereo, the things in cans in the kitchen cupboard, cocktail sausages and sardines, that he sucked when he watched television. She slowed down and became more methodical, opening closets and cupboards one by one and receiving from each new shock of revulsion fresh confirmation of her newly discovered emotion. Each and every thing redolent of him she could regard, did regard, with an impartial and inexhaustible hatred; she proved it in every corner of the house. At length she sat down in the kitchen again, breathing heavily, as if she had been running, and waited, hoping that something would happen to efface the clarity of her discovery. It was the largeness, the absoluteness, the incredible implications of the discovery she could not bear. It was as if she had suddenly discovered herself to be heir to a kingdom or gifted with genius—discoveries admonishing action and responsibility, which could not be ignored but must be acted upon at great personal sacrifice. It is at great personal sacrifice that I hate you, Mahonri. To hate you is a great personal sacrifice.

She felt this. It was too great a sacrifice. The longer she sat in the sacred presence of her kitchen, whose clock ticked off moments until the children, some of them, would come home, and whose windows disclosed plump, happy William in the back yard eating cookies, and whose stove shone and

156

whose cupboards stored the pledges of her love and good will and good intentions—jars of pickled watermelon, jars of minted pears—the longer she sat in this presence the more she was reassured that she would not have to make the great personal sacrifice. Some are spared. She was soothed slowly. The discovery, clear enough moments ago to embroider on a sampler, began to be effaced; the colors ran, the stitches frayed out, the motto was no longer readable. The click-click of the cooling iron asserted itself. The hum of the freezer asserted itself. Childish scuffing footsteps on the front sidewalk asserted themselves. She got up, tired and empty, but feeling that she had, for the moment at least, been spared a horror, the nature of which she was no longer, for the moment, quite sure of.

When I saw her, she still looked as if she had seen a terrible specter, but she couldn't describe it. She was blanched and vacant, her hair frizzier and her clothes sadder than usual. It didn't help that we were both adulteresses; I still didn't have much to talk about with Joan, though I tried to say soothing things.

I didn't want to go around and see Patty, though I knew I would have to sooner or later, but she, all sweet and unknowing, called me up on Wednesday to ask if I would sit with Mark and Eric while she went to a La Leche board meeting, and of course I said yes.

I got what I deserved, too. I felt deceitful and more. I felt jealous. Patty was waiting for me in the back yard, where Mark was splashing in the wading pool and the baby slept in a basket on the doorstep. There was a settled air of comfortable domestic tranquillity upon the scene. Acute discomfort settled on me. All I could think of was Patty and Sebastian in bed, in the embraces of sacred matrimony, and they seemed to be getting on very well. It didn't even help to think of Sebastian thinking of me while making love to Patty. And worst of all, I learned that my fantasy life had been forever ruined by my one brush with reality. I could no longer imagine any scene, in any context or with any characters, that did not take on the aspect of Joan and the furnace man.

These first impressions passed, of course, and then a worse feeling came—arrogant pity for Patty because she didn't know. I understood for the first time the way in which sin corrupts, not by creating an insatiable appetite for more, but by inducing such contempt of honest people. I felt unhappy when I saw Patty because I felt I could not feel contrite.

"Hi," I said, pushing open the gate to the back yard. Kate and Toby ran screeching toward the wading pool. "Take off your shoes, Kate."

"Hi," Patty said. "I haven't seen you all week. What've you been doing?"

"Oh, you know, busy," I said, waiting tensely for those feelings of jealousy and embarrassment to dwindle. Patty looked pretty, calm, unsuspecting, the same. I looked the same too, though I had to glance down at my legs and feet to confirm it.

"I have to run, but I do want to talk to you," she said. "I'm in the midst of great decisions. Sebastian has finally come through, sweet man. Monday night, practically out of the blue, he said I could have a new dining-room table. He told me to go ahead and pick it out. So I've collected these manufacturer's catalogues—you might look at them while I'm gone. The other thing I'm trying to make up my mind about is whether to cut my hair." She pulled her braid. "I'm just sick of it this way."

I had never liked it long, and was about to encourage her to cut it, but then I had to stop and think. For the wicked, apparently, everything becomes a moral question. Perhaps I would be encouraging Patty to destroy something about her that Sebastian loved, and that would be a rotten thing to do. Or, if I encouraged her to keep it, dowdy and faintly passé as it was, perhaps I was trying to keep her from looking her best. Also rotten.

158

"I hate to think of being bothered with having it done and curlers and all that, but I am so sick of it this way." She jumped up to go. "Life is full of problems," she observed, and closed the gate behind her.

So it would seem. But when Patty had left, my discomfort left me, too, and a certain pleasure in life reasserted itself. It was paradoxical, but the more surely I knew that life is full of problems, the happier I felt with it. Only one thing marred my pleasure in the sunny back yard, in the sight of the children splashing, in the bright day: I had thought Sebastian might call me, but he had not.

Later in the day I found out why. Every thought was routed from my confident, self-possessed new consciousness by coming home from Patty's to find my mother-in-law sitting in my kitchen.

"Put the children down for their naps," she said. "You and I are going to have a talk."

I didn't even pretend I didn't know she meant a serious talk. Toby and Kate must have sensed it, too; they crawled into bed with cowed looks. Mother Fry had stayed at the kitchen counter. I was acutely aware that the dishes sat dirty in the sink, a book lay open by my empty coffee cup on the table, Katy's shoes were in the middle of the floor. Mother Fry had moved the open peanut-butter jar to put her purse down on the counter. Her eyes seemed to contain her intelligence of every detail of this mess, and, as she looked at me, her intelligence of me. She knew, I had the frantic thought. She knew about me.

"I suppose I've seen as much of life as anyone," she began. It was her usual vein. "I'm not ignorant or naïve. I know that people have troubles and temptations. Women as much as men." Her voice was flattened with dislike, as if she could not bear to waste a heightened inflection on me. In spite of this I could see that she was trying to speak kindly. She had not come to accuse, but to advise. My relief at realizing she could not, of course, have known about Sebastian and me was still confused with the sense that she did know.

I sat across from her and felt my face congeal into expressionlessness, as it always did when I talked to her. My knees were weak; I could not have stood.

"And I've seen enough people to know that lives can be ruined. Misery and error, and a life is ruined forever. And not one life, but the lives of many. Lives of children. I don't presume to know much about you, Karen. I guess you didn't have some advantages. I don't understand a certain kind of person, because I don't come from that sort. I don't mean to talk to you about religion. I know there's no point in bringing that up. All the same, I'm talking about your immortal soul."

It was odd how Mother Fry always talked about anything by talking about herself. What was she talking about now?

"I'm sorry, but my immortal soul doesn't worry me, Mother Fry," I said. She leaned across the counter, very close to me, and I noticed she was wearing powder, which I had never known her to do before. In spite of it, her red face was redder than usual. She is an old woman, I remember thinking. Her lashes are white like her hair. Her pale eyes did not release my face. All at once I saw what she was talking about. She did know. How on earth could she have known?

"For better or worse, you married my son Garth. He isn't a perfect man; no man is. But Garth is better than most, and you are lucky. You know that. I don't say it because he is my son but because it's true. One of *the* promising young vascular surgeons, as everybody knows. Like any man, he needs a wife. And you can't seem to be one. I don't presume to know why. I'll never understand a girl like you anyway. Life seems so simple and joyous for a woman. Her duties are her joys; that's a blessing men don't always have. But you seem not to have any joys—you seem to hate the rest of us, hate your life, bring down one trouble after another on yourself and Garth and the children."

"I don't think that's true," I said.

"Your life will always be a burden to you," she said. "You deny your womanhood."

"That is not true," I said.

"I've come to suggest, Karen, that you get some help for yourself if you can't handle your problems. Professional help." She drew back, keeping me in her gaze. "I don't think anything so serious has happened yet but that you can't save yourself and Garth and the marriage, but you need insight, emotional maturity. Remember you have the children to think of. I'm sure—we haven't discussed it with him—Garth will agree. If he understood these things fully, he would insist."

I guessed she was saying that Garth didn't know about it yet, that she wouldn't tell him if I went along to the doctor like a good girl.

"I know you don't have religion, and you can't seem to talk things over with me the way Joan and Patty do. Just having someone to talk things over with would do you a lot of good."

"I don't know, Mother Fry," I said, as bravely as I could. "I think the real trouble is that I think what I do is dumb and boring, and I don't believe in it, and sometimes I think I ought to go learn to be something else. Then I could hire some imbecile to do the things I do."

Her face twisted. She stared at me for a long moment, so angry that I had to think over what I had just said, for fear I had said something more.

"How dare you say a thing like that!" she spat. "You are a stupid girl, and you don't know anything. You have contempt for the lives of millions of fine women. Who are you to be contemptuous of something you can't even do? It's wicked to despise the lives of others. I . . . that just makes me so mad, I . . ."

I had not meant to hurt her feelings. She is an old woman.

"I just meant, I'm no good at it, I ought to do something else," I said. "I just seem to get into trouble, sitting around."

161

"Why don't you get to work, then? Work in your home, the way women should. You don't know anything; you know nothing of work and satisfaction and life. You'd better learn, Karen, because only bad can come of it otherwise, and I don't want to see Garth and the children caught in it. You are a selfish, self-centered, vain, vain person, and you'll be miserable all your life."

"No, I won't, Mother Fry," I said. "I am determined not to be miserable." Then she turned her head, as if she could no longer bear to look at me, and left the house.

Chapter 17

I watched Mother Fry out the door and then walked upstairs, feeling, more than anything else, relieved. Now I would leave Garth. Not to avoid exposure or a psychiatrist. It was simpler than that. I would just leave because it was time, and it would avoid unpleasantness, and I was, after all, a guilty wife. I did wonder how they had found out. I believe it was that, more than anything else, that I thought of as my feet carried me around the house on ineffective little errands of preparation. I got crawlers and shirts for Toby and packed them in a plastic airlines satchel. I went into the bathroom and put some lipsticks, eye paint, Kate's and my toothbrushes, toothpaste, hand lotion, hair spray, aspirin, powder, ointment for Toby's rash, and, strangely, my diaphragm, into my biggest purse. Brave little woman setting out for a new life. I got a sweater and two dresses and some underwear for me and put them in my beach basket with some clothes for Katy. I put some of their favorite toys in a paper sack, Toby's blanket, five children's books, my nice edition of Shakespeare, my first edition of *The Bostonians,* my best jewelry, my childhood diaries, the latest *New Yorker,* two pairs of shoes, some letters, a pen, an address book, paper and ink, Kate's slippers, a little vase I've always liked, my good scissors, the photograph album, a favorite candlestick, warm coats for all of us, six unopened packages of stockings—forgetting anything to hold them up with—two carving knives my father had put the handles to, a length of expensive green wool I was going to have a suit made of, and the figure of a bear, carved in ivory by an Eskimo. Kate crept out of her bed and followed me interestedly.

"But where are we going, Mommy?" she kept asking.

"We're going to have a little vacation, mouse," I said.

"But where are we going?" And I had no idea, of course. We were just going.

For some reason Garth had driven a Citroën that morning, and for some reason I decided to run away now in his Porsche. It was hard fitting everything in it, but what didn't go in the trunk I stuffed into the space in the back of the rear seat. I put the top up in case Toby tried to leap out, and wondered briefly whether Garth would have me arrested for car theft. As we pulled out the driveway I heard the phone ringing. I didn't think it would still be ringing by the time I went back to answer it, so I didn't try. We sat in the car waiting for it to stop. It rang for nearly five minutes, and the children howled for me to go.

We went. A couple of hours before, I had gone into the house happy, and now I had come back out a fugitive. The world in the meantime had undergone a great change. I had expected it might seem alien, enormous, but instead it had altered in the opposite direction. Before it was impersonal, existing to provide my household, like a great store. Now it had shrunk; its corners and strange stairways were all places I might go; I might live on any of these streets. Everything I looked at was suddenly relevant to me in a new way. I saw more, and had the feeling that if I could maintain my augmented vision I would see everything. Some of this feeling of possibility infected the children, too. See the blimp, see the tandem bicycle, see the purple poodle. We shouted at wonders. Garth's car goes very fast, even between stop lights, and the tail pipe made a splendid roar behind us, as if we were

164

being escorted by the motorcycle police. See, see the fire engine, see the man with the long, long beard.

Where to go? You have the impulse to exert some kind of revenge on the people you have left by going someplace impossibly sordid, a trailer park or a downtown hotel. Another impulse is to go far away, where the surroundings will make up with their wild strangeness for the strangeness you feel inside.

The children wanted to go to the beach, and that seemed a good idea. The beach is inevitably soothing and hospitable, a natural place for people. My mind, which seemed clear and happy, was not working practically. I had no thoughts of food, shelter, money—only of having left home. I was doing what I ought to have done—the usual analogy about being pushed into cold water in which you have been dragging your toe best serves. Fortune clearly had directed me into the arms of Sebastian and prompted him to speak out afterward. Beyond this, I tried not to think of him much, because thoughts of Sebastian, strangely, hurt me more than thoughts of Garth did. It was not that I supposed he loved me—I don't think I hoped he did, really—but that I had thought of him as an agent of good. And he had hurt me; for I reluctantly concluded that it must have been he who told his parents, or confessed to Patty in a fit of remorse, or something.

I did think of Garth, too, of course. I found myself remembering, not our recent years together, but our wedding. We had run away for that, as I was running now, and were married in Las Vegas in something called the Little Chapel of the Orange Blossoms. I had never liked remembering our wedding, because it was, at the time, a disappointment. I had always wanted to be married in a white dress with all the fuss. What can I have been like, to have set such store by something like that? But I did. It seemed like a shame to have saved up my virginity for the Little Chapel of the Orange Blossoms.

The rest of it, our brief honeymoon, had been perfect, but

I tried to put that out of my mind completely. Idyllic honeymoon weekends are not what you should be thinking of when your character has been exposed and you have left your husband and taken your children, his car, and the family treasures. The beach is a good place for putting things like this out of the mind. It is beautiful at the end of the day, empty of all but a few walkers, barefoot people in old clotnes striding along the hard sand in the shallow water among the sea birds who come down to pick tiny creatures out of the sand. And a few people sit here and there on blankets to watch the sun set. I sat on the sand, too, while the children ran and chased birds. You couldn't sit forever on the beach, I knew, but it was peaceful and good now. And then I had a horrid conversation with an old woman, telling me secrets. As on secret-life days, it seemed, the world provides to him who will listen.

The children had been entranced by a small dog, who sniffed in the sand at their feet and led them, with little yaps, to the buried feet of its mistress, a stout old woman in a plaid jacket who was sitting on a mound a hundred yards from us with her feet in the sand as if in a bucket of water. She was gazing out to sea but appeared to think about her feet or some process going on within her big body; her smile was viscerally oriented. She paid no attention to the children at first, ignoring them so steadfastly that I began to fear they would bother or startle her when she finally did notice them. So I drew close and prepared to interfere in Toby's attempts to help the dog unbury her feet.

"Never mind. They love it; it's a game," she said without turning her head to look at me. She wiggled her feet, suddenly exposing the tips of her toes, like ten white pebbles on the sand. Toby shrieked and fell upon them with his shovel. I apologized.

"It's okay," she said. Now she looked at me, and I looked more closely at her. She had deep, deep eyes, set in caves, invisible in shadows, but the rest of her face was made of puffs and pads of plump old skin. Her untidy gray hair was bound up with a twisted nylon stocking. She wore a man's watch. When she turned her head a certain way, the low sun made her deep eyes shine out at me wickedly.

"You're late on the beach," she said. "Usually there's nobody here at this spot but me. Dog and me."

"I like this time of day," I said. "Do you live on the beach?"

"I wish," she said. "No, I come down in the car every evening. Are you having a vacation?"

"Actually we're running away from home," I said, liking the way this sounded. She seemed interested, making me feel by her knowing nod and look of sympathy that she had had a great deal of experience in running away, and I sensed she was going to say something important about it. I hovered timidly and then sat down near her. She made a moving-over gesture, though her wide bottom did not move at all.

"Your first husband?" she asked. I nodded. "It's a very exciting thing, leaving your first husband. Scary." The eyes looked at me sidewise out of the caves.

"Yes, but we're having a good time," I said.

"Good. You can do anything as long as you have a good time of it. I remember the day I left my first husband." She had had quite a few, as it turned out—like the Wife of Bath, whom she seemed at first to resemble. I remember only the end of the monologue, because it scared me.

"I've been in a lot of beds with a lot of men," she said, "but what I remember most is not that part. Not usually." The poodle turned tail on Toby, kicking sand on his head, so I had to rescue him and dust him off.

"What I remember is the showers. Baths and showers. You could always tell about a man, if you didn't know already, by the showers."

"How? What could you tell?" I felt it was something somebody on the brink of adventures ought to know. She folded her plump arms and resumed her sea-gazing, seeming now to see in the shapes of sunset clouds to the west a succession of clean pink lovers approaching out of the past.

"I used to think there was something not quite nice about a man who wanted to wash right off afterward, but I was wrong. The way they all want to stuff you into the shower, there must be something else about it, I figured. Probably some nice basic urge, like animals. Monkeys and elephants wash each other, I know. Love and co-operation. Watch out for the man who puts you in a cold shower, though. Like as not he simply wants to wake you up. Greedy types are one-night standers, believe me. After awhile I got to like it, the back-scrubbing, particularly. A gentleman will scrub your back. You scrub him, too, if you aren't too shy. Well, if you are, you shouldn't be there anyway."

I had begun to feel funny, apprehensive of this revelation, and did not really want to hear more of it. But I asked for more. "What else can you tell?"

"Observe the soap. Never marry a man—here's a rule—who uses the soap on his privates before you have washed your face. Well, actually, if you wear as much make-up as I used to—I was no natural beauty, believe me—you better not really wash your face. Leave the eyes alone and hope to Jesus he doesn't push you all the way under. Just kind of dab at your skin. But you're a pretty thing, no need to worry about that."

"Thank you," I said, since she paused and seemed to expect me to say something.

"I used to think a gentleman would let the lady wash first, but I'm not so sure now. There's something in letting him step in first and get the water adjusted. If he uses up the hot water, though, have nothing further to do with him. Either he's a cad or has bad judgment." She paused, turned and tapped me gleefully on the knee. "A gentleman always keeps track of his capacity." She laughed.

"Another bad risk is the man who takes baths. Though I was once in love with a man who took bubble baths. He was magnificent. He had a beard, and this beard, in the course of the bubble bath, would get foamy and sudsy. King Neptune, I called him. That's how he looked rising out of the tub. He was a god in several ways, never mind he took baths. For the main part, though, baths aren't a good thing."

Abruptly she grasped my arm and turned her old eyes full on me. "Make sure a man is clean," she said. "Be careful that a man is clean before you go with him. There's filth in the world, too, let me tell you."

She stopped and looked at the sea again. She had not let my arm go. It was then I became, all in a rush, full of dread, not at her touch, but at her words, which seemed to be about the world that I would find, and about things I was not prepared to deal with. When she got old, maybe Alma would talk like this, her hair bound up in a nylon stocking, not golden any longer, and she would have no memories but of filth. And it came to me that this old woman could be Mother Fry, too. Mother Fry's voice telling me the world is full of filth.

"I have to go now," I said. "I . . . it's been nice talking to you. I . . . we have to go someplace." She dropped my arm but did not look at me, and kept on gazing fiercely out at the horizon and did not say good-bye.

We had no place to go. The children were hungry, and so was I, so we drove along the highway toward town and stopped at a diner for hamburgers.

It is harder to keep hopeful after dark. People began to wear a nesting look, home-going, bed-going, tired. The luster of adventure and freedom was gone, and my view of the world began to tarnish, too—I felt restless, anxious to keep moving, to find reassuring evidence of hopefulness and beauty in things. After dinner we drove into town again and up into the hills to look out over the city. There the remoteness of the height, the distant lights, the blackness beyond, lent a certain peacefulness again. But then I looked at my watch, saw that it was nearly nine, and realized for the first

169

time, as if it were an inconsequential thing, that I had no money for a motel. Tomorrow, of course, I could cash a check at the market, but tonight I would have to think of something else. I wasn't alarmed at the prospect. This was the first test: Karen against adversity. And I thought again of Alma, who was always in adversity and didn't seem to mind. No money and no place to sleep would not have seemed so bad to Alma. Her troubles were always worse. She was hungry, or expelled from school, or, the last time I saw her, about to become an unwed mother. She was standing in the doorway of her horrible house, wearing a man's shirt stretched tight over her bulging stomach, her hair hanging damply in the terrible heat of that summer day, and she smiled and wished me luck because I was going away to college.

I came to a simple solution—we would sleep in the car, if I could think of somewhere to park it. At first I thought of a lonely road, but lonely roads have lovers and bushwhackers and police. Parks are locked at night. Parking lots are dark and solitary. It was finally clear that an ordinary residential street would be safest and best. I drove around, not very many blocks from my house, until I found a street that looked quiet and settled for the night. Amherst, very cozy-sounding. By the light in the living room of a tile-roofed bungalow I could see through the window pleasant things which suggested that I would like the people who lived inside. So we parked there.

"We're going to sleep in the car," I told the children. "Won't that be fun?" Miraculously they thought it would.

"Is it the middle of the night now?" Kate wondered.

"Yes, so you see why we have to go right to sleep." She peered up and down the quiet street and was impressed by the dark windows, the silence. I covered them up with jackets and sang them lullabies, and felt guilty that they never thought to challenge my right to make them sleep on public

170

streets in cars. Toby dropped away to sleep right away, but Kate lay looking alertly at the car roof and at me.

I sat in the driver's seat watching up and down the street, feeling afraid someone would come along and look in the windows at us. It was not harm I feared, but discovery. There was a restless sense that we would not be allowed to sleep in a car, and that if anyone saw us they would call an ambulance or the police, would wake us up with flashlights and noise. Then, trying to think of some means of protecting us from this, I hit on the idea of draping the car with the heavy plastic cover Garth kept to protect it from moisture at night. Expensive sports cars are commonly swaddled this way, so the sight would attract no attention, and passing people couldn't tell if we were underneath or not.

When Katy had at last fallen fitfully asleep, I opened my car door quietly and crept into the street. No one was in sight. I was afraid the cover might not be in the trunk, but it was. I unfolded it and threw it over the roof of the car, from which it fell to the hubcaps, making a blue plastic shroud over us. When I was sure nobody was watching me, I lifted one corner, opened the car door, and ducked back inside. Inside was black and stuffy, like the inside of a pup tent, and I kept thinking of people being smothered by plastic.

I folded my jacket into a pillow and put it on the armrest on the driver's side, and then put my head on that. It was impossible to stretch out altogether, but with my knees bent it was possible to make most of me horizontal. One trouble was the space between the bucket seats, which gave the feeling that I was sleeping between two chairs. I wondered if anyone had ever slept in a Porsche before, and I remember thinking as I wriggled down under the steering wheel that if the children cried I'd just have to let them cry, and if someone came and snatched off the cover and raised an alarm, I could do nothing but lie there blinking up at the gathering crowd, the way a creature washed up on the beach stares philosophically up with lidless eyes at the ring of people. And

171

they would gaze down at me with that mixture of revulsion and fascination with which people always regard sea creatures, and then I would be harpooned or something, or die of fright.

I lay still but awake for a long time. It was horrifying inside that shrouded car; it was like that primitive fear of being entombed before you are dead. We seemed to have breathed up all the oxygen, leaving only a dank and sticky darkness. Wave after wave of anguishing maternal compunctions swept over me each time the children stirred or moaned, which they did quite often; but miraculously they never woke. How can you bring your sweet babies into this miserable condition, sleeping endangered and malnourished on Amherst Avenue? Someone will take them away from you. Someone should, irresponsible and neurotic woman.

There were noises. A block away on Santa Monica Boulevard a siren, heavy trucks shifting down for the stop light. It was cold. I wanted to sit up and make sure the children were covered, but I was too inert, even frightened. I pulled my jacket out from beneath my head and put it over me.

But my shivering was mostly fright, apprehension. It is hideous to hear things but not see them, near noises—footsteps coming up the street, causing my heart to pound. But of course they passed. Nearby I heard a door open, voices, the door closing. "No one would know we are under here," I said to myself. Faint noises, crickets, night birds. These seemed strange in a city. Music barely heard—the ghost of the Ninth Symphony, skeleton high notes only, above the traffic noise, my mind supplying the whole tune. Other radio ghosts, and, from far away, laughter.

Music and laughter make life in the cold front seat of a smothered automobile seem bleak and arbitrary and foolish. My mind tried to cling to the romantic aspects—outcast little family living in its car—but I always fell down on how cold it was, how cramped, how illegal, how absurd. I realized that I was terribly tired, and that probably I would sleep.

172

"Mommie, Toby keeps pushing me," Katy suddenly said. I struggled to sit up. "Try not to mind. Lie down and I'll tell you a story. But we must whisper."

She slept again after awhile, and I was more wakeful than ever. Now it seemed not cold but hot, and I was seized by increasing claustrophobia. By reaching above and behind me, I could touch the window crank and let some air in, but it didn't really help; it only made it cold again. Our shroud had begun to flap around the bumpers in the newly risen wind. I wondered if I could snap it some way, or if there were ties.

It was soon clear that the cover would have to be secured in some way. It would be impossible to sleep with the fear that it would blow off without our noticing. I extricated myself from the wheel and half sat up. After bringing myself to the point, I crawled outside again. Again there was no one to see me. The street lights were bright, but most of the houses were dark now. At the corner some headlights turned in, and I hid between the car and the curbing, crouched like a fugitive until it had gone by. My watch said nearly one, which surprised me. I tied the long strings at the four corners of the cover around the tires. I didn't really want to crawl back in the car again yet, so I sat on the curbing with my feet in the gutter under the car, and considered myself. Gone twelve hours and in the gutter already.

Then I heard something far down at the end of the street, slow footsteps walking up toward me from Santa Monica Boulevard. I felt the dilemma of the mother animal—should I rush into the burrow to protect my young, or should I walk in the other direction to mislead the predator? Whoever was making the footsteps was nearly within sight. I tried to master my fright, and to remind myself that while it was odd for a woman to be out alone at one in the morning, it was not usually dangerous on a pleasant residential street. I had only to walk calmly along as if I were confident and safe. If you look a criminal in the eye, I remembered hearing, he will not attack you. He will attack only if you falter and drop your

173

gaze. If it is a criminal coming up the street, I told myself, I am bound to be falterish. I remembered what else you do— you walk up the safe steps of someone's house as if you lived there. If someone pursues you, you ring the doorbell and scream and scream.

The man—it was a man—visible under the far street light, walked slowly and unsteadily along the sidewalk toward me. I was apprehensive, but I walked toward him with a steady gaze. He was indeed watching me. I grew more frightened, tried to make my walk more unconcerned, purposeful. Then, suddenly, when we were twenty yards from each other, he turned into a yard between two houses. I did falter now, wondering if he meant to lurk there while I walked by. It also occurred to me that maybe he was walking up the safe steps of someone's house, in fear of me. Or maybe he lived behind that house. Perhaps he meant to jump out at me from that dark yard.

I walked more slowly, then stopped altogether to listen. I hadn't heard any door open. He was still in the dark side yard between two houses, waiting there. I stopped under the street light, as if nothing could hurt me there, and hoped for another car to come by.

Another faint sound, that of water being poured upon the ground, thirteen seconds of this. So I understood why he had stopped between the two houses, and I laughed at myself. I had linked one arm, I noticed, around the street lamp, as if to anchor myself against a wresting force, and peered with the fearful calmness of dread into the dark.

There was no movement, none for so long that I began to wonder if he was drunk and had passed out in the bushes back there. Then, a rustle, the snap of a kneecap or a stick. I swallowed, shivered, listened. The man came out, thirty, then twenty feet from me onto the sidewalk, near enough within the periphery of the street lamps to be seen. He was a middle-aged man in a sport shirt and windbreaker and old creased shoes. He walked toward and past me. His pants were unzipped; he had exposed himself, but his gaze was averted, and he did not look at me.

So, I thought, the world *is* a dangerous, terrifying place full of sex maniacs, exploitation, loneliness, and death. My fears were suddenly consolidated, satisfyingly concrete. I held my breath while he walked unnoticing past my car, and listened a long time to his footsteps, until they were out of hearing up the street. Then I climbed back with my sleeping children, writhed and wriggled back under the steering wheel and stiffly lay, tired and hungry, suffocated with sadness and pity for myself, and for the whole airless, homeless world. Looking back, I suspect the poor man in his drunkenness had merely forgotten to zip up his pants; but one has to take symbols at face value, as they come.

Chapter 18

I woke, feeling drugged, to the distant and then more immediate sounds of sobbing and wailing. It took me a few seconds to realize that my children were both sitting up in the back seat crying. Gray light somehow penetrated the shroud, telling us it was morning, very early in the morning. I soothed the children and hushed them, and then crawled out of the car to untie the tarpaulin. Up ahead a man in a business suit was unlocking his car and staring at us. A cat slunk home across the lawn of the house where we were parked. Heavy truck noises came loudly from distant freeways. It was six-thirty. My back and head ached miserably from the discomfort of the car.

On Pico Boulevard we found a coffee shop that opened at seven, and waited until we could go in for breakfast. I made the meal last as long as possible. People began to come in, talking, and the street filled with cars. The morning haze was burning off by eight o'clock, promising a hot day, and I felt spiritually better, though the headache was still there. After awhile I'd get some money at the market and we'd drive to some pleasant place like Santa Barbara. Coffee made me feel better. Toby and Kate love eating in restaurants.

Later I cashed a check for two hundred dollars, bought a few groceries, and in the dime store things like soap and cheap dishes, and thin rayon blankets of fake fleece. Planning an expedition distracts the mind from real troubles—I understood Joan better when I came out of the dime store. Toby and Kate were miracles of cheer.

The hours passed. I suppose I was comatose, sunk from reality in thoughts of Sebastian and Garth and the Frys and the future, so that I seemed to have little notion of how long to take at things. It was noon before we loaded up the car again and set out in the direction of Santa Barbara on Sunset Boulevard, trying to feel purposeful and really feeling aimless.

Pacific Coast Highway was too familiar—I could find no new responses in me to old sights—but this did not discourage me at first. My spirit must settle in a bit, I thought. I must soothe the children with uneventfulness. So we stopped and had ice cream in Brentwood Village. We went inside Will Rogers' house in Will Rogers' Park, and watched two lovely young girls work their ponies on his polo field. I had an ignoble twinge of wishing to have been that kind of rich competent pretty creature when I was sixteen so that I could have gone on to more important things by now.

I have only one accomplishment. I can walk on my hands. I learned it after hours of practice and much vigorous bruising—from Alma, of course. Alma could do back and front flips as well. In acrobatics as in everything she far excelled me, but she was willing to teach. She held my feet for weeks and weeks. I am not sure why I cared about this, but I do know standing on my hands was the first thing I thought about mornings; it occupied every spare moment, and I cared nothing for the aches it cost me, not even that it meant spending time with the by then disreputable Alma.

On the grass at the end of the polo field I stood on my hands. It is apparently something you don't forget. Kate and Toby stared, at first. From upside down I watched them blink and try to understand. Then they began to laugh and run around me. I walked in this strange fashion a few steps toward Toby before wobbling and bringing my feet down.

177

Then I had to hold the children's feet while they walked around. Thus we passed the early afternoon.

I was, I knew, temporizing. It would be necessary to view the world right side up, straight on, soon—we could not sleep in the car again. But I was troubled now with an unwanted, intrusive thought: perhaps all this was crazy. Why *was* I here with my diaphragm and my childhood diaries? Who would drive car pool to nursery school in the morning? How could I take my children away from their home into a motel wasteland? But I struggled against these thoughts.

I suppose it was the need for encouragement that developed in me a powerful desire to see Alma Phelps again, or at least to learn about her. I found myself looking around me on the polo field for her, and telling myself it was not impossible—everyone comes to live in Los Angeles sooner or later. I became convinced, almost, that I would find her name in the phone book, or that I could get her address from someone. It was not impossible—my mind clung to that. The mind in trouble seeks omens, and rarely gets them. Even news of her would be welcome.

I tried to think of somebody to call about her, but all names evaded me. Then a few came, Charlotte, Janet, Barbara Benz. Whom had these girls married? Did any of them still live in Bede? I even found it hard to imagine a Bede existing apart from my memories of it, but of course it must be there, with its brick streets and frame houses, and, probably, new supermarkets. Laura Hoaglund. Peggy Lofting, who had married Tommy McCarthy. He was a Catholic, and her folks had been upset; I remembered that bit of gossip from somewhere, some Christmas card. The McCarthys must still live in Bede, because he was due to inherit the Chrysler agency. I would call Peggy.

I became excited, talked carefully and plainly to the operator lest she think my frenzy was drink, and, disapproving, refuse to place the call. But her neutral and obliging

178

voice inquired along elaborate circuits for Mrs. Thomas McCarthy, drawing me out finer and finer in expectations along two thousand miles of wire. Then someone said importantly that they were ringing, someone rang, a strange, pretty voice said hello. I didn't know if I had the right woman—maybe Tommy had another wife. But no, they were Catholic. And then there was something in the voice at the second hello, and I remembered it.

"Peggy?"

"Yes." Cautiously.

"Peggy, this is Karen Coe. I'm calling from California."

Surprised, impressed, curious silence.

"Karen? Hello, how are you? It's nice to hear from you," she finally said.

"How are you?" I don't know why I asked this.

"Why, we're fine. Well, you found me. I guess you knew Tommy and I had married. Are you married now?"

"Yes, I'm Karen Fry now. I have two children."

"I thought I heard you were married. We have three. Did you read about Tom running for state senator?"

"No. That's wonderful. Congratulations. Good luck, I mean," I said.

"I thought maybe that's why you were calling," she said.

"No. You'll think it's funny why I'm calling. I wonder if you could tell me what ever happened to Alma Phelps?"

Another pause. "That *is* funny. Alma. I hadn't thought of her in a long time," she said. "I hadn't thought of you in a long time either. And I had another echo from the past— Grace Williams and her children were visiting here last week. They live in Monmouth, Illinois. She moved away our sophomore year, remember?"

"Do you know where Alma is?"

"Alma's been dead a couple of years now. She died right here in Bede. Some sort of drug reaction."

"Drugs?" This couldn't be right.

"She was allergic. It was penicillin, I think. Dave Etley

179

was her doctor, and he was pretty upset. Frankly, I think he used to . . . when we were in high school."

"What was she doing? Did she live in Bede? What do you know about her?"

"Well, not much. Alma wasn't exactly my closest friend." She sounded as if my questions offended her. "She came back to Bede a couple of months before it happened. Somebody just saw her, in the market. She had a couple of little girls, but I never heard if there was a husband. I think they may have been visiting her mother. Old Mrs. Phelps cleaned up quite a bit after Mr. Phelps passed away. She's worked at Freddie's for years now. Anyway, Alma had a sore throat or something, and Dave gave her penicillin and she had a reaction. They barely got her to the hospital before she died. They said her face was swollen twice its size. Couldn't open her eyes. Twenty-four years old. It makes you realize."

"You don't know where she had come from? How did she look?"

"Terrible, I guess. Blue, with her eyes swollen shut. Marilyn said Dave was a wreck over it."

"I mean before. Was she well? Happy? Would you say she had made a success of, well, being alive?"

"Honestly, I never heard. Why? Are you doing some survey? I always thought it would be a good idea if someone followed us all up, and found out what everyone was doing now. I bet there would be some fascinating things. Maybe we should do it for the tenth reunion. You're coming for that? You said you're in California?"

"Did you go to her funeral?"

"Well, she wasn't ever a particularly good friend of mine. I only saw her once, actually, a couple of weeks before her death. She looked all right. She always was a pretty girl. That was her trouble, as my mother always said. Her girls look just like her. I think somebody took them to Chicago. Marilyn said Dave even talked about adopting them. That's how responsible he felt, though it wasn't his fault. In a way

180

he's too sensitive to make a good doctor. But Alma looked all right. She had nice clothes, as I remember. I didn't have a conversation with her. Nobody knew anything about her life, as far as I know. She was just in Bede on a visit. I think she might have been some sort of waitress. Or maybe that's her sister I'm thinking of. Yes, the oldest Phelps girl was a waitress at the Antlers Inn on the highway to Bloomfield."

"Three minutes," the operator said.

"Well, thanks, Peggy," I said. "Say hello to Tom. I was just wondering about Alma, just an impulse."

This did not seem enough. I wanted to do something for Alma, to make it all right. Tears gathered in me. Nothing I could do would make it all right.

"I was really calling for a friend. It was just one of those funny coincidences. I heard this story from a friend, a famous French diplomat, about a beautiful woman named Alma whom he had loved, and she disappeared two years ago, and, I don't know, it just sounded like our Alma. She never told him that she came from Bede. They met in Paris."

"Alma in Paris?"

"Yes. Apparently she was the mistress of some European movie director, and they lived in Rome or somewhere, but they were in Paris. She was going to have an exciting life, only . . . only . . . She was very beautiful, he said."

"I didn't know anything about her," Peggy said.

"Yes. And now a tragedy. I have to hang up, Peggy. Thank you."

"It's nice to talk to you, Karen," Peggy said, her voice wistful. "Is your husband in the movie field? Are you coming to the reunion?"

"I'll try," I said. "Thanks again." And hung up. I supposed she would find flaws in my Alma story, but I hoped not. I could believe it myself, almost. Dead Alma. I felt dead myself, and tried to cry over her, or over my loss of her, but it is hard to cry out loud in a drugstore, on a sidewalk, putting the kids in the car. I managed an awkward sob, an aching throat; the infuriating picture of Alma dying managed to send tears to my eyes, but they were tears for myself, of disappointment. I had wanted inspiration and had gotten a grim reminder: courage and independence and beauty and wisdom get you no place in the end. But that was no news.

"Lady, you have to put some more money in the phone," a clerk cried, running after me into the parking lot. "The operator rung back."

Nothing gets you anywhere in the end, so it's how you kill time until then that counts. I could see that, all right. There was no reason to think that Alma had wasted her time. She had been cheated, but you have to expect to be cheated, you have to play watchfully, and hope to palm a little pitiful ace or two while the divine dealer nods in his beer. Ha. Alma had aces and eights, that's all. She had too good a hand. I kept trying to tell myself it was all right for Alma to be dead, but it wasn't.

"Are you crying, Mommy?" Kate asked.

"I'll be all right," I said, but I wasn't so sure of it.

It was only three o'clock, and I didn't feel like checking into some dingy motel quite yet—I was going to have to do something soon enough. We went to the park instead. Just our plain old same old park. I hoped I wouldn't meet Patty. Toby happily dug into the sand, and Kate went to the swings. I just sat in a dumb heap, sick and unseeing on a bench, trying to make some sense out of what had happened to Alma and what was happening to me. And I did make some sense out of it. It came to me very clearly that though the world, and life, were frightening and brutal, nothing bad would happen to me, or to Toby or Kate, or to anyone, as long as I could—the thought became obsession—as long as I could eat a popsicle.

That was the answer. The desire, which one part of my mind knew to be ludicrous, consumed that part, engulfed my flat grief, my lonesome fears. I dwelt ravenously on the icy sweetness, the idea of the cold of it tempering some heat within me. I was new, strong, and nothing could hurt me if I could just have a popsicle.

That meant one for Kate and Toby, too. Thirty cents. We were going to be all right. Kate wanted orange. I got out the money and stood up to walk over to the alley where the Good Humor truck was parked. Children clung like wasps to the fence, sticking their dimes through. I felt funny. Walking in sand is always funny; you sink and slip, but I felt more slippery than usual. My face was on fire with the desire for a cool popsicle. My poor head, with all that building and renewing going on in it, ached, hurt, objected.

"Three orange," I said, putting my hand through the fence. The popsicle man took my money. He peered forward concernedly. Mothers, peering, too, drew their children away.

"Are you all right, lady?" the popsicle man asked.

I opened my eyes. "No, no, I'm not all right at all." I started back to my bench. Someone offered to help me.

"Here, somebody, give her her popsicles," the man cried. Somebody thrust three popsicles into my shaking hand, as if they would make me well. With my last strength I got my children over to the car.

"Are you crying, Mommy?" Kate asked. "You look all funny."

I did. My face in the rear-view mirror was red; my eyes were moist and bright. The surface of my skin seemed to be comprised entirely of pain receptors, and it hurt where my clothes lay even lightly upon it. My head was not being rebuilt inside at all; it simply hurt crazily. I had a fever. It must have been a high fever.

I tried, although in pain and increasingly weaker, to fight off a tendency to slump into the seat and just lie there hoping that Kate would call someone to come help. Surely they, someone, would take me to a hospital or something. Then what remained of my sense prodded me upright into the appearance of competence. A horrible thought, borne, no doubt, of my Bede, Iowa, upbringing, suggested that because

183

I was leading an irregular life, I might have caught an irregular disease somehow—how?—and if I took it to the hospital, I would be apprehended. No haven for the wicked. But I had not thought I would be struck down so soon.

The children sensed that something was wrong, and they were still and anxious. I managed the thought that I must get them to safety, perhaps to a room somewhere. But what if I were to die and they were left alone there with my body? I thought of a doctor, the hospital again, even thought of calling Garth to come and get them. But something would not let me do that. Finally I thought of Mrs. Pratt.

It was a reviving thought. I had more strength than I had imagined, enough to start the car and drive to the Pratt Foundation. It was an awful drive, a tortured progress through a jungle of malign metal animals whose awful roaring dented my agonized brain. Cars seemed to come at me and miss me miraculously. The green and red lights, at which I stared with such care, fearful of mistaking them, seemed to burn holes in my brain. I nearly cried when we reached the safe Pratt road, but I was too weak to. Funny, I thought as we pulled up outside the mansion, I hadn't expected to be struck down this soon. If God lets me live, I thought, I'll go home to Garth. Just let me live and I'll do everything I'm supposed to. I'll pick up the peas, clean house. I promise to do what is right. This running away was all very silly, I thought. I hoped only to live.

Chapter 19

I lived, obviously. I was limp and barely aware of things for a couple of hours while gray shapes bustled around me. Then, as in a dream or romance, the room gathered from random strands of color and music into a comprehensible pattern of wall, drape, overhead beams, and in this landscape I perceived, without recognizing or understanding, an unearthly face, pale and anxious, bending over me. From the edges of my attention I received the impression that I was lying on a sumptuous bed, baronially hung in blue. The beautiful lady, whose clothing also seemed to be out of Dumas Père, bent closer and finally spoke.

"How appalling. It just makes me itch to look at her. Isn't there something we can do? Baking soda or something?"

"I don't think one itches particularly. It only seems as if one would," came a strange voice with a heavy New York accent.

"I think she's waking up," the beautiful lady said. I closed my eyes, taking stock of the recognitions—Mrs. Pratt and a little young woman I had never seen before—and wrestled with small decisions, such as whether I should wake up just then. I felt weak, but somehow intrinsically sound. Probably, although I couldn't be sure, I was not going to die. I opened my eyes again.

"Oh, I've wakened her," Mrs. Pratt said. "I'm sorry!" I

smiled at them, weakly, I suppose, and began to feel like lifting my head. "Do you itch?" she asked.

I didn't itch, but I could see what they were talking about. My arms and what I could see of my chest were covered with a flat red rash, like prickly heat. I was puzzled but not alarmed. My hair had not fallen out, or anything like that.

"I'll look in later," Mrs. Pratt said, and faded out of my line of vision. The young woman came over to the bed.

"How do you feel? This is her guest room. That lovely smell you smell is oil of apricot kernel. I know for a certain fact, from snooping in her bathroom, that she anoints herself with oil of apricot kernel. And now she's gone to take my husband for his walk. She says that walking co-ordinates the body with the soul, and he says walking is a metaphor for painting. Fancy that. It warms him up for painting. When they walk they never talk; imagine them wordlessly trudging around this big place. My husband says it opens the faculties. It seems that was what he was always trying to do in the park, only our little boy was always breaking into the requisite isolation. They do talk; I've heard them. They talk about the requisite isolation, also the pacification of the sensibilities. I cannot tell you how maddening it all is."

"Could you tell me, please, what have I got? What's the matter with me?" I interrupted.

"Measles. Your little girl, too. Only you're much sicker." Relief. God does not send measles as a punishment for wickedness; you just *get* measles.

"She says he paints like walking, that is, by selecting in a straight line across visual experience. I heard that with my own ears," the girl said. "And my husband said how clever of her to understand that."

"Where *is* my little girl?"

"Having supper. She isn't in bed or anything. She was apparently nearly over them." My head sank back again, unable to support the horrible thought that I hadn't noticed

186

my own child's measles. Obviously I was not a responsible person or fit mother. I wanted to go home.

"Where's Toby? My baby."

"At Sebastian Fry's house. His wife is watching him. He had a measles shot, and they don't think he'll get it. They wanted to keep him away. The doctor said you're to stay in bed for a few days. An adult can get complications. So stay in bed; there are maids and things. I have to go cook supper. It was me that found you."

"Well, thank you for tending to things," I said.

When Mrs. Pratt came back, I was sitting up, feeling quite strong, and prickly, and silly. She sat on the edge of the bed and leaned forward.

"What *have* you been up to, anyway?" she asked.

"What do you mean?" Because I myself hardly knew, I didn't feel able to explain.

"We called your husband, of course, and he sounded most relieved to know you were up here sick with measles. He said he had been frantic—his word—because you and the children had been gone all night. And he seemed to think that you'd been here the whole time, so I let him think so. But, of course, you haven't."

"I was running away," I said. "I left him. A silly thing. But I'm saved now, I suppose."

She frowned. "What do you mean by *that?*"

"I mean I've realized that you can't run away from your problems. You have to face them."

"Oh?" Mrs. Pratt said.

"It seems so clear to me now. I wasn't facing reality. I was being—I don't know—a dropout, like a high-school dropout. A marital dropout. When in fact you have to persevere and graduate."

"Well," said Mrs. Pratt.

"Millions of fine women . . ." I said.

"I don't know," Mrs. Pratt said.

"I *love* my husband," I said.

187

"We must talk about this when you are stronger," Mrs. Pratt said. She patted my hand and rose. Her expression was one of concern, and disapproval, which I knew I deserved, dropping out like that.

Garth agreed with Mrs. Pratt that I should stay at the Foundation a couple of days to recuperate. He sounded pleased at the notion. He visited me briefly after dinner and was very solicitous, so I knew he hadn't been told about my transgression. That was nice of the Frys. Perhaps, I thought, I had been wrong about them, and my own hostility had kept me from seeing that they didn't dislike me as much as I had thought. I was repentant, chastened, willing to try some more with them.

And the next morning, when I was stronger, I felt even more repentant, and full of good resolutions, so I knew these had not been the simple products of debility. I had been shown the dreadful face of freedom and now was being given a chance, another chance. I would go to a psychiatrist, to learn why I had done all these strange things. I hoped a psychiatrist could also explain why I did one more thing, a terrible thing, to my nice friend Patty on Friday afternoon. I think I did it because of my anger at Sebastian, but that is no excuse.

It is delightful being an invalid in the mansion of a millionaire. All that beauty, and servants, and great food, and being made to feel a precious, delicate plant to be coddled into health. I was almost literally carried downstairs into the library after lunch so that I could read and enjoy the faint breeze through the French doors from the lawn. All at once, Sebastian stepped through them, quiet as a cat burglar. My heart, as they say, skipped a beat, but from sudden rage. Sebastian the traitor. It had not occurred to me until that moment that he didn't love me.

"What happened?" he asked.

He must have seen surliness cross my face, because he hesitated before stepping closer.

188

"I left Garth. Just an accumulation of things. I left, but then I got sick, and here I am," I said.

"Did Mother scare you? She told us she had gone to see you. The rest of us were up there for supper after the ladies' quilting thing they go to, and Garth called to say he couldn't find you. So Mother, looking knowledgeable, told us how she and Father had heard a dreadful rumor about you, and how she, in her anxiety—she said—went to tell you as best she could that she wanted to help you. It was plain to us all that you'd run away, and we had to decide whether, or how, to tell Garth."

"But you never did tell him?"

"No, I got them to . . . we decided to wait."

"So now they all know—Patty and Joan and Mahonri, too?"

"Yes."

"Do they know about you?"

"No," he said. "I . . . there didn't seem to be any point in that."

"Then how did they find out in the first place?"

He hesitated. "Mrs. Pratt told them, indirectly. It's hard to explain. I don't always understand her reasons for doing things."

"But you told *her?*"

"It . . . yes . . . it came out. She meant to help you."

"You and Mrs. Pratt," I said. I cannot describe how angry all this made me, how tricked feeling.

"Yes." He looked handsome and grave and concerned, like a minister.

"I always wondered if you were Mrs. Pratt's lover," I said.

"I am your lover, too. I mean in the sense of loving you, caring about you. I'm sorry because what happened has got you in hot water now. Sorry and not sorry; it's hard to explain. I'm aware that it's not the place of the villain to tell you what's good for you. I sound defensive, but . . ."

189

"Never mind," I said. "I've thought it all out. I've just been going through a dumb, rebellious thing. Maybe everybody has to go through one, and this was just mine. I'll be better now. It's probably better that everything has come out in the open, relatively. What did they say about me?"

"Who?"

"Oh, Joan, Mahonri."

"Well, Joan said you mustn't be judged too harshly, and Mahonri said he always suspected you had the morals of a whore." He smiled for the first time.

"Mother and Father Fry?"

"Mother said she wished Garth had married a nice Mormon girl, and Father, as usual, said only that things would undoubtedly work out. Mother thinks your sin will be punished with misery."

"With measles. It's expiated already." It did seem a very distant sin. Even though he stood near me, he seemed strangely separate, and I could no longer conjure up how his body had looked or felt.

"I suppose I've been very much wrapped up in my own life. I haven't been a very good wife to Garth. That's probably why he buys all those funny things. He needs someone to be interested in him."

Sebastian looked at me. "Do you really mean to go back?"

"Oh, of course. A person can't just say to hell with things. I have learned that. It's childish."

"I suppose," he said. "Well, you're brave to go back and face them all. And maybe, as you say, things will be better once you face them down. Face up. Whatever. It's hard to tell you what I really think, because it seems to involve wishing hard things on you."

"This will be hard enough," I assured him.

"We'll talk about it," he said. "Maybe now isn't the time." Then he touched my hand and left me. The good, warm, loving confidant. We'll talk about my little problems some other time.

Perhaps it was the memory of his conversation that made

190

me do what I did to Patty. It seemed an act of anger and hurt pride. Yet at the time, I thought I had forgiven Sebastian, and that he was an agent of good. I sat in the deep chair, like a cripple powerless until my anger had seemed to slip away, and I thought to myself that I had forgiven him. But then Patty came to visit, after lunch.

"Hi," she said, very casually. Her cheeks were faintly pink against the clear olive skin—she looked embarrassed to be seeing me. I wondered briefly if Sebastian had told her the whole story, but then I realized she was just embarrassed because I was in disgrace; it was like visiting a loved relative in prison. I contrived to look as cheery and normal as I could, but was aware of looking bedraggled and wan and much chastened. The wages of sin.

"Toby is fine," she said. "He misses you. He talks quite a lot, doesn't he? More than Mark did at that age." This was indeed amiable, this unmotherly concession. "As soon as you aren't infectious, I'll bring him over. Nowadays they don't feel children should get measles. There's just too many serious complications. More children die every year from postmeasles complications than used to die of polio."

Her tone became faintly admonitory, and reminded me of a social worker who once visited us when I was a child. Ignoring the fact that our house was perfectly clean, she gave us a lecture on sanitation and personal hygiene, with a patronizing air which social workers usually do not have. Patty gave me the same feeling—she was being diplomatic and kind, and I felt myself slipping into the resentful and irritated stance of the disadvantaged, watched the kind lady and thought my own thoughts.

"And he's good as gold, and not one toilet accident. You've really trained him well." Again, the faintly condemnatory tone, a suggestion that I had probably traumatized Toby by training him too early or too rigorously.

"He's just one of those kids; once they train themselves, that's it," I said.

Suddenly Patty leaned forward. "You've had a chance to

191

kind of see what goes on, haven't you? Around here, I mean. It must be a fascinating place, so much happening, artists, famous people visiting."

"Yes, a great place to convalesce," I said.

"Do you see much of Sebastian?" she asked. The voice was innocent, but I immediately felt wary.

"He pops in and out," I said.

"I'm going to ask him to show me around. I parked in back and came up through the kitchen, but from what I could see, it's a beautiful place. Do you see much of Mrs. Pratt?"

"I've seen her a couple of times. She's an interesting woman."

"I'd love to see her some day," Patty said. "Ah, how long do you think you'll be here?"

"I don't know."

"Will you . . . I mean, have you seen Garth?" She said this in a rush, having got out at last what she had wanted all along to ask. "I wanted you to know I hope everything works out."

"Thanks, Patty. It will, I suppose."

"And no matter what, I hope we'll continue being friends," she said. This did annoy me. It was like what Sebastian had said, irritating from him and infuriating from Patty, as if they had agreed between them on the family policy toward me. But of course, I had to keep reminding myself, Patty did not know that Sebastian had made love to me.

"It's psychologically very understandable," she was saying. "Things have been hard for you, with the family, and not being in the church, and Garth is a difficult person in many ways, I can easily see. In a way it was bound to happen." If you were poor you were bound to be dirty. She did sound just like that awful woman.

"I hate your deterministic view of psychology, Patty," I said. "If I had committed suicide, would you have said it was bound to happen?"

"Well, no . . ."

"It wasn't bound to happen. I wanted it to happen. I'm just as as glad it's out in the open, too; it certainly does clear the air. Whatever I've done, I decided to do, for a change. And I decided to have everything out in the open. Tonight I'm going to talk to Garth."

"I can't help feeling you should have done more of that," she said, leaning forward, infected by my flicker of spirit. Patty, the passionate champion of communication. "If only you'd been able to talk about some of your troubles more openly. You never could, at least to me, and Garth doesn't seem like much of a listener." Patty the psychiatric social worker. "I don't mean to preach, but we've always been so close."

I sat there listening. Patty went on.

"I've always believed—this isn't Mormonism, exactly—but I believe anyway that morals are a matter of you can do whatever you like as long as you don't hurt others. Being unfaithful is something that hurts others. That's the sin—it's not so much the act itself."

"You don't think it's true about what people don't know doesn't hurt them?" I asked. The evil thing was almost on my tongue; I felt it coming.

"It does. It hurts them as much as if they knew. And you shouldn't keep from a person that you have hurt him. Otherwise it just rankles inside of you and makes you hate him."

"Then you probably ought to know about Sebastian being in love with Paris Pratt," I said. It came out very easily.

"Sebastian?" She seemed to crumple out of that pose of kindness and assurance. Self-disgust consumed me.

"It really *is* a good thing to get these things out in the open," I said, bolstering myself. "Mrs. Pratt taught me that. As you said, deceit never helps anyone. I know I sound like a tattletale, but . . ."

"You've been around here, I suppose you can see it plainly

enough," she said. The color had gone from her face, and she looked muddy. "Are they having an affair, I suppose?"

"Oh, I don't know, Patty. I just think it's a thing you ought to recognize as a possibility. He seems to love her."

"It isn't anything I haven't known, I suppose. Underneath." She got up and wandered, Ophelia-like, to the door, looking as if all the recollected confirmations of my suggestion had seeped into her head at once and addled her.

"Patty, I didn't say that just to be mean . . ." I began, but she had sadly shut the door. In a minute I could see her crossing the lawn, wringing her hands like an actress. I tried, wretchedly, to return to my book, but in a minute something made me look out the doors again. Patty was coming back across the lawn. I listened and stared, but could hear and see nothing. Then Sebastian came in, frowning, with a stricken expression, and motioned me to be quiet.

Now that we are friends again, Patty has told me how she felt during her interview with Mrs. Pratt, but I could have guessed. Sebastian and I could hear the whole conversation, which took place in the adjacent room.

Chapter 20

Patty stood restlessly at the big carved door, angry about the disadvantage of waiting to be let in or shut out, like a tradesman. She was not even sure, because the house was so big, that this was the front door. She allowed her apprehension to focus on the awfulness of having come, perhaps, to a service entrance.

Her real apprehensions were too diffuse to capture and name. She had gone to her car, and turned around and come back, a moment's decision, but now she was afraid of appearing a cartoon wife, fisted, irate, rolling pin in hand. And what on earth was she going to say to Mrs. Pratt? The phrases that came into her head were so pitiful and strident. Give me back my husband. You have everything—why do you want him, too? She tried to empty her mind, as she used to do at Morris College before an examination, in the hope that the correct things would bubble up from an unconscious depth when the moment required them. She felt consciously bottled up now, corked but unlabeled, a brew of emotion and rage fermenting within. She hoped that whatever came out would be civilized, drinkable, potent.

She had to wait; this caused her rage to build up and overcome again her momentary qualm. A maid answered the door, and she gave her name, sent it echoing martially around the foyer and up the stairs. Mrs. Sebastian Fry. The maid repeated it respectfully, and led her to a sitting room. Patty grew stronger every moment.

In the sitting room she had to fight against returning qualms. Everything around her was chosen, exquisite, expensive, rare, so that to stand for aggression there was to feel yourself crude and barbarous. It occurred to her that the assemblage of these beautiful things was Sebastian's work, but her skin still heated with the involuntary, shameful sense that a woman who loved and could pay for the splendid Braque was somehow better than one who made mosaics, however cleverly, with bits of found glass, that those who have the finest of everything have somehow deserved it. Did Mrs. Pratt deserve Sebastian, too? Patty stiffened herself against this nonsense and thought resentfully about accidents of birth. It must be easy to be perfect if you are rich and never have to battle against shabbiness. You can just point with fingers like wands to this and this, great works of beauty. You would only need to think of the why of things. Why shouldn't we make love, Sebastian? Why shouldn't we have a Picasso if we want one? You would never have to worry about *how*—how a dining table could be bought, how to fix hamburger some new way, how to bring up children, how to be a good wife.

Wife. She suddenly hated the badgelike sound of the word; it had about it a pitiful air of self-importance, like a twenty-year gold pin earned for running an elevator. Service and security. Wife. That, she saw, was a credential Mrs. Pratt would despise, as one might a medal from a third-rate Central American government. No, she would never use wifehood as a claim on Sebastian.

What claim did she then have? She pictured a Jamesian scene: Mrs. Pratt and Sebastian and others on the lawn, brightly witty, talking of aspects of morality, perspectives of truth, attitudes of love. And then herself, red-necked and looking her worst, bursting in upon them with embarrassing incoherencies about Sebastian come home. She dimly saw the incongruity of her new feeling that she must not disgrace Sebastian by saying to Mrs. Pratt anything poorly phrased or gauche. It *was* incongruous; after all, who had wronged whom? It was pride, now, that made her want to be poised and cold and haughty, assured, amused, and condescending. "Sebastian isn't much, I admit, but I am used to him; he is a trifle, of sentimental value only, but please return." This was the tone she wanted to take, but the fomenting emotions within her, the dry hurting headache of impacted tears, suggested that as soon as she opened her mouth, something like "Give me my Sebastian, I am his wife," would rush out of it. In the glass of a carved mirror she could see her own pinched face, and, suddenly, the figure of a woman, whose footsteps she had not heard behind her. She turned.

She was disappointed that Mrs. Pratt was not more beautiful. A rival of divine and undeniable beauty would be, like an act of God, scarcely to be complained against, uninsurable. One could feel there was no need trying to compete. But Mrs. Pratt was more a matter of taste; that is, not to Patty's taste and evidently to Sebastian's. She must have been forty, had the beginnings of crow's-feet and a gaunt face, and she was wearing a curious but not unfriendly expression, timidly welcoming, like a sweet saleslady.

Patty could just make out, within her, a spring of primitive jealous rage, something that made her want to shriek and stab and curse; but it lay too deeply buried, like a jewel glittering out of reach at the bottom of a lake. She was all cold water and inhibition, would have no notion how to begin shrieking. The tear that sprang to her eye was for the repressive depths of civilization.

"I'm Patty Fry," she said in a well-bred voice.

"Hello, Mrs. Fry," Mrs. Pratt said. "It's nice to meet you. I've seen your picture and heard a lot about you." Her voice was pleasant, maybe even docile, speaking banalities. They stood. Patty drew the cork on her bottled-up angry speech, but heard no encouraging pop. Nothing emerged, not even

197

the smallest fume. Nothing would flow. She couldn't think of anything to say.

Mrs. Pratt touched her arm, smiled, gestured at a thick sofa. "Sit down," she said. "It was bad of me, now I think of it, not to ask you to come and see me years ago. I suppose basically I haven't wanted to."

Patty, not knowing whether this was said belligerently or in a mood of self-reproach, responded by saying "Oh" in a voice perfectly poised between question and answer, smile and frown.

"Keeping Sebastian at such odd hours and duties, it's better for one's conscience not to picture his forlorn wife and sweet lonesome babies home alone waiting only for him. While one keeps him late playing Scrabble or something. I've probably repressed you, been a Scrooge, selfish."

"I haven't minded at all. I'm used to his hours," Patty said.

"That's good. Sebastian says you're a resourceful and self-sufficient person."

"I am, up to a point," Patty said, wanting to bring the matter up clearly before Mrs. Pratt did. Now that she was sitting, as if her blood, when released from the task of keeping her in an erect and imperious posture, refueled her brain and concentrated it to its task, she was able to survive Mrs. Pratt's frankness. "I don't exactly like the idea of him having an affair with you," she said. Mrs. Pratt blinked her big round eyes like an owl startled awake and pressed her hands together against her breast, as if in delight with Patty's statement.

"I'm glad you've mentioned that," she said. "I know I'd hate it, too. I mean, there you are scrubbing and what-all, and little children are so tiresome, I know, though I don't have any myself, and all that cooking and housework, and then your husband cares for someone else. It's very unfair." She was watching Patty sympathetically.

Patty, confused, felt herself resenting Mrs. Pratt's picture of her as someone disheveled and overworked, like Joan, but she did not feel able to say, "I don't work *that* hard."

"That's hardly the point," she said instead. "You just don't—it just isn't right of you."

"Of course you would feel that way," Mrs. Pratt agreed. "It isn't right as far as you're concerned. And of course for years I hadn't felt it would be right for any of us. But now I don't know. It may be, after all. Of course, that doesn't help you, that's very true. Do you want me to stop having an affair with Sebastian?"

Now Patty did feel tears, but they were tears of exasperation. "Of course, yes, you should. It's just wrong. That's why I'm here, of course," she said.

"It must be difficult having to come ask another person not to interfere in one's domestic affairs," said the maddening Mrs. Pratt. "Such a feeling of impotency." She leaned closer to Patty and peered with compassion at Patty's tears. Patty mastered them.

"It's not so much that I mind what Sebastian does, but think of his own good. He's had two marriages, he should try to stay with this one, there are the children. He cares for his home and for us, You are just wrecking his life."

"Why?" Mrs. Pratt asked, as if she didn't really know. "I think Sebastian is happier now than he has been in a long time. He seems very happy."

"It's bad enough that he's your servant, and now he's a paid lover," Patty cried. "What do you think that does to his self-respect?" Something quivered, hurt, in Mrs. Pratt's expression.

"Self-respect is something a man can only judge for himself," she observed. "Since I don't think of Sebastian as a paid lover, or a servant, it hadn't occurred to me that he might consider himself so." Her voice dropped reproachfully; the implication was clearly that Patty was the only one to disrespect Sebastian.

Patty saw, without admitting it, the truth in this, and came a little closer to shrieking. She wondered how she could get away from Mrs. Pratt.

"In a way, it was more necessary to his self-respect, I would think, for him to become master of this house," Mrs. Pratt said. "I'm sure you can understand that. What you're saying, after all, is that *you* will ruin his life—leave him, break up his home, take away his children."

"Yes, but it will be your fault," Patty said.

"No, you don't need to do all those things to him. Your vanity is hurt. You aren't thinking of Sebastian."

"You don't understand," Patty said. It seemed so strange that this calm woman could be so stupid. She wanted to tell her; something stirred in the depths, sending up the first felt words. "I love Sebastian. I . . . . it hurts me to think of him making love to you. I can't even say it. When I think of it I'd like to kill you both. It's so wrong and greedy of you, when you have so much. Sebastian is happy with me. He loves me, our sons. Perhaps you have no one to love you, and that's bad, but Sebastian has me. If you only knew how I feel when I think of it, how I love him . . ."

"Oh, my dear," Mrs. Pratt said, "you don't know, do you? You have no idea."

"What?" Patty asked.

"There is no such thing as love." Mrs. Pratt, frowning anxiously, got up and stared at Patty like the bearer of difficult news. "There's no such thing as love, just as there is no such thing as happiness, and wise people have always known it, and they have conducted a gigantic conspiracy to keep people from finding it out. Because it's much better if people behaved as if there were. But there isn't; there isn't, and you mustn't expect it. There are all kinds of other feelings—responsible, protective, dependent, acquisitive, lonely. Love is always one of these, or a lot of them, disguised. This is the bad thing. What I do best, I suppose, is to keep people from finding it out, and here I am telling you. Well, you mustn't expect love. It is only people asking for what they need."

"Oh, that's a lie," Patty cried out. "What about children?" Mrs. Pratt was smiling sadly. She had not made the deplorable world.

"And so you must just give people what they need, and not expect anything. It isn't so bad," she said.

"You are a terrible, terrible woman," Patty said, full of fear. "I know what you need. You use Sebastian."

"I suppose so, in a way, and he uses me," Mrs. Pratt admitted. "Reciprocity being the closest thing to love, I suppose." Her face was not taunting or triumphant, but Patty heard the word "love" as a taunt.

"Sebastian loves me! I am his wife!" she moaned, not even hearing the words. Mrs. Pratt reached toward her.

"Please don't hurt Sebastian," she was saying. But Patty ran out of the room, trying not to hear another word the dreadful woman said.

She sat in her car a long time trying to sort out all the words. Nothing had been said, really. Only, some phrases kept coming back to her. There is no such thing as love. She kept thinking about that.

Sadly she dried her tears and drove home. It didn't come to her until after she had paid the baby-sitter and poured herself a glass of the sherry it was permitted to keep for cooking that she did, suddenly, inexplicably, feel a whole lot better. There is no such thing as love, she kept repeating to herself, puzzling over this. Finally, she had it. It meant, of course, that because there was no love anyway, she wouldn't have to give Sebastian up.

Indeed, she realized, she felt better, suddenly better than she had in quite a while. Perhaps Karen had been right about clearing the air. She seemed to herself now to have a better understanding of things between her and Sebastian, better than she had had in a long time.

Mrs. Pratt came into the library where Sebastian and I had been listening. Sebastian was watching Patty walk out to her car.

"I hadn't wanted her to be hurt," he said. "I hadn't planned to let that happen."

"I'm sorry," I said. "Sorry and ashamed."

"It's always better to know things," Mrs. Pratt said. "It will be better. But I didn't mean to scare her."

"Paris, do you really believe all that?" Sebastian asked in a minute.

"That I didn't mean to . . .?"

"That there is no such thing as love."

"Yes," Mrs. Pratt said. "Almost. I believe that there are a lot of other things that are called by the name of love. Real love, the disinterested, pure conception, is rare, I think. A fugitive feeling, and people, when they have once glimpsed it, have a way of digging traps to secure it. Marriage and money and promises and demands. They catch it and destroy it. I don't know anybody who has love, do you?"

"No," I said, though nobody was talking to me.

"Yes," Sebastian said. "You have mine." Not talking to me.

Mrs. Pratt smiled. The expression of her big eyes was unmistakable. "If that were so—if that should prove to be so . . ."

"It is and will be," Sebastian said. "It's the one thing about myself I understand."

"Then, my dear, we'll have pulled something off. Something very rare. We . . .." Sebastian had walked over and put his arms around her. She held herself stiffly within them.

"The conditions are right, anyhow. I hope you will have a better opinion of love someday, Paris."

In a moment she laid her head against his shoulder and closed her eyes. With the glowing eyes closed, she looked older and tireder. It was an odd, dependent gesture, but Sebastian seemed not to notice that. He drew her more tightly to him.

"Perhaps," she said. "Oh, I hope so, Sebastian."

202

Chapter 21

I was quite well by Saturday night, and sat upstairs listening to Sebastian and Mrs. Pratt play duets on the cello and piano. Sebastian was still there when I went to bed, but I heard a car leave about two in the morning. He had not mentioned what happened between him and Patty when he went home on Friday, and I had not mentioned what happened between Garth and me, because nothing had. He stopped in briefly Friday night, and was impatient about my measles—with him no pathology signifies unless it can be cut away. And I had no impulse to introduce the subject of our marital pathology, because, in the light of my new resolutions, it didn't signify either. Everything would be all right. The Frys would know, and I would face them down, but Garth needn't know. And I would reform. He had a busy day on Saturday and did not get by, but he said he would take me home first thing Sunday morning.

I woke up on Sunday morning not dreading but even looking forward to my new role, erring wife, at family dinner. It was Joan who woke up Sunday morning full of dread. She woke early, when the faintest dawn light showed in the sky, and lay in bed, like a ticking watch, breathless with fear, listening within herself for the tiny cog sounds and whirrings of a new life. This mechanism she could all but hear beneath the skin of her belly before it was drowned out by the striking of great chimes of dread in her ears. She gasped and tossed. Still again, a ticking inside her again. She pressed both hands against her belly, as if to press the life out of it. But it was alive, ticking, waterproof, shockproof.

She tried to think of an approach, a rationalization. She could be brave. The idea of herself as cheerfully courageous relaxed her, as it had often done before. She would survive, subdue; people would admire her. Eight children and does her own housework, admirable. By her lifted chin she would discountenance the ordinary and become a captain—at the helm, she felt, of something important, above pity, an Ahab to life. Like a favorite of God you had but to command a sea of admiration and respect to rise, and then you floated on that. Joan tried this kind of rallying thought, but it was little use.

Her spirit sank, was replaced by a more likely fantasy, a mother of eight drowned in a nursery in Westwood. People said it was suicide. There was no note, but the survivors, small children clinging to floating bits of shoe and comb, testified that their mother had been despondent, had not spoken for weeks except in tones of hysterical command, shrill imprecations on tooth-brushing. Joan thought again of something that had happened in the drugstore the day before; the clerk had told her that toothbrushes do not come in nine different colors, and this had nearly dissolved her into a heap of inexplicable despair. The incident became central to her fantasy: mother of eight drowned in a nursery, and found floating in the wreckage two red toothbrushes, one with a string tied to the handle. The identity crisis, touching but inadequate.

Perhaps there was no baby beginning in there, and that slow stirring was the dissolution of its nest. In the bathroom she folded toilet paper, dabbed at herself, and stared for blood, but no stain came. In anger and anguish she got a chair and climbed up to where the very poisonous medicines were safely hidden to prevent accidents to small children.

Some compound to cause an accident, some dislodging dose. Of what? Useless antibiotics, dried-up cough syrup, aspirin, soda mints, sulfa. What did one take? She didn't know, had never heard. She was not even acquainted with a single old wife to ask. Then she felt slightly dizzy and had to steady herself with a hand against the cupboard to keep from falling off the chair. Dizziness was a sure sign. She thought of casting herself down off the chair. But they said that falls really never do help.

Then she realized that Mahonri was standing in the bathroom door looking at her. His face was redder on one side, where he had slept on it, and his pajamas clung to his fat body damply, as they always did, as if he had sweated all night.

"Are you all right?" he asked, his face concerned.

She wondered what he would do if she flung herself off the chair and broke her neck and lay at his feet dying. It would almost be worth it to see him gape and cry.

"Getting an aspirin," she said. Then she thought she might as well tell him her suspicions. They would probably make him gape and cry anyway, some compensation. She climbed down and told him in a matter-of-fact voice, as they dressed for their Sunday activities, that she would give him an eighth child.

My morning was more peaceful. It turned out that Garth could not come to get me Sunday morning because he had an emergency operation to do, so Father Fry came, after Sunday school. He was full of good wishes about my health, and said nothing more. He and Garth are just alike, I thought. They ignore trouble. But perhaps that is the pleasantest kind of husband to have. My scarlet-letter apprehensions were almost dispelled by the kind pinkness of Father Fry's face as he talked about a concert he had heard, and about the excellence of as much as he had seen of Mrs. Pratt's collection. But the sky was dark. It seemed possible we would have our first September rain.

205

We stopped at my house so I could put Sunday clothes on me and the children, and unload my car. It was the same house, maybe cleaner. I guess Garth had a cleaning lady in, or, more likely, Joan and Mother Fry had come to his rescue. We drove up the hill, and for the first time in six years I was happy about going to family dinner. Except for a few qualms, I was absolutely eager to appear in my own face and not mind the criticism I had earned. I could imagine liking them all better now. Their house was the same, unchanged; it is odd that nothing else changes when you do. I felt a prickle of fear at seeing Mother Fry and Patty, but it went away. Nothing had changed. In fact it was anticlimactic, it was baffling, because as we arrived it became clear that everyone was going to behave as always.

"Well, Karen," Father Fry said as we crossed the patio, "Mother is in the kitchen, I think."

And in the kitchen I was handed a paring knife. You might have thought that one privilege of disgrace, or at least of illness, might be to be excused from your regular duties, but I guess that only happens if you are locked up. At large, I was at work. Patty was quiet and steady-eyed, and I could tell nothing from her face of what had happened between her and Sebastian. Something threatened us all, like the dark sky, but we continued, like optimistic picnickers, to go about our preparations for the feast. Mother Fry was cheerful, ignored me as usual, and often spoke to Kate in tones of conspiratorial friendliness, as if to hint that there would be fun times ahead for the two of them as soon as I was out of the way.

Because we didn't talk much, dinner was ready sooner than usual, even without Joan, who arrived with Mahonri and the children just as we were dishing up. So did Garth. He would never permit an emergency to encroach upon family dinners.

Joan looked terrible and tragic, as if some fearsome plague had ravished off all her young, only of course there they were, noisy and hungry, all seven of them. Joan's face was

206

puffy, her lips were bleached, her hair was limp—she looked like a woman who has decided to revenge herself upon the world by affronting its eyes. Mahonri seemed his usual self, which made me suppose it some private disturbance of Joan's and nothing to do with him, the children, or the rest of us, though I had feared for a second, when I first saw her face, that she might have been caught at one of her little adventures. She looked as serious and miserable as that. Of course nobody paid any attention to it.

Father Fry said a blessing on the food and remarked on the beautiful performance of Mahler's *Kindertotenlieder* he and Garth had heard the night before. Mahonri and Sebastian expressed regrets at having missed it. Mother Fry pronounced briefly on the advantage to children of a stimulating home cultural environment. We ate our soup. Then Mother Fry disappeared into the kitchen and came in again bearing a proud smile and a platter of mushrooms.

"A special treat," she said. "Did you ever see such beauties?" They *were* beautiful, whole, tender, steaming slightly, green-flecked with herbs and moist with juices. It was ten dollars' worth of mushrooms. I wondered irrationally if they were in celebration of my return. Mother Fry laid them with proprietary tenderness before Father Fry, and stood behind him a moment to admire.

"The delicate white color means that they're very tender," she said.

"This looks very nice, Mother," he said, not seeming to realize that they were an uncustomary extravagance. He plunged his serving spoon eagerly into the base of the mushroom heap.

"You'd think someone would have noticed them long before this," Mother Fry said. "Right there outside the Home Ec Building. It just goes to show you how much good an academic degree does some people; they still can't tell a food product in its natural form."

A silence. We all looked more closely at the mushrooms.

"These mushrooms were growing outside the UCLA Home Ec Building?" Father Fry asked. "But Mother, how do *you* know they're all right? Mushrooms can be very poisonous."

"One of the ladies in Relief Society's brother is a botanist, and she told me about them," Mother Fry said, clearly annoyed at having to admit the existence of another authority. "They gather them all the time."

"I never saw mushrooms as pale as that," Mahonri said. "You don't catch me eating them." Garth picked one up from the plate and turned it over, sniffing.

"Serve them, Jacob," Mother Fry said with an edge to her voice. I had never before heard her use Father Fry's Christian name.

"Well, Mother, if you're sure . . ." he said.

"You'd have to be crazy to eat these," Garth said. "We none of us know anything about mycology."

Her face was growing redder. "I don't know what's the matter with all of you. Give the girls some, Jacob. You men and your scientific silliness."

"It might be safer not to, Mother," Garth said. "If you've ever seen a case of muscarine poisoning . . ."

"None of you are going to eat these mushrooms, is that it?" Mother Fry asked. "Nobody trusts me. You think I intend to poison my own family."

We protested in chorus.

"Serve me some mushrooms," she said. When Father Fry hesitated, she ladled a plateful for herself and picked up her fork. She glared at Garth. She pressed her lips and frowned. We all watched quietly, a conclave of Caesars, while the accused poisoner ate. I think we half expected to see her writhe and die. The redness in her face faded. We leaned tensely forward. She made defiant sounds of gustatory pleasure, and ate and ate. It appeared that she intended to eat every last mushroom.

"They look delicious," Joan said suddenly, and reached forward to help herself from the platter.

"Honey," Mahonri said, catching her arm, "maybe you hadn't better do that." His mother looked at him, swelling with wrath.

"It's just that we think Joanie is expecting again, and I don't think she should take a chance that these might disagree with her," Mahonri explained.

"Don't tell me!" Mother Fry cried, dropping her fork and throwing up her hands in an ambiguous gesture of approval or shock.

"Number eight," Mahonri said, his head bowed with modest pride. The rest of us were producing a chorus of suitable roars, with individual variations of congratulations and horror being lost in the over-all noise.

"That's our Joan," Father Fry said with a wide smile.

"Jesus Christ," Garth said.

"Your grandfather was one of eight children," Mother Fry said.

"I hope it'll be a little girl," Patty said.

"Early February," Mahonri told us. "Joanie just told me this morning."

"Oh, it's thrilling. I do love little babies," his mother said.

"Wonderful, wonderful, Joan," Sebastian said hesitantly.

"I think it's terrible," she answered in a flat voice.

There was a brief, disbelieving silence, and then several people tried at once to interpret this remark in a charitable light.

"It always is a shock at first. I remember when Garth was coming," Mother Fry said.

"Joanie is a little stunned. I must say, no more than me." Mahonri chuckled uncertainly.

"Terrible, terrible," Joan repeated, her voice rising. Her eyes held uncanny desperation, and for some reason, perhaps because this contrasted with their customary expressionlessness, she all of a sudden seemed quite handsome.

"Eight is such a nice even number," Mother Fry said.

"I can't see where one more would make much difference," Garth said.

"She's just getting William old enough for kindergarten," Patty explained sympathetically.

"I can't think of parents better fitted to have a large family. Joan is such a wonderful mother," Father Fry said.

"Well, I won't have it. I won't have it," Joan said, her stoical face contorted now. She pushed back her chair.

"Joanie is a little upset by it. William just ready to start school and all. But I've told her, this will probably be the one to support us in our old age," Mahonri said.

"You have it, then," Joan screamed. We all stared. Father Fry was on his feet, thunderstruck. Joan now began to cry, great screeching hysterical sobs; but her eyes were dry and furious. Father Fry impotently waved his napkin at her.

"Oh, goodness," Patty murmured, and went to the children, who were eating in the kitchen because of the threatening rain. She closed the door behind her.

"Joan, dear," Mother Fry was saying urgently over and over. Sebastian stared into his glass, and the rest of us stared at Joan.

"Now, honey," Mahonri was trying to say.

"I told you this would happen, Mahonri," she screamed. "I told you. Oh, damn you, damn you, damn you!" Mahonri's face went radish color.

"Now just shut up, Joan, that's enough," he said.

"I told you, I told you, oh, damn you," she wept, and covered her face.

"She's got to get control of herself," Father Fry said firmly to the rest of us. Mahonri came around the table and began to shake Joan.

"I think God just wills these things," Mother Fry was saying.

"Well, I won't have it. You'll see, you horrible pig," Joan wailed, pushing at Mahonri.

"She's out of her mind," Mahonri said to the rest of us. Joan uncovered her face, now bloated with passion, and looked at him.

"Ha," she said in an ominously changed voice. She wrenched the napkin from Father Fry, who was still proffering it in a limp hand.

"It may not even be yours," she said to Mahonri, mopping at her dry eyes.

"Honey, you'll love the baby. You'll see," Mahonri said.

"It may not even look like you, Mahonri; it may not be yours," Joan said, beginning now to laugh. Mahonri looked imploringly at us, as if asking us to dash cold water in her face or cart her off.

"Psychotic," Garth said interestedly. It was so seldom we had a medical emergency at family dinner.

"You better believe me," Joan said, mastering the shuddering laughter. "I have lovers, Mahonri, only, only when I want to."

"What am I going to do here?" Mahonri asked his father.

"Lovers in the afternoons, Mahonri. You never knew, did you? Ha." The laughter seized her again. "Ask Karen. She saw me. Ask her."

In spite of himself, Mahonri looked at me. I said nothing. Then Joan dropped back into her chair, as if her knees had buckled, and, oddly, picked up her fork.

"Just tell him, Karen, what I do in the afternoon."

"Karen has been filling her mind . . ." Mother Fry said. "You might expect . . ."

"What is she talking about?" Mahonri said to me. I did not know what to do or say.

"I want him to believe me," Joan said.

"What is she talking about?" Mahonri demanded in a louder voice.

"I don't know," I said, frowning at Joan. It was not good that they should know about this.

"Tell them, Karen. She saw me, walked right in and saw me." Joan laughed. "Was she surprised!"

"No, no, it's a mistake," I said.

"Nice Karen, you don't need to lie."

I suppose I looked like a liar as I shrank in my chair. And it would have been interesting to see Mahonri's face; Joan evidently thought so, too. But I couldn't tell on her.

"You've seen her with another man?" Mahonri said.

"She just wants people to look as guilty as she is," Mother Fry said, speaking, I think, of me.

"Did you see my wife with another man?" Mahonri shouted.

"Go ahead and tell him," Joan said. I gave a shrug, to mean I would not say, but Mahonri interpreted it otherwise and roared, and looked split and purple, as if he had been electrocuted.

Joan continued her loud laughing, and the rest of us sat sickly.

"Someone ought to take her out. She should lie down," Father Fry said.

"Get rid of her. I'm getting out of here. I'm taking my children out of here," Mahonri said. "My wife is a whore."

"Mahonri," his father said sternly. Oddly enough it was Garth who gently took Joan's arm and led her out of the room. Her laughter rose madly.

"Whore is right," Mother Fry said.

"Get rid of her, that's right," Mahonri said.

"Mahonri," Father Fry said, "Joan is a sick girl. She needs help."

Mahonri turned an incredulous face. "Help? Did you hear what she does? I couldn't even stand to look at her now. She can go find help somewhere else if she wants."

"She's a sick person, Honn," his father said. "The strains, the stresses. We have an obligation to help her." This was talk in a strange vein, taking the rest of us by surprise. Mother Fry had a horrified face. Mahonri, shaking his head, sat down again in his place at the table.

"I just don't want to have anything to do with her," Mahonri said. "It makes me sick."

"She's emotionally disturbed. She's had a hard time of it.

It's your duty to stick by her now," Father Fry said. Mahonri raised his eyes.

"Hard time of it! Hard time of it? So what about me? Do I go around laying my secretaries? I've had a hard time of it, too, but I don't do that. What about me? Fat old Joan, old cow tits. Every year another damn brat. 'Fulfill me, Mahonri, my destiny as a woman.' Kid after kid after kid. Who am I? The stud and the meal ticket. Does anybody ever talk to me? Sure, I like a clean house, anybody does, but how about talking to me? Shut up and play your stereo, Mahonri. Damn right I don't change diapers; I didn't ask for all those kids. But I take care of them, don't I? She does her job, I do mine, ha ha, the perfect wife. I thought she was. She never complains, Joanie doesn't, just like my dear mother. These are strong women, you have to respect them, but I never wanted all those fucking kids."

"You were blessed with them, Mahonri," his mother said. "Joan was blessed. I never had but three; your father didn't want *that* many."

"The children are the point, Mahonri," his father said. "You have seven children, remember. That's a big family. It would be a great blessing if their mother could be restored to health. A mother is the proper guardian of her young."

"I wanted an operation, I was really going to do it, but the wife has to sign the paper, too. Joanie wouldn't. Now I know why. Ha ha."

"Jesus, Honn," Garth said sympathetically, coming back in from wherever he had put Joan, "why didn't you ask me? I would have done it for you. It's a very simple procedure. . . ."

"You're not whacking on my balls, buddy, not you—you've been out to get them long enough, everybody else's, too," Mahonri said. There was a sputter from Sebastian, maybe laughter. Garth smiled.

"What your father is saying," Mother Fry interrupted in a calling-to-order voice, "is that it will be hard to find somebody else to take care of seven children. You'd better get the slave labor back on its feet. Your father has a very practical view of wives."

"That *is* what you mean, isn't it?" Mahonri said. "I'd better not throw old Joanie out. Live with the poor sick darling. It'd be damned expensive to replace her. Maybe impossible."

"You could always get married again," Garth said, with what I hoped was irony. He had an odd, concentrated expression.

"I'm trying to point out the practical implications. I understand the emotional reaction Honn is having. He of course feels betrayed, disgusted. But he does have an obligation to those children. And Joan's behavior is so unnatural as to indicate she badly needs help. In a way, she isn't responsible. Honn as an attorney can certainly understand the legal and moral implications of responsibility."

"I think that's contemptible," Sebastian said suddenly.

"You'd turn the poor girl out? All those motherless children?" Father Fry said righteously.

"No, no, I would not, but your reasons are contemptible. The expense and scarcity of household help, let's face it," Sebastian said.

"Didn't anybody ever think maybe Joan doesn't want to stay with Honn?" Patty suggested, speaking for the first time. "Why else would she—behave that way?"

"She'll stay with Honn all right. She'll do her duty. You girls are just whores nowadays. You don't know much about responsibility. I thought Joan was better than that, I thought she was the best of you. I've always done my duty, that's certain. 'And the woman shall spin and toil and work and work. . . .' I have nothing to reproach myself with."

"So why did she want all those damn kids?" Mahonri asked dazedly.

"Which is more than your father can say. You men—you boys are the same way—you want to be comfortable, you

214

don't care who scrubs the floor. Did any of you ever say thank you to me? Look at these hands. Hi, Mom, you look wonderful, Mom. You'll live forever, Mom. You're self-centered. Oh, I don't say it wasn't my fault. I spoiled all of you. And then you had your father's example. One of the great economists, and I don't say it hasn't been worth it. But don't you boys make the mistake of thinking it's easy for a woman."

"It does seem to me we'd all better calm down a little," Father Fry said, looking uncomfortably at his wife. "Everyone is emotionally overwrought, quite understandably."

"The great economist suggests the economical solution, Honn," Garth said. "Where are you going to find someone else to take care of your eight kids. Seven kids. Well."

Mahonri gave him a look of hate, then swung it around on me. "This is your doing, isn't it? Garth's slut of a wife. Well, he's taking *you* back, and Joanie is worth ten of you. I should have charity." I had not expected this attack, and braced myself against Garth's surprised look.

"Joan has always been easily influenced," Mother Fry said. "How I cried when you brought this girl into the family, Garth. I knew then that it meant heartbreak for all of us."

Garth was looking at me dumfounded.

"Joan is, in some ways, a real woman," Mahonri said. "I've had my faults, haven't always been too sympathetic. I didn't realize the extent to which she had become emotionally disturbed."

"A real woman. That's the problem," Mother Fry said with a laugh. "It takes guts to be a real woman, to bear the burdens. You don't get thanks for it, but you have served. There's the satisfaction."

"Joanie has served, apparently," Garth said.

"Shut up, you bastard," Mahonri said.

"Karen is afraid, she's a coward," Mother Fry said. "I am strong. I am the only strong one. None of you knows it. None of you has ever taken the trouble." Something in her voice

215

arrested the chaos of murmurs, phrases from the rest of us. Her eyes and cheeks were bright and hot.

"I don't say my life has been a waste," she said. "I have been useful. People have depended on me. Except you, Jacob," she said.

"Of course I depend on you, Mother," he cried jovially, watching her with careful eyes. "I always have."

"Karen thinks she's important," Mother Fry said. "Joan thinks she's important. Patty knows, you have to keep the perspective. I have always fulfilled my responsibility."

"You're a wonderful woman, Mother," Father Fry said.

"I have been of use. I was once of use," she said. "I don't say my life has been a waste. I brought three sons into the world and raised them into men. For what that's worth. But I don't make the mistake of thinking I'm important. Joan, too. Patty knows, you have to keep things in perspective. Do my sons listen to me now? Do they trust me? Well, I sound like one of those complaining mothers now. I am not complaining, I . . ."

Suddenly Mother Fry stood up. Her hands were over her mouth; above them her eyes were terrified. She rushed toward the kitchen. Garth leaped after her.

"The mushrooms," he cried. We followed him in a herd to the kitchen, shouting. Mother Fry sagged over the sink, vomiting and retching horribly, great agonized barks. I remembered that one dies quickly of mushroom poisoning, and apparently everyone else knew this, too, because we stood, rooted, compelled to watch, supposing she was going to fall dead before our eyes. For minutes we did nothing, except Garth, who rooted through the cupboards pulling out mustard and oil. Finally Father Fry stepped to the telephone—he has always been calm in crises—and called an ambulance. Now Mother Fry was gagging and belching awfully; her stout body writhed and contracted. Garth was back at her side, supporting her, but in spite of this she sagged to her knees in front of the sink. Sebastian and Mahonri tried to help her up,

216

but it was unnecessary; it was clear that her stomach contained nothing more. They got her to her knees again, a lump in a print dress. Garth came forward with a glass of something. I cannot now remember what I felt, besides fascination. Real emotions were suspended in us all, I think, until we knew what would come next.

Then Mother Fry was quiet, her eyes open and panicked, her body limp. Sebastian and Garth picked her up—one holding her under the arms, the other under the knees—and lugged her off, a soggy dead weight. The rest of us trooped after to see her laid on her bed. Then Garth sat down on a chair by the bed and began to take her pulse and peer into her eyes. Seeing Garth in his doctor role always made me feel proud and admiring of him.

Father Fry pushed us all back into the hall, stepped out of the bedroom himself, and closed the door on Garth and Mother.

"She needs quiet," he said. Accordingly we tiptoed along the hall to the living room, tiptoed, too, past the door where Joan had been put. Here we stood awkwardly, like guests who want to leave and can't. We were more dazed than worried. None of us knew how to feel. Patty's stewardess training continued to show as she heroically took over the children, who, having seen their grandmother fall sick, were reacting chaotically. Joan's Petey had himself thrown up on the children's table. Kate and her cousins Judy and Nephi were shrieking gleefully that Petey and Grandma both were going to die. Margaret, Joan's oldest girl, was sobbing onto Patty's breast, and Brigham was shouting, "I'm going to throw up, too. I feel it, I feel it coming up!" The rest of us stood around. Every minute or so Father Fry walked to the front door and looked out for the ambulance, which seemed to be hours late. Then it did come, almost without our noticing. There had been no siren, but suddenly two men and a rolled-up stretcher appeared at the door and were motioned inside by Father Fry.

217

"I'm going to! I can feel it coming," Brigham shouted from the kitchen.

"Don't you throw up on me, Brigham Fry," Katy screamed. Wide-eyed the stretcher men ran down the hall.

"Petey's going to die first," William cried. Father Fry opened the kitchen door to ask, in the crossest tone I had ever heard him use, if Patty couldn't please keep the children quiet.

Things kept getting madder and stranger. The stretcher-bearers came back into the living room bearing Joan, who lay loosely covered with blankets and looked wildly at us with the face of someone who expects she is being taken away to be operated on without anesthesia.

"Petey's dying! See how red his face is!" Kate called from the kitchen.

"My baby!" Joan screamed, sitting up suddenly, changing her center of gravity, so that the stretcher man behind dropped his end. And my response to this, Sebastian's, too, was inappropriate but reflex: when you see someone dropped on her rear you laugh. So we laughed, but because of the strain and oddity the laughter got out of hand. I could hear my own become shriller and more hysterical, and my stomach ached with uncontrollable paroxysms, and Mahonri was shouting, "That's the wrong woman, you fools," and Joan had scrambled up and rushed off to the kitchen, and Father Fry was trying to explain in a reasonable way to the ambulance men that they ought to go down the hall again and get the other lady, and the men were clearly wondering if they were needed in the kitchen, where all the screaming was, and Sebastian and I infected and fed each other's silly wild laughing, gaped and cried.

Suddenly Garth appeared, pale and grave, and we all, even the ambulance men, were instantly silent, as if in the presence of the angel of death.

"There doesn't seem to be anything wrong," Garth said. "She's fine now. I don't really think she's been poisoned at

218

all. Or it was a mild form. We can take her over to the hospital for observation, but I don't really think that's necessary." He had an apologetic smile for the ambulance men.

"Are you sure everything is okay?" one of them asked Father Fry. Father Fry seemed momentarily uncertain, then gave a brusque affirmative wave and told them to send him a bill. The men gratefully fled.

Everything was quiet in the kitchen. Patty had handed around another batch of ice-cream cones. Father Fry closed the front door, and we listened to the ambulance drive away. Then we all became aware again of the presence of Joan.

She stood, rumpled and diffident, by the door, wearing a chastened face and a certain wary squint that suggested she was wondering how a plea of temporary insanity would go over with us. Mahonri looked at her briefly, and turned away to Garth.

"You say Mother is all right?"

"There's not even a sign of systemic illness, no pupil changes, no motor changes. Certain mushrooms are emetic without being fatally poisonous. She must have got something like that. Or it could have been psychosomatic—we must have scared her with our suspicion of her mushrooms. Or it could have been caused by—" he looked embarrassed and tried not to seem to mean Joan—"some emotional upset."

"Probably something wrong with those mushrooms, just as we said," Father Fry agreed.

"What happened?" Joan asked, tentatively, apparently unsure whether she would be answered. Now Mahonri looked around at her again.

"Mother's mushrooms disagreed with her. It's just as well you didn't eat any." His face reflected the progress of his feelings—the anger, the marshaling of forces of humanity and practicality.

"Yes, they didn't look just right to me," Joan said, and sat down weakly on the nearest chair.

"You can't take chances with these things," Garth said.

That was when I saw the future clearly, how it was all going to be. I stood up. My legs felt weak, perhaps from all the laughing and fear, or maybe with apprehension about what I was going to do now.

"Good-bye," I said. "I'm really going now."

Garth and Sebastian, but nobody else, looked at me.

"Wait awhile. I want to watch Mother a while longer," Garth said.

"I'm much better," Mother Fry said, tottering into the room. Her sons dashed to her, bringing chairs, shouting for her to go back to bed. She did sit, gray-faced, wearing a smile of grim enjoyment at the fuss. Her entrance had dissipated the force of my announcement, but I felt obliged to go on with it.

"I mean, I'm leaving forever," I said in a dramatic loud voice. Now people did listen. Then they all began to speak to me at once.

"I would, if I were you," Joan said.

"Don't be stupid," Garth said. "We'll talk about it later. I want to watch Mother a few more hours. We'll get things straight later."

"She ought to go," Mahonri said. "She's brought us enough trouble."

"That's what I think, too," I said to him. Then there wasn't anything to do but go, so I walked across the living room toward the kitchen, where Patty was still tending the children. She had heard.

"Oh, it's a mistake, a mistake," she cried from the kitchen door.

"No, get her out of here," Mahonri said. Garth made no move either to get me out of there or to stop me. He was taking his mother's pulse.

It was Mother Fry who came after me. She took her wrist from Garth's grasp and stood up. "No," she said. Her step was pained, and her shoulders were bent, but her face was purposeful. She put out her hand and grabbed my upper arm.

I was surprised by her, and by being physically detained. Her fingers held me tight enough to hurt.

"This girl will stay like the rest of us," she said.

"No, I'm going," I said, and tried to pull my arm free. Her grip was strong, though she was trembling.

"You are not allowed to walk out on this life," Mother Fry said. "We are none of us allowed. You will learn that."

"This is silly, Garth," I said, and pulled at her again. Nobody did anything. Suddenly she put her other hand on my shoulder and, coming very close, made me gasp at her size and strength, and at the horrible reek of her sickness. She was dragging me into the hallway toward the music room. I was towed by her like a fearful child being pulled to the doctor.

"Mother!" somebody said, but nobody did anything. I thought of pushing at her face, but she is an old woman. Terribly strong. She shoved me into the music room so that I fell against the piano. I heard her lock the door.

"I hate that girl," I heard her say to the others. Then there was a general murmur of voices, from which I could not distinguish individual words.

I didn't do anything. Mainly, one feels astonished. People don't lock you in rooms, except, of course, they had, and now were talking outside in a muddle of voices, and were not coming to release me. No one came. And I simply sat there trying to imagine what they were saying, and wondering what would happen next.

But then the sounds, the voices, the pale-blue carpet of the music room, all that recorded culture and refinement in the cabinet, and, from the big window the view of the city stretched out below, the freeways curving out of sight, and the broad sea to the west, all worked on my resolution. I opened the window, pushed away the screen, and climbed through, dropping out into fuchsia and natal plum. Dropping out after all. The bushes scratched a little, but it was otherwise an easy escape.

I went around the side yard to the driveway. The children

221

had been put on the patio. I collected Kate and Toby and drove off in Sebastian's car, the only one with the keys left in.

First we went to our house. All the things I had packed for my first adventure lay neatly stacked on the garage floor where Father Fry had unloaded them that morning. I put them in Garth's mail truck. Then Katy and Toby and I walked around to the front yard to have a last look.

It was the finest sort of California evening, a pale, long dusk, the sun hovering over the sea like a lover reluctant to leave, and the land lying content and warm under the last pink caresses. Our sidewalk was wet where someone's lawn sprinkler drained along it. Mrs. Burke's poodle, mad with the joy of freedom, romped by, his leash dragging, and was captured when he stopped to lap at a puddle by the driveway where I stood. Our cat, Thomas, ran to me in alarm, so I gathered him up and stroked him. The fascinating French diplomat, as he slowed to pull into his garage, spoke to me for the first time. My hopes started; here was a good omen.

"Zat ees a nice car you have there," he said with his heavy accent. I supposed he was talking about one of Garth's Citroëns parked at the curb. Probably it stirred a patriotic memory. "Aren't you afraid someone will steal it? Running around loose like that. It looks quite valuable." I thought perhaps the problem lay in his imperfect knowledge of English idiom.

"It's so old, I'm sure no one would bother," I said. "Besides, there's no more room in the garage."

It was his turn to look puzzled. "Does it eat much?" he asked.

"About twenty-five miles to the . . . oh." I realized he had been talking about the cat, not the car.

"Not much. Are you fond of cats?" I asked.

"Not personally, no," he said. "There ees always something I have wanted to say to you." He leaned out his car window, and my hopes raised again. "Eet is not good, the color you have your hair now. Too yellow. Needs a little darker shade. Also, you should not do this yourself. At my shop we are experts in this, hair coloring. Eet has just bothered me, those dry ends of yours. Eet is perhaps irregular to speak out this way in the street . . ."

"I didn't know you had a salon," I said. "Are you French?"

"Armenian," he said, "but trained in Paris, definitely."

"I know you're right about my hair," I said, and thanked him, and he pulled into the garage.

It was just as well to lose my very last illusion. In the real world there are no fascinating French diplomats, but it doesn't make any difference.

Garth's mail truck doesn't go very fast, but we got to the beach before the light had faded entirely, and after we had set up camp, we ate pretzels and oranges, and watched the moon rise.

Chapter 22

And that is how I came to be living out here at the beach. It's lonesome at times, but other campers come, an occasional beachcomber, terrifying teen-agers on parties. Living by yourself in a mail truck at the beach is infinitely more arduous and often more boring than the life of a respectable housewife in West Los Angeles, but it demands new qualities of self-reliance and self-knowledge. I fortify myself with Thoreau. And the children like it here. They have grown very brown, and their blue eyes are star-tling, like the legacy of English pirates upon an island people. Of course the weather won't hold much longer, and then I'll have to do something. I don't know what, but I have decided it is to be interesting.

Patty and Joan and Garth and Sebastian all come to visit me. They preach at me, and tell me their secrets—there is apparently something about my mail truck akin to the con-fessional. I am not sure, from the way they talk to me now, whether they feel I am no longer one of them, am remote and a safe listener, or whether they feel I belong to them still. I am more hopeful about Garth than about any of them, perhaps because I need to be, to avoid feeling guilty.

He said a strange thing. "You know, Karen, at first I didn't know how I'd get along without you to take care of me, but I find I do pretty well." He seemed pleased as he said this, not reproachful.

I was caught by surprise, because I saw, and said, that I had never taken care of him at all. "That's where I failed you. I was awful. I didn't do anything. For you."

"That's for sure. That's what I'm saying. So I take my shirts to the laundry, and Mother gives the house a once-over every week, and I'm turning into a terrific cook."

"And you kind of like it?" I suggested, hoping so.

"That's what I'm saying. Of course I'll be glad when your wits return to you, but meanwhile I'm doing very well."

As for the others—I don't know. Sebastian says he and Patty have spoken only once about Paris Pratt. It was on the way home from Sunday dinner, the awful day everything happened. He had been almost grateful for the confusion, one more thing to take up conversation. Her silence about what she knew, and about her visit to Mrs. Pratt, and about his infidelity, about everything, had him nearly demented, but he had been avoiding a talk as much as she had. Now they were alone together again, and he felt his apprehensions return.

Patty put Mark and the baby in the back seat of Mother Fry's car, and then got in front and moved over close to Sebastian the way they used to do when they were first married. He glanced at her sideways. She was tugging at the unfamiliar curls above her ears. Unconscious of his eyes, her face sagged. Sebastian headed off any serious discussion of their own situation by talking volubly about the family troubles, the mushrooms, Mahonri and Joan, my escape in their car.

"We have to stop at the market," she said, interrupting him. "We need milk for breakfast."

He relaxed. Presumably they wouldn't discuss Mrs. Pratt in the supermarket. But *why* hadn't Patty brought it up yet? Why didn't she? He felt like the quarry in a spy movie, or a mouse, in spite of the fact that she seemed to have no catlike deliberation, no sadistic game with him.

"It was awful, wasn't it?" Patty agreed, returning to the subject of Joan. Her face and tone were blank, uncomprehending, as if she hadn't really understood any of it yet. "Such misery. Such awful misery. I didn't know whether to feel sorrier for Joan or Honn or Mother Fry or who. There just isn't anything to say, is there? It's hard for me to understand how people can, well, get themselves into situations of such misery."

"It was like the tent collapsing on a circus," Sebastian said. "Things happening, screams, dashing around."

"No marriage is perfect. People don't seem to realize that. There's good and bad in every relationship. People can be very unrealistic, that's the trouble. I always knew Karen was unrealistic; Garth, too. That is, he is a little weird. But Joan has always seemed so stable."

"She is, in some ways. But emotions are facts, too. Realism takes emotions into account, too. A marriage . . ." Sebastian began, seeing glimmers of his own future defense in the argument he was about to advance. Sometimes you just can't help falling in love with someone else.

"I can only think of once you really disappointed me. I mean, that's when I first learned that everything isn't always the way you want it. You have to be mature. But I didn't turn around and have affairs because you'd disappointed me. Of course, Joan has other pressures, all those children."

"How did I disappoint you, Patty?" Sebastian said, asking for it.

"Just pull into the Food Queen here. It was the statue."

"The statue?" Sebastian parked and tried to remember the statue. He couldn't. They got out, each took a child, and they picked up a cart in the parking lot.

"The Rodin statue. Don't you remember?" She smiled with a touch of triumph, as if his blankness proved her point.

"The one I found? Oh. Certainly I remember it."

Patty stared at two boxes of soap flakes, chose the red-and-yellow one. "You gave it to Mrs. Pratt. It only cost a quarter. I mean, *we* could afford a quarter, you could have brought it home. But you didn't, you gave it to Mrs. Pratt."

"But the collection . . ." Sebastian tried to say. He realized he hadn't even thought of bringing that statue to Patty. "Why didn't you say something at the time?"

"I don't know." Patty put milk in the cart. "It was only later, when I thought about it. Although I was pretty dumb even then; I didn't exactly see what it meant."

This was the time. She had to be told things.

"Patty, I was in the next room when you came to see Mrs. Pratt, and I happened to hear. I listened."

She looked at him and then turned her face away. "I'm embarrassed about that. I was just so angry and upset when Karen told me, and I saw it must be true. I wish I hadn't done it."

"I felt pretty wretched, I assure you," Sebastian said. "It seems to be my natural mode lately, feeling like a bastard, hurting women." They wheeled into the check-out stand and he got money out. Patty was automatically watching the cash register.

"Tide is on special," she said. "Forty-seven." The checker, annoyed, peered at the box and then at a sheet pasted on the stand. She frowned and called loudly for someone named Perry. A man in an apron appeared, was consulted, and confirmed Patty. Sebastian was embarrassed.

They walked back to the car. Sebastian impatiently waited while Patty deposited the children again.

"You have to be realistic," she said as she climbed in. "I can understand how you would be attracted to Mrs. Pratt. She's glamorous and rich."

Their house, to him and apparently to Patty, looked meager and dark. A little gray home in the west. Patty was looking wistfully at it but made no remark. Neither of them said anything until they had gone inside and put the children in bed.

"What I'm trying to say," Patty began again, sitting down by him in the living room, "is that I'm very disappointed but

227

I can forgive you. A person has to be realistic. But it would be silly of me to pretend I'm not hurt and disappointed."

Her voice had a tactful poise which Sebastian now realized masked worry. She was handling him, was being careful not to enrage or irritate him. This made him feel powerful and at the same time remorseful, sad that she could mistrust him or think him capable of doing her some further harm if she weren't careful.

"Nothing has changed," he said. "Nothing will change." He thought it only fair to tell her this, but he could not quite bring himself to say more explicitly that he would continue to love Paris. He hoped she would understand that this was what he meant.

"At first I was afraid that you meant to leave me, but then I saw you would have done it already if you meant to," she said.

"Perhaps you will want to leave me," he said.

"No. I can forgive it," Patty said. "There's more involved than my pride. The children, our home."

"I am still in love with Paris Pratt," Sebastian said, making sure she understood this. It was becoming clear to him that she was not going to leave, and that everything would continue as it had. He felt both regretful and relieved.

Patty seemed not to hear him. Her face had assumed a distant, resigned expression, like the mother of a difficult adolescent, whose childish passions, she assumes, will one day burn themselves out.

"I was hurt at first, and thought of leaving you. But I know you love me and our family."

"Yes, of course I do," Sebastian said, "but I'm trying to be honest, trying to make sure you understand. . . ."

"In a way everything is the same, except that I know now what I should have known all along," Patty said, and Sebastian saw, with a coward's relief, with manly regret, and with a sigh of acceptance, that this was probably true.

Patty went into the dining room, walking toward the

228

kitchen. "And I've changed my mind about the table," he heard her remark. "I guess I'm more attached to it than I thought. And it was a wedding present. Those were happy times."

Sebastian stayed in his chair and looked around him for something to happen. He was thinking how strange it was that people could make great decisions, declare themselves, defy, and nothing was altered in consequence. Now he felt powerless and puzzled. Nothing happened. He picked up the Home Section of the paper and began to try to read it, and wondered if the subject, the great and dreaded subject, was now closed. His thoughts left it and drifted to Paris. Her face, looking down on him from her house, seemed in his imagination to brighten and glow, like a taper lit by his ardor. He supposed it would be colossally tactless to make some excuse to Patty and go see Paris tonight, so he contented himself with just thinking about her, and this was in itself an intense pleasure.

And that was all that was said. I am still surprised at Patty's restraint. She has said nothing to me except that she is redoing her kitchen. We sit on the sand and discuss the psychological effects of blue or yellow.

Perhaps Sebastian and Paris Pratt will always be lovers. Perhaps Sebastian can eat his cake and have it, too. If so, he will have got away with something. But I hope he does. For me, I suppose, things are bound to be harder.

Of all the family, it is Joan who has come most often to see me. She comes at unexpected times; I look up and see her walking toward me, lifting her bare feet high like a cat off the hot sand, and her children teeming around, scampering after my children to the edge of the water. Sometimes we talk, but sometimes she just stretches out in the sun and appears to sleep. Her pregnancy does not yet show, but her psychotherapy does. Her insights are not startling, but she has already developed an intensely subjective way of seeing things. And she has gotten that deceptive candor that enables

229

psychoanalyzed persons to tell you all their awful secrets as a way of making friends. She has told me, for example, that she had had a "college widow" period, before she met Mahonri, that she had completely repressed. "I seem to have a sexual reaction to psychological stress," she explains.

The Fry family assumes Joan's problem will soon be fixed up, and in the meantime she is enjoying her invalidism, I think. Mahonri has bought her a new washer, and a cleaning lady comes twice a week, and the psychiatrist is helping her not to feel guilty about this.

"It will give me some time for personal development," she said, and I wasn't sure she wasn't being ironic. I am not as sanguine as Mahonri and the others about her prompt return to emotional health. She says ominous things like "Psychiatry doesn't really change your behavior, you know—it just makes you understand why you do things." But probably she doesn't make such remarks to Mahonri.

Of course I have thought most about Garth, though I daresay not as much as I ought, because I find it too confusing. Because he has stood so close to me, my view of him has been obscured, and has grown no clearer now that he is remote. He is a remote person anyway, and I hope he was not just being gallant about being quite happy without us. He gives me what money I need, and spends the rest on strange collections, and putters in the garage, and goes to concerts with Father Fry. Most things about him—love-making and moments of fond parental co-operation and quarrels—I remember with a kind of distant affection. It is astonishing how quickly a person fades from you if it is you who have put the distance between. It is the deserters one longs after.

It is hard at any rate to think about the past when the beach and the sun are so palpably present and so fill our days. We continually make discoveries here. Yesterday was the finest thing. We were up before six, when the tide was low, and walked along the beach to a new cluster of rocks, a virgin limpet field, to gather this most delicate and wondrous creature for our food. It was a splendid, fresh morning. The sun brightened the colors of things, brown and pink on the moist sand, blue over the water, warm on our skin in spite of the early breeze. Coming back we stopped at the inlet where a shallow stream empties into the sea, and the sand along its banks was hard and flat as wet pavement, good digging sand. Here we began to build.

Our first project was modest, a low pyramid of sand with a deep trench around it, in which water came up for a moat. We flew a bathing-cap strap from its peak, and incised little windows with a stick. Then, while the children patted its sloping sides as smooth as stone, I attempted a tower at one side, a knee-high stalagmite, astonishingly sturdy, the sand being in a condition for building, just wet enough, and incredibly cohesive. I stacked sand waist high, a firm pillar, broadened its base, and built it higher. It could be shaped, sculptured with a shell into a square tower. The children laughed, astonished.

Possibilities. We began to build in earnest. Toby and Kate dug sand into their buckets by the edge of the water and dragged it to me untiringly, like ant children. We heaped a mountain as high as my shoulder of perfect sand, packed it firm, even Toby beating it with his shovel. We were more than an hour amassing this colossal sand heap. The sun went higher, became warmer, and we had to bring water to pour over the drying surface. Then with my shell tool I began to carve us a castle, a cathedral, some fairy-tale monument with thin spires and buttresses and crenelated towers, splendidly tall, the tallest tower nearly as tall as I, firm as a pillar, and a deep arch carved out for a door, the whole tenderly watered and packed and watered again.

We knew we were doing an important thing. This knowledge possessed the children as it possessed me. We praised ourselves endlessly, and worked another hour, two hours, building, extending. Our thoughts, outrunning us, leaped to a great walled city.

Two little boys, aged perhaps twelve, came along the

beach with buckets, and stopped. Although we did not ask them, they saw what was needed—more water to preserve the tallest towers against the drying sun and more wet sand brought from the edge of the water. With four to help, the work went faster, tower after new tower, until at last the tide was almost upon us again, and I saw that it must be nearly noon.

I did not mind the tide, for it seemed, suddenly, that we had done our work. We watered the whole and firmed up all the surfaces, and then climbed the low cliff by the highway to look down upon it. From this vantage I truly saw what an extraordinary, inspired sand castle we had built. The children, like me, were content to sit and watch the waves come closer. We were not at all regretful.

We, or our castle, drew other watchers, two carloads of them, children and grown people who had pulled off the road and stood behind us pointing and exclaiming. Several of the strange children slid down the cliff bank and ran around the castle, shouting but not touching it. A woman near me put her camera to her eye. No one asked me if the castle was mine, but, of course, it was.

So our days go, and other things seem remote in consequence. Garth and the rest say I am simply running away from life, which, in the eyes of many people, is something immoral and suspect. I'm not sure of that, or even if I'm doing it. People are always telling you to find a purpose in life and then stick to it when the going gets rough. That's probably not bad advice, but it does seem that people usually pick a purpose wrongly and too young, below the age of consent, the romance of people and purposes being therefore more like statutory rape. In this regard I've just regained my virginity, and if I'm running away, I'm running to protect it.

No, I am not running, nor am I waiting. I am reorganizing. The good weather will not last much longer.